UNLIGHT
CHANDRA SHEKHAR

UNLIGHT

Chandra Shekhar

Science and Prose
PRINCETON, NEW JERSEY

FIRST EDITION November 2018
SECOND IMPRESSION January 2024

Cover designed by Jeff Brown Graphics
Layout and Typesetting by Hari Ravikumar

www.ScienceAndProse.com
Science and Prose, Princeton, NJ

ISBN-13 978-0-9988137-1-4

Dedicated to Jeff Hoyle and Carl Sagan,
two brilliant astronomers who were also gifted writers

1

Flight

"**S**O THIS IS what a dying planet looks like."

Anna's exclamation was lost in the roar of the helicopter as it carried her and the other four passengers westward toward the Australian desert, its engine struggling in the near-cryogenic conditions. After leaving Simpsonville and its surrounding expanse of fields behind, they had skirted the hamlet of Balindoo and were flying over a vast, arid expanse devoid of even a dried shrub or a leafless tree to relieve the sandy monotony. Behind them, instead of the golden blaze of the morning sun, a muted glow bathed every object in a ghastly shade of brownish crimson and turned the barren landscape into a sea of clotted blood.

As Larry flew the chopper, his passengers gazed in horrified awe at the frozen wasteland underneath. Anna put a hand on his shoulder and shouted: "How much longer?" Larry's reply was drowned out by the helicopter's engine noise and whirring rotors.

Larry took his eyes off the control panel and glanced at his passengers, four shapeless hulks swaddled in layers of improvised winter clothing. Beside him sat his fiancée Nicole and, in the seat behind, her mother Elizabeth. Next to Elizabeth, clutching her grandmother's thickly gloved hand, was Anna, Nicole's older daughter. And with her face almost jammed against the other window sat Anna's younger sister, Jessica. The women's ashen faces bore witness to the horror of the past few weeks, all their warmth and vivacity gone.

They trust me, Larry told himself. *I won't let them down.* And at that moment the motor started sputtering.

"What's that sound?" cried Nicole.

"Engine stalling. Too cold for the fuel to ignite. But we're almost there. Look!" Larry pointed to an assembly of giant rust-colored balloon-like objects near the horizon. As they drew closer, a vast structure on the desert floor that seemed a cross between a techno-art installation and an advanced alien spaceship came into focus before the women's astonished eyes. At the center of this structure the metallic surface of a perfectly hemispherical dome as tall as a three-story building glowed a ruddy orange in the fading light. Six evenly-spaced corridors radiated out from it, each terminating in a dome about a third smaller than the central one. Tunnel-like structures connected these peripheral domes to each other, creating an overall assembly like a giant six-spoked wheel with studs.

"What the hell is that?" Anna shouted.

"The Shell."

"The what?"

"The Shell," Larry shouted. "It's where we're headed."

"But what *is* it?"

"Home."

A sudden loud metallic rattling shook the cabin and its passengers. The helicopter swayed and bucked so violently that Larry had no choice but to bring it down for a landing. As they neared the ground the engine cut out completely. In the sudden silence, the chopper fell like a stone. It hit the ground with a deafening metallic screech, its chassis twisting and shearing. Everyone screamed. For a long moment, the chopper leaned over with its nose in the sand, its still-rotating blades slicing into the desert floor and whipping up a mini-sandstorm. Then it slowly righted itself.

For a few seconds nobody moved or spoke. They sat still, gasping, hearts racing.

"Everyone okay?" Larry finally asked.

"No," said Nicole. "Not okay at all. But alive."

"No bones broken, I think," said Anna. "Jess?"

"I'll live."

"Grandma?"

"I'm fine, dear. All shaken up, but unhurt."

"Then let's get out," said Larry.

With great difficulty they kicked a door open. Anna and Nicole jumped out. Jessica and Larry freed Elizabeth from her harness and helped her down to the ground before jumping out themselves. Larry's legs nearly gave way as he landed.

The temperature had fallen below minus 50 degrees Celsius. Torn out of the relative warmth of the helicopter cabin, the five of them began shivering violently. *We are minutes away from freezing to death*, Larry thought.

They had already begun to move toward the nearest peripheral dome of the Shell that loomed like a ghostly bubble half a kilometer to the west.

Way too far. We can't make it.

Larry tried to keep the panic out of his voice. "We can make it if we run."

They began a desperate scramble across the desert. Their lungs burned from the frigid air and their feet sank into sand that felt like liquid ice. Their eyes struggled to focus in the somber red glow that seemed to obscure rather than illuminate. Anna and Larry, both athletic and fit, managed the best. Jessica, screen-addicted and sedentary, found the going tough, her legs and lungs barely equal to the challenge. Nicole needed all her grit to keep going, though her legs felt like they were being amputated without anesthetic.

Elizabeth knew she wouldn't make it. Unused to anything but warm weather and gentle domestic activity, she knew she couldn't survive long on this nightmarish tundra. After the first few meters, she could no longer feel her limbs, and every few paces she stumbled and fell.

"Please, leave me and go," she begged, but nobody seemed to hear her. The moment she flagged, faltered, or fell, one of her companions propped her up and urged her forward with hoarse words of encouragement. And when she collapsed a few dozen meters from the dome, Larry simply lifted her up and staggered the rest of the way with his load.

In this fashion they finally made it to the dome. They wheezed and panted, struggling to catch their breath, feeling as if their lungs were on fire. Larry twisted a handle and pushed hard. A door swung open. The moment they stepped inside the dome, Larry swung the door shut. They were out of the desert and inside the Shell.

And they were as shut in by the deadly cold outside as if a jailer had turned the key.

2

Entry

INSIDE THE DOME, air at a relatively balmy 10 degrees Celsius caressed them. Recessed lights illuminated a curved room resembling the interior of a planetarium. Bottles of water and boxes of energy snacks sat on a low rectangular table in the center of the space. The rest of the room was bare. Airlock-style doors to the left and right and a regular door on the far wall interrupted the smooth monotony of the dome's interior.

"Is everybody okay?" Larry asked between deep, hoarse breaths. Nicole and the girls nodded, shivering, too out of breath to speak. Everyone looked anxiously at Elizabeth until she gave a weak thumbs-up sign.

"Then help yourselves," said Larry, pointing to the items on the table, and for a few minutes, the only sound was that of food and drink being ingested amidst noisy inhalations and exhalations. Finally, Nicole put down her bottle of water and gripped Larry's hands. "Honey, we'll thank you later, but first, some explanations. What the hell is this place?"

Larry cleared his throat. "Well—"

"Is this what you were working on?" Elizabeth cut in, her breath still wheezy. "All this time when we barely saw you?"

"We thought you'd forgotten us," Nicole said.

"How could you even think that?" Larry exclaimed.

"I told you we should trust him!" Anna said, turning to the others.

"Is this where we're going to live?" asked Jessica.

"Yes and no. This is part of our shelter, but only a peripheral building, the Entry dome. Now that you've had a chance to catch your breath, I'll take you to the Central dome. That's where we'll live."

"Is it a real house?" said Nicole. "With a kitchen and living room and everything?"

"Absolutely. And a lot more."

Larry's words had a cheering effect on the group. They still trembled from the shock of their narrow escape, but the prospect of finding themselves in a comfortable house calmed their nerves.

"I can't wait," Anna said.

"Me too," Larry said, smiling despite the tension that clenched his gut. "But we need to clean ourselves up first."

"Clean ourselves? Why?" Nicole asked.

"Bugs," said Larry. "We can't risk taking in any six or eight-legged friends. If they hitched a ride with us, we might never get rid of them. The Shell is a pesticide-free ecosystem."

"That's not really—" Jessica began, but Anna cut in quickly: "Something like that happened in Biosphere, didn't it?"

"Why is that relevant?" Jessica demanded.

"Well, it too was a sealed, self-contained ecosystem."

"But what's Biosphere? And what happened there?" Nicole asked.

"It was an experiment in Arizona where people lived in a closed ecosystem for two years. Some species of ant got into the facility and wouldn't leave."

"That's right," said Larry. "We don't want that to happen here."

"But how do we clean up?"

Larry pointed to a door on the far wall. "There's a bathroom just outside."

The others found the mention of that mundane convenience oddly reassuring. Though life as they knew it had ceased to exist, here was something familiar.

"Ah, a hot shower!" said Anna. "Half an hour under that will hit the spot. Who's first?"

Larry shook his head. "No, it's not that kind of shower, I'm afraid. It's just a ten-minute rinse."

Anna's face fell. "Oh no! Ten minutes each?"

"No, not ten minutes each," Larry said. "Ten minutes in total."

"Just two minutes each? Are you nuts?" Jessica snorted.

Larry looked to the older women for help.

Nicole laughed. "Eight minutes each, maybe. Perhaps even five. But two minutes? What were you thinking?"

"Unfortunately, the tank holds just ten minutes of water."

"Bad planning," said Jessica.

Larry shrugged his shoulders. "Probably. But we can't change it now."

Nobody spoke for a few seconds, and then Elizabeth, still breathing hard, said hesitantly: "I have an idea."

Larry turned to her eagerly. "Yes?"

"Why don't we shower together?" she said.

"Are you kidding?" gasped Anna. "No way!"

Nicole, after an incredulous laugh, warmed to her mother's idea. "I guess that's one way to do it."

Elizabeth looked at Larry. "Would you mind?"

Larry colored and looked away for a second, then made a quick decision. "Yes, let's go for it. In fact, let's leave our clothes and shoes here before entering the shower. It'll reduce risk of bugs even further."

Seeing the girls hesitate, Nicole said: "Larry, turn the lights off. Make it less embarrassing, man! Anna, come on, don't make a fuss. Let's get this over with quickly."

Anna groaned. "Ok, Mummy, if you say so," she said and began to unzip her jacket as Larry dimmed the lights and then stripped himself down. After some hesitation, Nicole and Jessica followed suit and helped Elizabeth, who was struggling with stiff fingers to unzip her jacket. Soon they all stood in the nude, shivering and avoiding each other's eye in the chilly dimness.

"Give me a second, and then follow me," Larry said, passing through the doorway. The women heard the sound of showers being turned on, and in seconds a thick, inviting cloud of steam emerged. "It's ready!" they heard Larry shout. They needed no further urging to feel the delicious rush of steaming hot water on their shivering bodies. The washroom had several dozen showerheads spraying water down with great force. The horror of the past several days—the storms, the freeze, the riots, the destruction of almost everything they held dear—receded from their minds. *Feels like soaking in very hot, heavy rain on a moonlit evening,* Anna thought incongruously. Soon the women were ecstatically soaping themselves, their embarrassment forgotten. Even Elizabeth forgot her fatigue and aching muscles. They laughed and giggled, nudged each other and pointed to Larry, who stood huddled in a corner with his back turned to them. Far too soon for the women, and not a moment too soon for Larry, the water flow dropped to a trickle, and a minute or so later, even that stopped. Hot dry air then blew through openings on the walls of the partition.

"I know how much you were enjoying this, but I'm afraid we've run out of water," Larry said, handing out towels. "The hot air won't last. Let's dry ourselves quickly before we start shivering."

Once the steam had dissipated and everyone was dry, the women's bashfulness returned until Larry handed everyone a thick hooded robe and padded slippers to match. The snug robes held and enhanced the warm glow from the shower.

Larry then led them to an airlock door on the far side of the washroom. "We have an unheated corridor to cross. Let's do it quickly."

The door swung open, and they stepped into a dimly-lit tunnel about twenty meters long. Larry slammed shut the door behind them. It was bitingly cold.

"Hurry, now." Larry urged the women along. A few seconds later, just when the glow from the shower was wearing off and they were starting to shiver, they found themselves at the end of the tunnel. Larry opened another airlock and ushered them through.

"Welcome to the Central dome," he said. "We're home."

3
Central

THE CHAMBER THAT greeted them was similar in shape to the Entry dome, but there the resemblance ended. Unlike Entry, Central was warm and commodious. On one side of it overstuffed couches cradled a medley of cushions and bolsters in leather, wool, and velvet. The wall behind sported an assortment of Indian silk tapestries of elephants, peacocks, and symbols from Eastern traditions, interleaved artfully with impressionist landscapes and Dutch still-life paintings. Small round rosewood tables nestling between the couches bore delicate porcelain vases in white and cobalt, smiling brass Buddhas, and regal Ganeshas fashioned from ivory, teak, or marble. Larry pressed a switch, and a bowl of amber liquid hanging from the ceiling bubbled gently and wafted fragrances of rose and sandalwood.

Another side of the chamber boasted an array of computers, electronic displays, and data banks scattered amidst glass-topped desks and wire-mesh chairs. The remaining third of the room hosted a cavernous tent, open at one end, lined and carpeted with thick layers of fur-like material.

Central dome evidently housed a snug living area, a high-tech work space, and a warm sleeping spot, but that was not what made the visitors gasp.

From windows on the far side, bright sunlight streamed into the room. It wasn't the dim, sickly, blood-red glow that bathed the desert outside. This was the real thing—golden, gleaming, resplendent with the joy of life. The women stood in silent awe, marveling at the spectacle.

Anna was the first to recover. "Well, *that's* one sight I thought I'd never see again!"

Nicole grabbed Larry's arm. "What is this?"

Seeing the awestruck look on their faces, Larry's proud smile turned sheepish. "Actually, it's not really the sun."

"Then what is it?"

"It's a full-spectrum lamp behind the wall. And the wall itself is just a transparent electronic panel."

"So your sun is fake?" Jessica asked.

"I'm afraid so. Just a digital creation."

"Who cares?" cried Anna. "I love it. Don't you, Mum?"

"Of course."

"How about you, Jess?" asked Anna.

"Too bad it's not real."

Larry looked slightly crestfallen. "I'm sorry …"

Elizabeth rushed to his support. "If it's an illusion, it's a lovely one," she said. "It brings joy to my heart."

She sank into a couch, sighing with pleasure, and the others followed suit. Larry put his arm around Nicole as she nestled against him. They sat in silence for a while, basking in the warm glow of the make-believe sun.

Elizabeth then turned to Larry and clasped his hands. "Larry, I know how modest you are, but would you allow us to thank you? For saving our lives, for—"

"No, no, please stop," Larry said, red with embarrassment.

Anna came to his rescue. "Enough with the hero worship. The guy has some explaining to do."

Nicole smiled and nodded. "If we're going to start thanking him, there'll be no end to it." She turned to her fiancé. "Honey, you've been a mystery man for too long. Start talking."

"Yes, Chief, time to come clean," said Anna.

Larry grinned for an instant, and then his expression grew somber. "It all started two years ago, as you know, when they first spotted a strange object entering the solar system. My friend Fred Walcott gave me the inside story."

4

Discovery

WHEN AN AMATEUR astronomer spotted a mysterious object 400,000 kilometers in diameter outside Pluto's orbit early in January 2020, almost everyone scoffed. The largest known asteroid, Vesta, was barely a thousandth as big.

"Amateurs!" said Fred Walcott, director of the James Webb Observatory in Palm Springs, California.

But the Webb Observatory's own telescopes soon confirmed the find and showed it to be a gigantic cloud of fine carbon particles. Astronomers worldwide went into a frenzy of excitement.

"This is for real," Walcott admitted once other measurements confirmed the finding and estimated the intruder's trajectory. "The good news is, it has too low a density to have substantial gravitational effects. It might cause the tiniest wobble in the Earth's orbit, some seismic anomalies, maybe even a tsunami or two, but nothing worse."

"And the bad news?"

"It's nearly opaque, and it's headed our way."

Walcott summarized the findings in a report titled *Impending Planetary Threat* and requested an emergency meeting of the US National Security Council, expecting all major military and civilian leaders to attend.

The NSC meeting that took place the next day proved to be a low-key affair. Unwilling to cut short his snorkeling vacation in the Cayman Islands, the US President had ignored the astronomer's urgent plea to attend the meeting. His lack of interest had rubbed off on other top officials as well; the Vice President and other senior leaders in the administration had decided to skip the meeting. The Armed Forces were poorly represented as well—the highest military official attending was a one-star general, John Hector, director of public relations at the Pentagon. His counterpart at the White House had sent a low-ranking aide in her stead. Most of the other attendees were minor officials from various government agencies—FEMA, National Guard, and the police. The sole attendee with scientific credentials was the President's Science Advisor, Harry Graham, a former petroleum industry executive whose claim to fame was a book attacking climate science.

Swallowing his chagrin at the poor attendance, Walcott went ahead with his presentation in the hope that the message would eventually reach the White House.

He had barely started when General Hector cut in. "Well, what's this nonsense about a comet?"

"Dust cloud, General—"

"Whatever. It's not our job to worry about all that. Don't we give you guys enough funding?"

Walcott glared at him. "The threat to our planet from this object is so grave that we at the Webb had no choice but to alert the authorities."

"What's the big deal here? Some chunk of rock passes through the solar system, and suddenly it's doomsday?"

"General, this dust cloud is huge, and it's heading toward us."

"So what? Worried about dust on your furniture?"

Some of the attendees chuckled. Walcott flushed, struggling to control his anger. "It's not the dust itself that's the problem, it's what the dust will do. When this cloud hits us it'll wrap itself around our planet like a blanket and cut out all sunlight to us. Without sunlight, the Earth's surface temperature will plummet to far below zero. And when this happens—"

Hector raised a peremptory hand. "Whoa there. Slow down. You mean *if* this object hits us."

"It doesn't have to be a bullseye. All it needs to do is to brush past us. And that is virtually certain to—"

Hector raised his hand again. "Hold it right there. How big is this thing compared to the solar system?"

"Its diameter is roughly one ten-thousandth of the solar system's, but a hundred times that of the Earth."

Hector laughed incredulously. "So this teeny little speck entering our solar system is going to exactly strike an even teenier speck? Tell me, Walcott, have you ever played the Lotto? You have a fortune awaiting you there!"

This time, there was an even louder chuckle from the audience. Feeding off its energy, Hector continued. "Let's assume you win the lottery, and this collision does take place. How do you know that the dust will hang around here, and how do you know it'll block the sun's light? Have you ever seen this happen before?"

"Yes, in the aftermath of volcanic eruptions, for example."

"Well, we survived them, didn't we?" Hector grinned at his audience.

"Yes, General, but this event is of a far greater magnitude. Our models show that—"

"Are these the same models that predicted a five-degree rise in temperature unless the President put a tax on carbon, which he wisely refused to do? And now you're using the same models to predict a *fall* in temperature? Man, you tree-huggers crack me up!"

Walcott bent his pencil so hard it snapped. "Goddamn it! The astronomical models we use to predict the outcome of this collision have nothing to do with the geophysical models used to predict climate change."

"Easy there," said Hector. "Yelling won't help. And you're talking too much." He turned to Graham. "You've been very quiet, Harry. As the President's science advisor, what do you think of this … global cooling scenario?"

Graham smiled. "Dr. Walcott's theory is intriguing, very intriguing." He spoke in a suave, bland voice that he had cultivated during his petroleum industry years. "But he seems to be overlooking basic physics."

"What exactly am I overlooking?" Walcott demanded.

"Simple energy balance. As you know, the Earth gets about 240 watts per square meter of energy from the sun in the form of shortwave radiation—that is, visible and ultraviolet light. It also radiates out into space the exact same amount of energy in longwave infrared, i.e., heat. Thus, the Earth is in energy balance overall and doesn't heat up or cool off. Agreed so far?"

"Yes, that's basic stuff. What's your point?"

"The point is this. You're now saying that the Earth's input energy from the sun is going to be cut off. Fine, let's assume that's true. But won't the same mechanism also block the outgoing infrared radiation? It's the same principle as wrapping yourself in a blanket—it'll block energy from outside but will also prevent your body heat from escaping. Ergo, you won't cool off, and nor will the Earth!"

Nods of comprehension and agreement came from around the room. In his many skeptical talks on climate change, Graham had employed such simple homespun analogies to devastating effect. Many who heard him went away firmly convinced that global warming was a myth. Apparently, his present listeners had a similar reaction, and many of them exchanged broad smiles with Hector.

Walcott flushed with anger. "But that's utter garbage, man! A cold, diffuse cloud doesn't behave like a warm, dense blanket. Sure, the cloud will prevent the infrared from escaping directly into space, but it won't reflect this energy back to the Earth like a blanket would. It'll simply absorb the Earth's heat radiation, that's all. It might eventually radiate a little bit back to us, but most of it will go off into space."

Graham shrugged an expressive shoulder, while the eyes of the others had started to glaze over on hearing these details. Hector took over the attack.

"Okay, let's assume that a cloud around us is bad news. Fine. Let's also assume that the Earth and this cloud run into each other. How fast is it moving, according to your estimates?"

"About one hundred kilometers a second."

Hector uttered a sharp bark of laughter. "A hundred freaking clicks per second! At that rate, it'll swing by so fast you'll miss it if you blink!"

"No, it won't, not all of it. Some of it will decelerate as it passes us, enough to—"

"Let me get this straight," Hector interrupted. "You're saying that a monster cloud speeding faster than a bullet through space is slowing down just to make a pit stop on the Earth?"

"No, I'm saying that a tiny fraction of it will plunge straight down our planet's gravitational well. Can you guess what will happen then?"

Nobody responded.

"It will form a near-opaque cloud around the Earth that will blot out almost all sunlight. We've already started referring to it as the Shroud."

Hector snorted. "Shroud, eh? I guess Armageddon was already taken." This drew another chuckle from the audience. "Just to humor you, when will this … thing happen?"

"It should reach us by the middle of next year and then wrap itself around in a few weeks. Once that happens, it'll get cold. Very cold. Lethally cold. For ten to twenty years, or however long it takes for the carbon particles to burn up or drift down to the surface. And do you know what that means?"

Hector and Graham exchanged quizzical glances, but neither responded.

"Extinction, that's what it means!" Walcott shouted, springing up. "Two years from now we'll all be gone!"

"Sit down, Mr. Walcott," Hector growled and, after the astronomer had slumped back in his seat, looked at the others in the audience with upraised brows. After a brief and uncomfortable silence, the White House aide asked a question. "How did you find out about this dust cloud, Mr. Walcott?"

"An amateur astronomer in southern India was the first to spot it."

"An amateur, eh? From India, too. Sure it wasn't a speck of dust on his telescope?" Hector said, and everyone except Walcott laughed. The astronomer's shoulders slumped in resignation. He remembered how he himself had scoffed when the discovery was first announced. The meeting broke up soon afterwards.

After several such meetings, the decision taken by the authorities was to do nothing except maintain strict public silence on the matter. The implications of the dust cloud were so staggering that most leaders were simply unable to wrap their minds around them. A complicit media, after an initial spurt of curiosity, joined the consensus to downplay the event. Astronomers did care but, as with climate change, could do nothing to convince the people with power—governments, corporations, media—to act.

In any case, there was nothing much anyone could do.

5

Refuge

"SO THAT'S WHAT got you started," said Nicole.

Larry nodded. "My company had just gone public, so I had a billion dollars to play with."

"Lucky you," said Anna. "And how did you then go about designing the shelter?"

"I left it to the pros. The experts in ecology, spacecraft design, material science—you name it. I told them it was for a nuclear winter."

"I remember the headlines," Anna chuckled. "*Billionaire Spins His Wheels* and *Shell of a Genius*."

Larry grinned. "Yes, the press had a field day."

"Unbelievable!" said Jessica, who had been listening to the discussion with a deepening frown. "You people are just incredible."

"Sorry?"

"Planet destroyed. Billions dead. Horror and devastation everywhere. And you're talking and joking like nothing's happened!"

Larry's face fell, and the two older women looked at each other in consternation. Everyone's mood darkened.

20

"It's true that something terrible has happened," said Elizabeth after a pause. "So terrible that we can't even begin to grasp it."

Anna grunted. "Yes, and some of us are trying not to think about it."

Jessica's voice rose to a shout. "How can you say that? Doesn't it matter to you that Jerry's dead? That Callista's dead? Lukas, Nirmal, Fatima, Uncle Peter … everyone we knew is gone." Her voice cracked and her eyes began to glisten. "How could they let this happen?" She sobbed loudly. "They could've stopped it."

Elizabeth held her close and rocked her gently. "There, there, dearest. My little baby."

Nicole kissed her daughter's forehead and made soothing sounds, while Anna and Larry gazed at them, looking troubled. Suddenly, Jessica stopped crying and glared at Larry. "Why didn't *you* do anything? With all your money and contacts? You could've made the government sit up and take notice."

"I …" Larry faltered. "I tried. Fred tried. But nobody listened."

"Excuses. You should've tried harder."

"Yes, perhaps—"

"Oh, let it go," Jessica sighed. "Doesn't matter. It's too late, anyway."

An uncomfortable pause ensued until Jessica broke it. "For crap's sake, don't sit there like dummies. Go back to your stupid discussion." She seemed to be back to normal, at least for now.

Larry stayed silent until Anna prompted him: "You were telling us how you built the Shell."

"Why *Shell?*" Nicole asked.

"Acronym," said Jessica. "Southern Hemisphere Energy Location Laboratory."

Larry stared at her. "I'm amazed you remember that. It got barely any mention, and I did my level best not to publicize it."

"But why the secrecy?" said Nicole.

Anna snorted. "Who cares? He made it happen, didn't he?"

Elizabeth nodded emphatically. "Yes, and thanks to him we're alive and safe." And for Jessica's benefit, she added: "We should be eternally grateful, not finding fault."

Nicole muttered an apology and kissed Larry on the cheek, but Jessica persisted: "Twenty million about to die in Australia, and the five of us were all you could save?"

Larry stood up and paced the carpet. "I wanted to save many more. Hundreds, thousands." But simple calculations had shown him how impractical that was, he explained; with the time and resources he had, he could house at most six healthy adults for the expected duration of the Shroud. "A shelter is like a lifeboat. Take too many on board, and everyone sinks."

"Ah, now I understand the need for discretion."

Larry nodded. "Since I couldn't take more people here, Nicole, I kept the project under wraps."

"See?" Anna said. "There's a good reason for, like, *everything* he does. Look around you, Jessica!" She gestured around the room at the elaborate and lavish provisions for working, living, and sleeping, and pointed at the ceiling with the blazing ersatz Sun climbing toward its zenith. "Could you have even imagined—"

"Fine, but what about the people who worked on this place?" Jessica broke in. "Masons, engineers, architects, laborers? How could you hide it from them? Didn't you care that they'd soon be dead?"

Larry winced and took a step back, accidentally knocking an ivory elephant off a small table. "Yes, it was morally wrong," he admitted, as he picked up the elephant and ruefully eyed a crack on its trunk. "I feel terrible that I hid the purpose of this place from … from the very people who were building it. And some of them would have guessed the truth anyway. But how could I have saved them? They were too many."

"And how should he have picked the ones to save?" said Anna, turning furiously on her sister. "By consulting you?"

Jessica ignored her and continued to fire away at Larry. "Okay, you misled others. But why hide it from us? You thought we'd post it on Facebook?"

"No, I knew I could trust you."

"Why, then?" asked Nicole. "Sorry for the inquisition, honey, but couldn't you have kept us in the loop?"

Larry sighed. "Yes, I should have. But until I was sure the shelter would work, I didn't want to raise your hopes. There were so many critical things that were untested until the last moment."

"Like what?" asked Jessica.

"Well, the heating system, for one. It couldn't be tested until about two weeks ago because it was too warm outside. I had to do most of the final work myself."

"Why?"

"Because I sent the workers away a month ago."

"To maintain secrecy?" asked Anna.

"Right. And there were last-minute glitches—doors that didn't open, vents that didn't ventilate, lights that didn't—"

"You could've fixed them later," Jessica cut in.

"True. I wasted precious time in tinkering instead of rushing to fetch you. And I paid for my stupidity. When I finally stepped outside the cold hit me like a body blow. All I had on was a light jacket. No hood, even. Within seconds I was shivering like a malaria patient."

"Oh, you poor dear!" said Elizabeth.

"So that was my state as I rushed out, dreading that I'd be too late ... that the rampaging mobs and militias would have destroyed Simpsonville, that you'd have fled from home, that you'd be dead from the cold." Larry's voice cracked.

"Dear Larry!" said Elizabeth. "I almost lost hope, but deep inside I knew you would come."

"Yes, me too," said Nicole. "You somehow found us in the chaos—"

"—and found us half-frozen but still alive," added Anna. "The rest of the story we know."

No one spoke for a few seconds. Then Anna stood up, came to Larry, and held his hands. "Larry Brandon, you are hereby entirely, completely, totally exonerated from the crime of neglecting your family," she said and hugged him in a tight embrace. One by one, the others came to hug Larry as well, Elizabeth warmly, Nicole passionately, Jessica shyly. All four women, even Jessica, wept and hugged each other. Soon Larry too had tears streaming down his face.

"Larry, you crybaby," said Anna at last. "Enough with the tears. How about showing us around our new house?"

6

Wheel

"**L**ET'S START WITH the floor plan," said Larry, pointing to a poster on the wall that showed an upper level called Wheel with circular rooms and a lower level called Honeycomb with hexagonal chambers. "We're here, in the Central dome, which is the Shell's living room." He pointed to a large circle at the center that linked via radial lines to six smaller circles connected by curved segments. "These smaller circles are the outer or peripheral domes. For instance, the Geo dome has the geothermal well underneath it."

The women studied the plan for a few seconds. Anna tapped on one of the segments connecting the domes. "And these are what? Corridors?"

"Right. Like the one we used to get to the Central dome."

Jessica shook her head. "More efficient to connect outer domes using straight lines."

"That's true," acknowledged Larry. "I chose arcs to make the arrangement look like a wheel."

"Aesthetics trumps function," Anna joked.

"Hexagons are more interesting," Jessica argued.

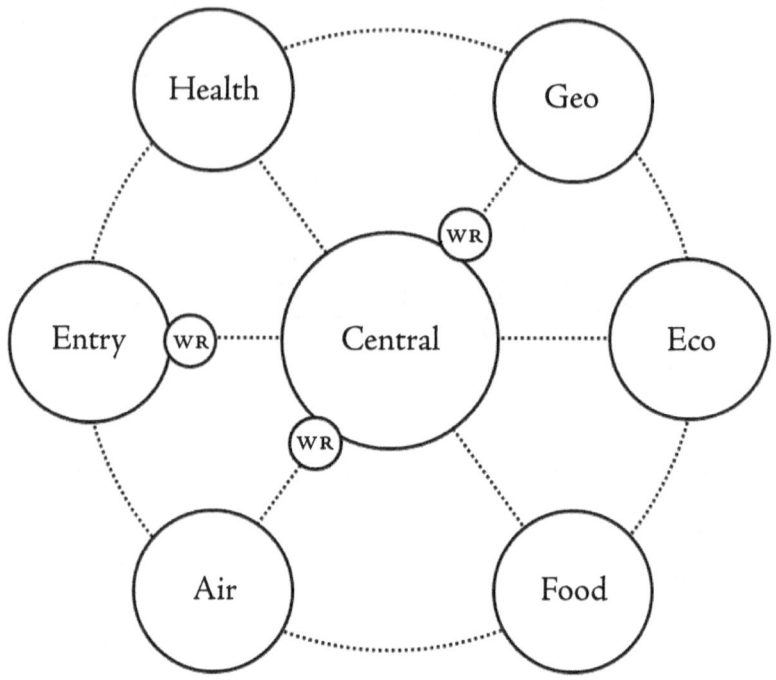

"Good, because that's what we have on the lower level of this shelter—hexagonal chambers connected by straight-line tunnels."

Jessica raced ahead to her next question: "Where do we get power and heat from?"

"From here." Larry pointed to the Geo dome. "It sits right on top of a geothermal well." He explained that the power plant in the dome generated about 2.5 kilowatts, just enough for their electricity needs, while the waste heat from it traveled via insulated ducts to the Central and other domes. "That's what keeps us warm."

"Why so many domes?" asked Jessica. "It'd be cheaper and more efficient to have just one."

"Cheap and efficient, yes. But not fault tolerant. What if we had a fire in one of the domes? This way we could seal it off before it spreads."

"Why not build the Central dome above the well?" Jessica insisted. "So much heat is wasted piping it to here!"

"True, but again it's a question of safety versus efficiency. It's risky living right above the heat source."

Anna snorted. "Jessica, you're welcome to live on top of a raging inferno, but I'll remain here if you don't mind." Jessica flushed and seemed about to argue the point further but subsided when her grandmother gently squeezed her arm.

"Well, it's nearly ten o'clock," said Larry. "I'll take you around the facility now. Our final stop will be the Food dome, where a home-cooked meal awaits you."

"You miracle worker!" said Anna. "How on earth did you arrange that?"

"It's one of the stupid things I lingered on while you were freezing to death in your basement. Feel free to kick me."

"Are you kidding?" said Anna, hugging him. "Let's get this tour over with quickly. I can't wait to sink my teeth into some hot food. I'm like *drooling* already."

"Right, then," said Larry. "Let's start with this dome. It's divided into living, sleep, and work spaces. The living space is where we are right now. Step over here, and we have the work space. It has everything we need to work or study—computers, projectors, and so on."

Jessica pointed to a large bank of servers built into a notch in the wall. "What's that, our database?"

"Correct. It holds about a hundred petabytes."

"What's in it?"

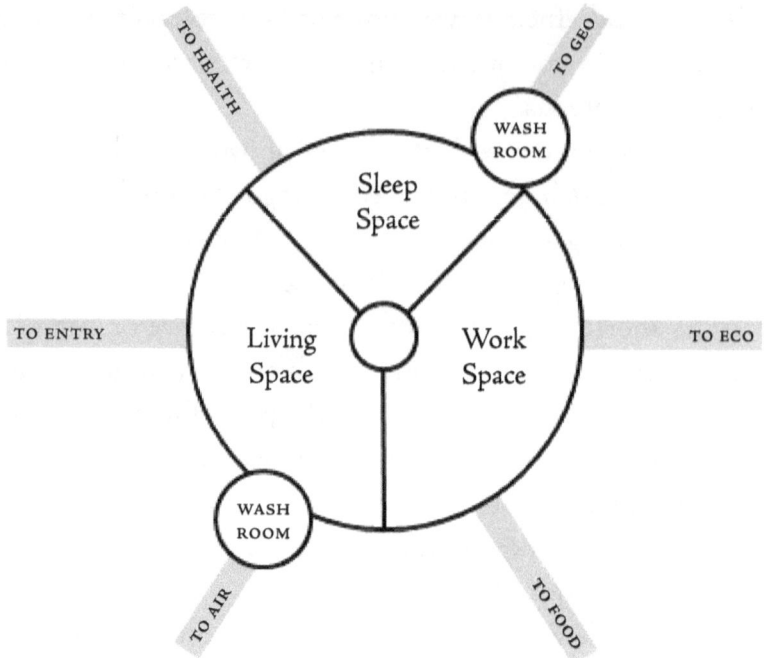

"History, science, engineering, medicine, home repair—the works."

"Cool, our own mini-Google," said Anna. "Does it have any movies?"

"Practically every movie ever made," Larry said.

"What's this?" Jessica pointed to a large console that displayed a table of numbers that changed from time to time. Most entries had a green check mark next to them, while two or three had orange marks. Larry explained that the console allowed them to monitor the functions of every system in the facility. "Take any system parameter, say air quality or temperature. If it goes outside safe values, it will flash red."

Jessica pointed to one of the parameters. "*Heat balance* is borderline."

Larry glanced at the number and nodded. "That's because we've used up some heat, air, and water during our entry. It should stabilize. Anyway, so much for the work space. Here," he pointed to the tent, "is where we'll sleep."

"It seems awfully cramped," said Nicole, following Larry into the tent. "And no beds?"

"No, we'll all sleep on the floor," said Larry.

"But why?"

"The heat turns down during the night to conserve energy, so it'll get really cold."

"Is that really necessary?"

"Perhaps not now, but we should anticipate future energy shortages."

"So we'll just huddle up to stay warm, like winter camping," said Anna. "I hope you don't snore, Larry."

"I'm not excited about being squished together like that," said Jessica. "No privacy."

"Fair point," said Larry. "But privacy is something we can't afford."

"Where's the washroom?" asked Elizabeth after they returned to the living space.

Larry pointed in the direction of the corridor leading to the Geo dome. "There's one right outside that door."

"Radio equipment?" Jessica asked.

"Over there, right next to the exterior temperature and light gauges."

Jessica went to the radio unit and fiddled with its dials and switches. Nothing came through, not even any emergency broadcasts. Only the hiss of static. She turned it off.

"Okay, for the next leg of our tour," Larry said. "The Eco dome."

They crossed a 20m-long corridor and stepped into a comfortably warm chamber filled with a vast, diverse array of potted plants and trees. Most were just saplings, but a few were in bloom and a couple even bore fruit. The labels on the trees indicated that they were dwarf varieties specially bred to grow in pots. A humid odor of flowers and decaying vegetation pervaded the room.

Her botanical instincts aroused, Anna ran around delightedly, examining the vegetation.

"What an incredible assortment! A Duke of York peach tree from England, a Temple orange from Florida, high-iron bean plants from India, even a Duc de Guiche rose bush!"

Larry smiled, pleased at her enthusiasm. He had gone out of his way to procure plants he knew she liked. He could justify the food crops from a survival perspective, but the flower bushes were purely for Anna's pleasure.

Jessica jumped on this. "Why roses? We can't live on flowers, can we?"

"True, dear, but pure survival is such a grim business," said Elizabeth. "It's good to have a touch of beauty."

"So we don't allow *privacy*, but *beauty's* fine?"

"Really, Jess—" Anna began heatedly.

Nicole quickly interposed. "What are these?" She indicated a set of large rectangular panels with textured surfaces stacked against a wall.

"Could you take a guess?" Larry asked Anna.

"Not sure … some kind of growing surface? For moss or lichen, perhaps?"

"You're close. Here, feel the surface. See how corrugated it is? Each panel actually has about ten square meters of growing area. They are for chlorella. Can you guess its purpose?"

"To make oxygen from the carbon dioxide we exhale?"

"Exactly! We'll activate the panels if we start having trouble with our air purifier." He informed them that the freezers contained several cultures of chlorella genetically modified to maximize their ability to fix carbon.

"But what *is* chlorella?" Elizabeth asked.

"It's a single-celled green alga, Grandma. It uses photo-synthesis."

"Oh, like plants?"

"Yes, just like plants, but, you know, much more efficient in its use of sunlight."

"Sounds good, but I hope we never need it," said Nicole.

"Amen to that," said Larry. "Okay then, moving along. Next stop, the power plant." He led them through an airlock door on their left and then counter-clockwise through an arc-shaped outer corridor to another door. Opening it and stepping inside, the visitors found themselves in a hot, steamy room with two large electrical generators in the middle connected to a vast array of pipes of various colors. A medley of gauges and other instruments lay scattered around the room.

"Welcome to the Geo dome," said Larry, "the place that will keep us alive and warm."

A dull roar came from underneath the floor, punctuated with frequent hissing sounds. The suffocating air reeked of sulfur.

Jessica made a face. "God, it's nasty! Not a bright idea of mine to live here."

Larry chuckled. "Then let's not linger. Next stop, the clinic."

They continued their counter-clockwise journey through another arc-shaped corridor to the adjacent dome. "Honey, this is your baby," Larry told Nicole.

In contrast to the torrid Geo dome, the Health dome lay cold and silent. One part of it boasted a mini-gymnasium with weights, stationary bicycles, and other exercise equipment. The other part contained the medical facility. Everything in it looked shiny, new, and state-of-the-art. While the others stood and watched, Nicole moved around eagerly, checking out the instruments and supplies. She opened a refrigerator and inspected the array of vials and bottles inside. "This place is better stocked than my hospital!" she said.

Larry smiled. "It's like the emergency clinics used by the military, only much more advanced."

Nicole walked around the room, handling the equipment and uttering cries of appreciation. "Looks like we can treat most common ailments, and a few uncommon ones too," she said after completing her circuit. "We can do basic surgery as well—I see you've got the best instruments money can buy, for anesthesia, surgery, rehab—everything!"

"It looks wonderful, dear," said Elizabeth, "but as with the algae, let's pray we'll never need any of it."

The next dome on the tour, cold and bare, looked oddly familiar, and then Anna noticed their discarded clothes lying on the floor. "So this is how we entered!" she said. "It feels like that happened ages ago."

"Yes, Entry dome. Nothing much to see here. Let's move along."

The dome that followed resembled the engine room of a ship, bristling with machinery. Most of the space was taken up by a system of pumps and gauges hooked up with colored tubing. The humming of motors and the opening and closing of valves combined to produce a subdued metallic din.

"This is the Air dome," said Larry.

"It cleans the air?"

"Yes, and keeps it from getting too dry or too humid."

They exited the Air dome and walked through to the next chamber.

"Welcome to the Food dome," Larry said. "Lunch is served!"

As his companions trooped into the dome, Larry's thoughts flashed back to his first meeting with them.

7

Simpsonville

*I*T WAS THE *sun that brought them together, in more ways than one.*

On the winding road to Simpsonville one cloudy autumn morning in 2020, Larry noticed a very pretty woman driving the sedan coming the other way. Dark haired, light-skinned, about forty years old. *I hope our eyes meet when we pass*, he said to himself. At that instant, the sun broke through the clouds and shone into the woman's face, causing her to swerve into his path. A collision seemed imminent. Larry frantically wrenched his steering wheel and somehow moved his SUV away from the sedan's direct path. Tires screeched and metal panels sheared as the two vehicles scraped each other and came to a jarring halt. Though the sideswipe had barely dented the SUV, it had nearly totaled the sedan. The woman who had caught Larry's eye and three other women stumbled out of the wrecked car, uninjured but shaken. They numbly accepted Larry's offer to drive them home. Once they reached home, numbness gave way to euphoria as the women hugged each other and thanked Larry over and over.

During a much-needed cup of tea they introduced themselves.

"Ladies first," Larry said.

The women looked at each other, and a girl of about eighteen took the lead. She had the same slim figure, dark hair, and attractive features as the woman who had driven the sedan. Sporting an impish smile, she showed no signs of the recent ordeal. "I'm Anna. I'm in the ecology program at the university. And this is my mother Nicole, who usually drives much better."

"But for your quick reflexes …" Nicole smiled at Larry, and their eyes finally met. He found her even more charming at close quarters.

"She's a surgeon," added Anna. "The male staff at the hospital would've been heartbroken if you hadn't saved us with that lightning-fast swerve."

"Anna, please." Nicole directed the attention toward the older woman next to her. "This is my mother, Elizabeth."

"I don't know how to thank you …" the woman began, speaking in a soft, deep voice. She held both Larry's hands and smiled at him, her brown, lustrous eyes calm despite her close brush with death. Her rich dark hair was lightly streaked with gray, but otherwise she showed no sign of age.

"She's half Maori," Anna cut in. "That's how she gets her lovely complexion."

Having elicited blushes from both the older women, Anna continued, "And this is my sister, Jessica." She indicated the other girl, a rather gawky teenager of about sixteen who had her grandmother's full figure, skin tone, and pleasant facial features, but lacked her soft voice or graceful movements.

"She's like the smartest person in Australia. A walking encyclopedia of science. And what she doesn't know about computers, you can write on the back of a silicon chip."

Larry smiled at each of the women being introduced and expressed his delight at knowing them.

"Okay, now it's your turn," said Anna.

"I'm Larry Brandon, and I'm an engineer," he said. "Not much else to say."

"Nice try," said Anna. "Now give us the full scoop. Your parents, education, work, love life—everything."

Under Anna's relentless grilling, Larry spoke about himself. An English citizen who moved to California for undergraduate studies, he was one-quarter Indian. While he attributed his athletic physique to his English ancestors, he credited his dark complexion, black eyes, and wide nose to his Tamil grandmother. In classic entrepreneurial style, he had been bored with university study and had dropped out of his Master's program at Stanford to found the first of his many companies in the USA. His initial ventures had foundered. He had first tried to market a mini-desalination plant that ran on solar energy but had failed to find any buyers. Some Gulf countries had expressed interest in the plant only to later reject it as too expensive and small-scale for their needs. His hopes ran high when a Chinese company bought a few of his units on a trial basis, promising to buy hundreds or even thousands of them if they worked as specified. He never heard back from the company but later learned that a cheap Chinese-made knock-off of his desalinator was selling by the thousand in the very countries that had rejected his prototype.

"The bastards!" said Nicole. "Did you sue them?"

"I just moved on."

Larry told them that he had gone on to make a tabletop reactor that turned used cooking oil into biofuel, hoping to capitalize on new automobile standards in the US mandating a 50-50 gasoline-biofuel mix. The device won the Consumer Electronic Show's design award for the best household appliance. Before it could achieve any commercial success in the US, however, a newly-elected Republican President and GOP-majority Congress had reversed the fuel legislation. Overnight, biofuel became a worthless commodity. Brandon's investors had pulled out and the company had gone bankrupt.

"What terrible luck!" said Anna. "You should've set up your company here. Our government isn't so stupid."

"Yes, I should have. But with my next venture, I finally got lucky."

Larry told them about a satellite he had developed for injecting sulfate particles into the upper atmosphere. By reflecting some sunlight back into space, the sulfate aerosol had proved to be a safe and effective method to combat climate change. When his company had gone public, it was one of the most sought-after stocks of the decade.

Anna stared at him with wide eyes. "Don't tell me you're Larry Brandon, of Brandon Satellite fame!"

"Guilty as charged."

Anna turned to the others. "Do you know who we have here? The guy who not only saved our lives today but who once saved the entire planet!"

So that was how Larry met the Millers and became a regular visitor to their household. Over the next several weeks, he got to know them much better, except perhaps for

Jessica, who had a way of going against the grain that seemed intentionally provocative. Direct praise, he found, embarrassed her, though she resented being denied credit. Likewise, although apparently too honest to deny her errors or faults, she seemed offended by criticism, however diplomatically worded. Larry, with his direct mind, was unable to connect with her despite his best efforts.

Unlike her sister, Anna put Larry at ease very early in their acquaintance. She was always in high spirits, and her sprightly, playful manner, the polar opposite of his own, tickled him enormously. Although initially tongue-tied in her presence, Larry learned to enjoy her banter and occasionally respond with a quip of his own.

He found Elizabeth warm and hospitable, and developed a deep respect for her serene wisdom. As for him and Nicole, their instant mutual attraction didn't take long to deepen into love.

And so Larry, who had been looking for a suitable location for his shelter, decided to build it in the Strzelecki desert, 80 kilometers west of Simpsonville.

8

Lunch

*A*ND NOW, *A year and eight months later, we are about to eat our first meal in the Shell,* Larry thought, shaking his head in disbelief. He looked around as if seeing his surroundings for the first time.

The Food dome boasted a superbly furnished kitchen, a fully-stocked pantry, and a tastefully appointed dining area. It was pleasantly warm and subtly redolent of spices. On a dining table stood bowls of fruit, a loaf of bread, bottles of red wine, and a large jug of water. Larry switched on an oven, and within seconds baking aromas filled the room.

Anna broke a long, stunned silence. "A dead planet outside and a gourmet feast here? I can't believe it."

"Surreal," said Jessica.

"It feels heartless to feast at a time like this," Nicole said. Seeing Larry's expression, she added: "But you know what? Screw that. I'm starving."

"I've never been hungrier," said Anna.

"Me neither," said Elizabeth.

Jessica snatched a peach and gobbled it, the juice dribbling down her chin unheeded.

Larry's pleasure at the women's reactions was mixed with an uneasy sense that he had once again gone over the top. It took a hug from Anna and a kiss from Nicole to restore his equanimity. "The lasagna and vegetables will take just a few minutes to warm," he said at last. "Let's set the table while we wait."

Soon they were all seated at the table with heaped plates and glasses of wine. For a while the only sounds were the clinking of silverware and the occasional sigh of pleasure. Jessica felt pleasantly woozy after her first ever glass of wine.

After a while, Anna finally laid down her knife and fork. "That was the best meal of my life!" she said. The other women echoed her sentiments and smiled at Larry, who colored, looked away, and murmured thanks.

The meal ended with apple pie and coffee, both declared by the women to be the best they had ever tasted. Larry had by then recovered his poise enough to deflect the compliments. "I just picked a good bakery and brand of coffee," he smiled.

They sat in contented silence for a couple of minutes, and then Larry said: "Well, this completes the Wheel part of our tour. Let's go back to Central and rest a bit, and then I'll show you the rest."

"The rest? What's left?"

"Everything below us. The Hexagon."

As they finished putting things away in the kitchen, Anna asked a question that had been on her mind throughout the meal.

"Larry?"

"Yes?"

"This meal was great, but ... we're going to be here, like, a long time, aren't we?"

"I'm afraid so."

"How are we going to feed ourselves for that long?"

"I was thinking the same thing," Nicole said, and the other two nodded.

"It's a natural question," Larry said. "The quick answer is that we're well provisioned. You'll see for yourself when we continue the tour later this afternoon."

Back at the Central dome, Larry pushed a button, and a digital cloud wrapped itself around the synthetic midday sun, casting a gentle shade over the room. The women stretched themselves out on the couches after helping themselves to duvets and bolsters from a heap in a corner. Normally, only Elizabeth indulged in siestas, but now the others too felt a delicious lassitude stealing over them. Exhausted from the anxiety of the past few days and the excitement of their trip, and sated from the meal, the women needed only seconds to start dozing.

Larry alone remained awake and vigilant, unable to relax. He walked over to the monitor and checked the gauges and external sensor feeds. Inside the dome, it was warm and snug. Outside, the desert would normally have baked under a blazing sun at this time. Instead, even the earlier dim red glow was gone; it was black as midnight and the thermometer showed minus 110 degrees Celsius. It was as cold, silent, and still as the dark side of the moon.

Larry's mind raced back to the months of uncertainty and denial that had preceded the final chaos.

9

Collision

B Y EARLY DECEMBER 2020, the Shroud slowed down to about 50 km/sec as it passed within Jupiter's orbit. Due to its position relative to the Earth, the dust cloud remained an unimpressive sight to untrained observers. Astronomers, however, noted its speed and trajectory with alarm and awe. That the two bodies would meet was now beyond doubt. Despite that, leaders of major countries were united in their denial of the cloud's significance. Under pressure, Walcott ceded his directorship at the Webb Observatory to a political appointee who clamped down on news dissemination; other observatories worldwide instituted similar policies. Anxious about jobs and frustrated about the scarcity of essential goods during a global economic slump, the public showed little interest in this celestial event. The mass media followed suit, ridiculing astronomers as scaremongers and relegating stories of the dust cloud to small columns on inside pages.

As if joining this conspiracy of silence, the Shroud made little visual impact when it reached the Earth on June 12, 2021. Since the initial contact was with the thin outer edge of the dust cloud, the naked eye could see nothing save a dull red patch in the night sky just above the horizon in the northern hemisphere. But the patch grew bigger, and by August it became visible in the southern hemisphere as well. An extremely fine, all-pervasive carbon dust caused certain types of machinery and electronic equipment to malfunction. Hospitals reported an unusually high incidence of asthma and other respiratory disorders. Still the public paid little attention. It was only when the patch covered nearly half the night sky that people started taking notice. This was toward the end of November, during a slow time for sports and entertainment, and speculative articles started appearing in the media when the situation changed dramatically. On December 21, 2021, the world experienced a peculiar kind of solar eclipse—a haze between Earth and Sun that gradually thickened over the course of the day. The following morning, the Sun was only dimly visible. The situation didn't change during the next few days. Temperatures started plunging everywhere.

Pandemonium set in. Schools and offices closed. Factory workers rushed home. The public demanded answers, but all their elected leaders could offer were banal platitudes that reassured no one. Astronomers suddenly found their star in the ascendant. Journalists, conveniently forgetting their earlier ridicule, sought answers from them, but all they got were variations of "we told you so."

Convening an emergency meeting on Christmas day, the US President, after making a brusque apology, asked Walcott what they should do.

"Do?" said Walcott. "After ignoring all my warnings, now you want me to tell you what to do?"

"I said sorry. Tell us, man, tell us."

"Since you've left it this late, there's only one thing left to do."

"Which is?"

"Pray, you stupid little moron. Pray!"

The President glared at Walcott. "Watch it, you creep!" he snarled, his face reddening and hands bunching into fists.

But the crude theatrics that had always cowed his colleagues and political opponents had no effect on Walcott. To him, even the most powerful human was laughably puny compared to the Shroud. "If you'd taken us seriously two years ago, you could've built shelters for millions." Walcott's voice dripped with contempt and disgust. "But you sat and did nothing—you and the other criminally negligent morons around you. And now it's too late."

The President gritted his teeth. "Why is it too late? Okay, you were right about this Shroud thing. I grant you that. But why can't we do something about it now? If we start construction on a war footing, we should have a thousand, a million shelters ready in a year."

"In a year?" Walcott laughed grimly. "At the rate at which the Shroud is advancing, it will cause a total solar block in seven days. Not a year. Not even a month. Seven days. A week or two more, and life on the surface will be impossible."

The President's eyes grew wide, and he fought to keep his jaw from dropping. "How long will this …" he groped for an apt word and failed, "… this thing last? Weeks? Months?"

"Weeks? Months?" Walcott mocked. "Try ten to twenty years. That's how long it will take for the sun to reappear."

"But what are you saying, man?"

"Extinction, that's what! We're going extinct. *Now* do you get what the fuss was all about?"

The President's jaw sagged. His arrogance and bluster now gone forever, he revealed himself to be just another pitiful, frightened human in desperate need of reassurance. But there was no reassurance to be had.

It was no longer possible to deny the truth about the dust cloud. Neither the government nor the media could control the message now. The panic and anger that political leaders had tried to evade by hiding the bad news burst out all over the globe. Now free from political shackles, newspapers and television stations vied with each other to air the direst predictions—even Armageddon couldn't dampen their lust for attention. But there was nothing anyone could say to reassure the billions who would soon perish. Most people huddled in their freezing homes, but many fled in terror without knowing where to go. Roadways jammed as people grabbed random belongings and rushed helter-skelter in the dwindling sunlight that cast a ghastly orange pall over the planet. Temperatures rapidly dropped into single digits even in the southern hemisphere, where it was technically summer. The combination of the warm ocean and the cold air gave rise to hurricanes of never-before-seen intensity that swept the globe.

Panic-stricken crowds went on a rampage, directing their fury impartially against government offices, security agencies, academic and scientific institutions, religious shrines, and anything else associated with authority or leadership. As public order broke down, hastily-assembled militias prowled the populous cities of the world in search of food and fuel, frequently engaging in bloody clashes with rival groups. In a few days, even the parody of organization offered by militia rule broke down and society was reduced to a collection of rampaging mobs and desperate families. A frenzy of looting, rape, and mayhem ensued in the big cities and population centers, reaching genocidal proportions and going far beyond. Hundreds of millions died in the havoc. Even more froze to death in the sub-Arctic temperatures that now plagued even the hottest places in the world, with the only respite from the bone-chilling cold coming from the countless fires that raged unchecked. But the bloodshed and chaos did not last long. By New Year's Day 2022, as Larry—after having squandered a week or more in checking and double-checking systems in the Shell—raced against time and temperature to fly his precious human cargo to the shelter, temperatures had fallen below minus 50 degrees even in the warmest regions of the world. Vehicles and machinery stalled, fires died out, and the roving mobs froze to death. Everything came to a standstill.

Human civilization had taken ten thousand years to bloom. In ten days, it wilted and died like a flower in a furnace.

10

Honeycomb

L ARRY KEPT HIS bleak thoughts to himself and greeted his companions with a smile when they woke up refreshed from their nap. He fetched a tray of coffee and cookies from the kitchen and passed it around.

"If you keep spoiling us, we'll think we're on a holiday, you know," said Anna.

Larry laughed. "That's the spirit. Enjoy your coffee, and then we can do the second part of the tour."

When the women had finished their beverages, Larry handed them an extra layer of clothing and led them to a corner of the workspace near the partition with the sleeping quarters. A switch on the wall opened up a small aperture in the floor. Lights came on inside the opening, revealing a spiral stairway that descended about three meters. At the base of the stairway they found themselves in a triangular space furnished with cabinets marked Office Supplies. It was much colder than the chamber above.

"We're now in the Central hexagon, or Central hex for short," said Larry. "It's right beneath the Central dome. Can you guess why?"

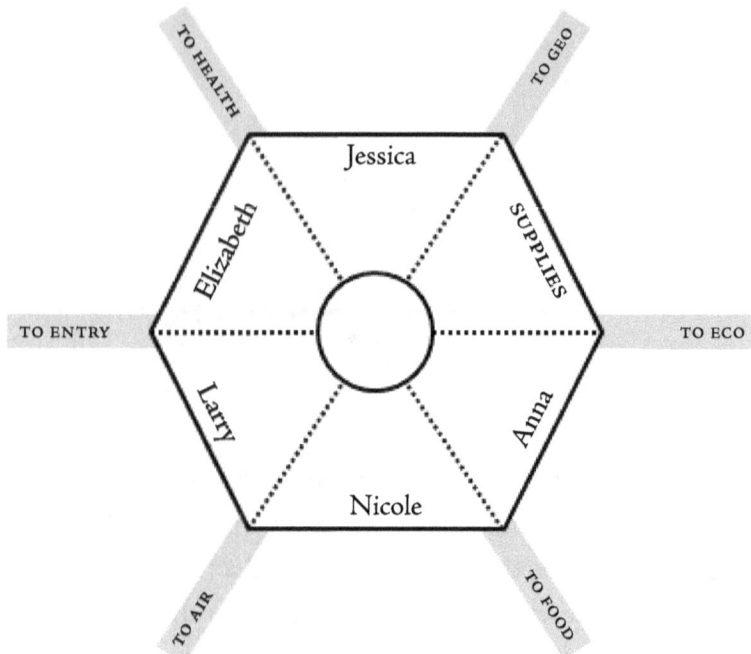

"Insulation," said Jessica.

"Exactly. The air in this room acts as an insulator. It's just like having a basement in a house—the room above doesn't get as cold because it doesn't touch the cold ground."

"No longer true," said Jessica. "The ground's now much warmer than the air outside."

"You're right for now, but with time the ground too will get very cold."

Jessica shrugged. "We'll have to wait and see."

"Fair enough." Larry led them through an opening at the apex of the triangle near the center of the chamber, through which they walked into a circular space about two meters in diameter.

"We're now at the center of the Central hex," he said. "Look around!"

In the circular wall around them stood five doors, each with one of their names on it.

"Lovely, we each get our own personal space!" said Anna.

"I hope you like it in here. All the rooms are identical. Let's go into Elizabeth's and check it out."

Elizabeth's room was another triangular section, sparsely furnished with a desk, chair, and a couch. As they entered, a space heater in one corner turned itself on, and the air grew warmer.

"It's pretty basic, but it might come in handy if you want some time alone," said Larry. "It uses extra energy, though, so we have to limit ourselves to an hour a day."

Jessica surveyed the room with approval. "I could use a quiet spot to read."

"Or meditate," said Elizabeth.

Anna shook her head. "Not for me, thanks. Too lonely and quiet in here. I'll stay upstairs."

"Me too," said Nicole. "I like being around people."

"Me too," said Larry, and thought: *We might be the only humans left on Earth. The last thing we need is solitude.*

Continuing with the tour, Larry led them through a narrow passage between two partitions that ended in the familiar airlock door. Beyond the door stretched a dimly-lit tunnel that ran for about twenty meters and led via another door into a smaller hexagonal chamber packed with various supplies—tools, chemicals, spare parts, gas cylinders, and the like. Larry told them that they were directly under the Health dome.

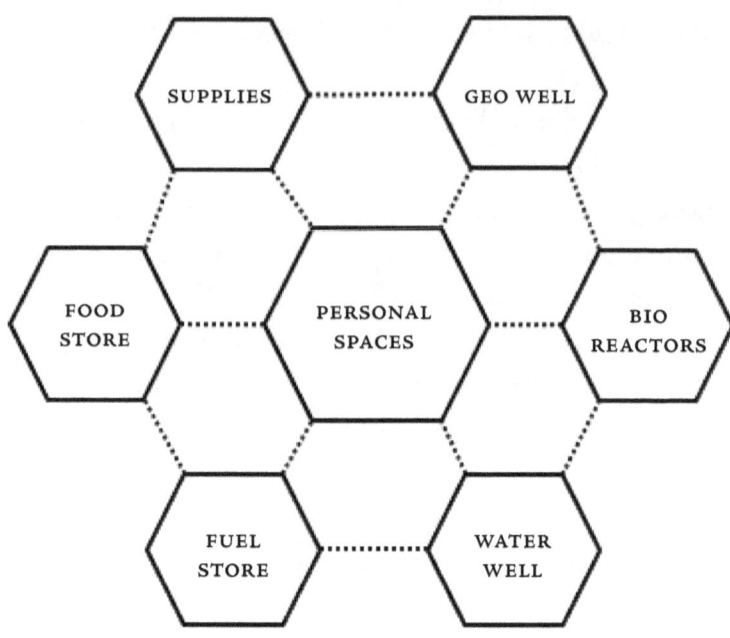

"This is where we keep a lot of the stuff we'll need to keep this place running," he said.

"But there's no food, water, or fuel here," said Jessica.

"Each of them has a hex of its own. Come, let me show you."

Another door, a stretch of tunnel, and they were in another similarly-shaped chamber. The women looked around in amazement. The room resembled the interior of a superbly stocked but extremely cramped food store. Food cans and packages stacked on shelves covered the entire space except for very narrow aisles. The intensely cold air bit like acid.

"Jessica, here's where we keep all the food."

"Lord, what a supply of eatables," said Anna. "It's like, you know, our personal gourmet market!"

"Won't things spoil?" asked Jessica.

"Yes, food will spoil," said Larry. "It'll oxidize and de-hydrate. It'll lose flavor. But at these temperatures, I'm hoping all that will happen *very* slowly. Remember, we are right under the Entry dome. We've just turned off the heat to this section. It's pretty cold here right now, but in a day or two it will be as cold as the outside."

"Cold enough to preserve even lab specimens forever," Nicole said.

"Right, so food spoilage is one less thing to worry about. Remember, though, to layer up really well before coming here and leave as quickly as possible."

Nicole nodded. "More than a minute or two here, and you're risking hypothermia, frostbite, or worse."

The next hexagon was equally packed from ceiling to floor, but with fuel rather than food. Most of the containers stocked diesel, but a few had kerosene, gasoline, or octane. The cold was intense.

"This is where we keep our backup fuel for heating, in case something goes wrong with the power plant."

"The diesel I understand, but what're the gasoline and octane for?" asked Anna. "Are you planning to take off with-out telling us?"

"No, I did that once already. I'm not going to make a habit of it."

"You know I was only joking, Larry, I'd never ..."

"I know," Larry smiled. "Okay, now a quiz question—which dome lies above us?"

"Air," replied Jessica promptly, and Larry nodded. "Yes, our air purifier is chugging away right above us."

"How did you figure that out so quickly?" marveled Elizabeth, mussing Jessica's hair. "I lost my bearings after the first corridor."

"It's like you've been here before," Larry told Jessica. "Remarkable!"

"It's nothing," she said, flushing uncomfortably. "Just kept track."

"Okay, here's a tougher one. What do you think we'll find in the next hexagon?"

"More supplies?" asked Anna.

"Nope," said Jessica. "Water."

"Right again!" said Larry. "That's amazing. How did you guess that?" The others looked at Jessica with astonishment.

"Simple elimination, people." Jessica rolled her eyes. "We've already seen where food, fuel, and supplies are kept. We haven't seen water. We've already visited hexagons under Health, Entry, and Air. That leaves three: Geo, Eco, and Food. Water can't be under Geo, because the geothermal well is there. It has to be under Eco or Food. Plus, there's one thing we haven't seen. Guess what."

"Well, let me see, maybe a facility for waste disposal?" Anna asked after some thought.

"Exactly. No hab can be without one. It wouldn't be under the kitchen—too gross—so it has to be under Eco. Perhaps it gets composted and fed to plants. The only hex left is under Food, next door."

"Oh, wow, simply awesome! I could never have figured all that out. Could you?" Anna asked Nicole and Elizabeth.

"Me, dear?" said Elizabeth. "I'm lucky if I can find my way to the washroom!"

"Same here," said Nicole. "We're lucky to have a prodigy in the family."

"Indeed," said Larry. "It's a relief to know that Jessica can run this place if anything should happen to me."

"Don't be silly!" Jessica said, extremely pleased with the praise, yet as always perversely annoyed with herself for her susceptibility to it, and illogically vexed with the others for her confused emotions. Her face went red, and it took a hug from Elizabeth to calm her internal tumult.

The water hex was very different from the ones they had previously visited. The visitors were prepared for vast aisles filled with containers of water, but what they saw made them gasp in astonishment. The water store turned out to be nothing but a large, nearly circular frozen pond almost right in the center of the hex. An apparatus that looked like a water heater spouted a thick pipe that rose up and passed through the ceiling into the kitchen above.

"How on earth did you manage to find a pond here in the desert?" asked Anna.

"There used to be a tiny waterhole hereabouts," said Jessica. "I saw it on a hike, but it was dry."

"That's the one. We're right on top of it." Larry explained that he had it dug until they hit the bedrock about 200 meters below, and then had the sides lined with bricks and mortar. Finally, it had been filled with a hundred truckloads of water.

He tapped on the water surface with a pole, and the sound reverberated within the hex. "It's frozen now at the surface and will probably freeze right through at some point." He pointed to drilling and ice-cutting equipment scattered around the narrow periphery. "We have machines to break off an ice chunk, melt it, and hoist it upstairs."

"We'll use this water for drinking, cooking, and showering?" Nicole asked.

"Right."

"Thank heavens," said Anna. "I was so afraid that we'd have to drink recycled waste water, you know?"

"Oh Lord, no," said Jessica. "Yuck."

"We might have to do that at some point," Larry admitted. "It all depends on how long we stay here and how much water we use."

"How long will this water last?"

"Long enough, if we're frugal."

"So we won't use waste water for now?"

"Not for drinking, no. But we'll recycle it for the toilets and the hothouse."

"Talking of the hothouse, when do we see the place where we process our wastes?" asked Anna. "Next on our list?"

"Good guess! You're catching on quickly too," said Larry.

"Well, I can't wait," said Anna. "There's nothing like a pile of rotting organic matter to get the ecologist in me all excited."

Unlike the other hexes, which were unheated, the waste recycling hex was warm. Bioreactors marked Bath, Sanitary, or Kitchen stood in the middle, gas cylinders lined the far end of the wall, and a hoist stretched to the ceiling. The bioreactors connected via pipes to what looked like air compressors. A mild stench wafted from the sanitary bioreactors. Larry warned them that the odor would get worse as they collected more human waste.

Jessica covered her nose and mouth with her sleeve, making sounds of disgust. Anna, in contrast, was happily opening the bioreactor to examine their contents. "How long do these reactors take to turn what we eliminate into useable manure?"

"About a year, I'm told," he said. "Provided we have the right mix of microbes, water, and organic matter at the right temperature. Perhaps you could figure out what goes on in there."

"I'd love to."

"The manure from here feeds the plants above?" asked Nicole.

"It's like a complete, closed ecosystem, Mum," said Anna. "We eat the plants, and the waste we eliminate goes back to feeding them. So, in a sense, the same carbon molecules cycle through our bodies repeatedly. We are essentially eating our own waste. Or, as one of the Biosphere dwellers put it, it's as if we are eating ourselves over and over again."

"Yuck!" said Jessica. "You could've spared us the details, Anna!"

Irked by this scornful attitude toward her pet topic, Anna burst out: "Why is it, Jessica, that you can't stand any talk about biological processes? Nature isn't all apples and roses, you know. Things have to die and rot."

"Okay, but why dwell on it?" Jessica retorted.

Anna exhaled and her frown relaxed. "I guess I got carried away a bit," she said, already regretting her loss of composure, afraid that her sister would go into one of her dreaded sulks and make everyone miserable.

"I'm not a big fan of this place either," Larry admitted.

"Oh, do you have a favorite hex, honey?" said Nicole.

"Yes, I do, and it's our next and final stop—the hex under the Geo dome."

The Geo hex resembled the one under Food in that it too had a well in the center, but there the resemblance ended. This chamber was stiflingly hot, the heat emanating from the geothermal bore hole that took up most of the floor space. A narrow bridge allowed Larry and his team to go across the well. Several thick metal pipes painted red or green came through the ceiling from the power plant above and plunged down the well until they vanished into its hidden depths.

Larry explained that the green pipes pumped cold fluid into a heat exchanger 2,500 meters below the surface, where it boiled and emerged as vapor up through the red pipes to drive the generator. "Then it condenses and goes back down."

"Oh, is that how we get our heat?" asked Anna.

"Yes, and our electricity too. This is the most complex and critical part of the Shell."

"Very impressive!" said Nicole. "How long is it designed to last?"

"The equipment should last forever, according to the engineers. As for the well, under normal circumstances it should stay hot practically forever."

"But our circumstances aren't normal."

"Right, so it's hard to tell how long it will stay hot. About twenty years is my guess."

The tour completed, the team found themselves back in the living space at Central. Larry showed Nicole how to work the coffee machine. It was just after 6:00 p.m., and the make-believe sun had now traveled all the way across the dome to hover just above the horizon on the other side.

"Now that you've had the tour, it's time for us to take stock," said Larry. "But let's take a rest break before that."

While Larry went to the console and checked the performance of the different sub-systems, Jessica and Elizabeth went downstairs to their private rooms. Nicole picked up the last edition of the *Simpsonville Weekly* and settled herself on a couch. Anna put on her headphones and listened to a violin concerto by Telemann.

It feels almost like a normal afternoon at home, Anna thought.

11

Meeting

ROUND 7:00 P.M., the Shell's sun set and soft indirect lighting came on, rousing Larry from his reverie. A few minutes later, Jessica and her grandmother came back upstairs. Elizabeth appeared refreshed, as she usually did after an hour of meditation. Larry arranged the couches into an inward-facing circle. He cleared his throat and began speaking.

"Folks, it's time for some planning."

"Oh, no," Anna groaned. "That sounds serious."

"Our holiday can't last forever," her mother said.

"Yes, we should start helping Larry run this place," said Elizabeth.

"Well, since we might be here for some time …," Larry began diffidently.

"How long, do you think?" Nicole asked.

While Larry hesitated, Jessica cut in: "It might take twenty years for the Shroud to thin out. That's how long."

Although the others were aware of the fact to some extent, they flinched at hearing it plainly stated.

"Oh dear …" Elizabeth's voice trailed off.

"Jessica's right," said Larry, his tone gaining confidence. "We might need to be here for that long."

"Twenty years!" said Nicole.

They sat in tense silence for several seconds. "Oh, well," said Anna finally. "It might not *feel* that long. It's so nice here, you know." Nicole and Elizabeth nodded in agreement, but Jessica snorted.

"Nice? What's nice about a prison?" she said.

Larry winced, and Anna turned red. "Don't be ridiculous!" she snapped. She gestured around her. "Does this look like a prison? Did the lovely meal we had taste like prison food?"

Jessica shrugged. "I call it as I see it. There's no freedom. Plush rooms and fancy food don't alter that."

Anna, furious, wanted to yell at her sister: *If you feel that way, you're free to open the door and walk out into the desert, you ungrateful brat.* But she bit her lip and said nothing.

Elizabeth observed the sisters with concern. "Twenty years in a luxurious place in the company of loved ones is not like prison, dear," she admonished Jessica. "Besides, what choice do we have? It's stay here or go outside and die."

"I'm not saying we have a choice. Just that it's not going to be much of a life here."

As if we didn't know! thought Anna.

Larry had recovered his poise. "Jessica has a point," he said. "Compared to what we experienced pre-Shroud, life is going to be restricted. No walks, no shopping, no travel, and no socializing outside our narrow circle."

"No universities, newspapers, seminars, concerts," Jessica added.

"Yes, all that's gone, perhaps forever. I tried to gather as much of the best art and culture as I could in digital form, but we might soon get tired of those. And there won't be anything new from the world outside."

"Exactly like prison," said Jessica.

"But on the other hand, we'll enjoy many advantages here."

"Yes, how lucky we are compared to everyone else," said Anna. "How incredibly lucky to be alive!"

"True, but that's not what I meant," said Larry. "I was comparing our present and future life with our pre-Shroud past. Sure, we're going to lack many of the things that used to enrich our lives, and we face an uncertain future with unknown risks. On the other hand, we'll also be spared much of the inconveniences and dangers that plagued us before—germs, pests, crime, weather, traffic, smog, noise ..."

Nicole nodded. "And no more pressure to earn a living, to compete, to maintain appearances."

"We need to focus on the positives, dear," Elizabeth told Jessica. "Life could be a lot worse."

"And death would be a whole lot worse!" said Anna.

Jessica laughed without mirth. "Sure, it's nice and pleasant here—for now. What if something breaks down tomorrow and leaves us to freeze?"

Anna couldn't hold it in anymore. "Trust you to always look at the dark side!" she shouted. "If you're so clever, why didn't *you* build a shelter instead of whining about what Larry has created?" She had never felt angrier with her sister. Here was her hero, Larry, who had saved them from certain death and brought them to this incredible place, a veritable paradise compared to the moonscape outside, and all her sister could do was gripe. She wished Larry would retaliate and put Jessica in her place, but he never did. She had noticed this before in Larry—he never showed any anger and responded to even the most unfair and nasty verbal attacks with calmness and compassion. Larry had explained his philosophy to her using a modified quotation from George Washington Carver: *Be tender with the young, gentle with the old, protective of the weak, and tolerant of the strong. Because someday in your life you will have been all of these.*

The problem was that Jessica didn't fall into any of these categories. She wasn't a child, but she lacked the maturity of an adult. With her social awkwardness, vulnerabilities, and neuroses, she wasn't strong, but neither was she weak—when it came to things that mattered to her, she could bulldoze anyone who stood in her path. Larry couldn't deal with her at all, Anna felt. He reminded Anna of a character in *The Razor's Edge*, also called Larry, whom the narrator described as "lacking that slight touch of ruthlessness that even the saint needs to earn his halo." Like his fictional namesake, the real Larry was simply too nice.

Nicole and Elizabeth exchanged a concerned look. Larry came to Anna and laid a hand on her shoulder. "Actually, we do need to talk about our long-term survival here," he said. "I was hoping to do it much later, but perhaps it's just as well not to put it off."

Larry returned to his seat and paused to gather his thoughts while Nicole ruffled his hair and kissed him. "A great many things have to work properly for this shelter to be livable," he began.

"Meaning a great many things could fail," said Jessica.

"True. It can get too hot or too cold, too dry or too humid. Carbon dioxide levels could rise to unhealthy levels.

Conversely, oxygen levels could drop too low. The central computer could die. We could run out of food or water. One or more of us might fall ill."

"But I'm sure you've figured out how to deal with all those situations," said Anna.

"I've tried to. Everything here has redundancy and fault-tolerance built into its design. If the main heating unit or power generator fails, an auxiliary one will take over until we fix it. Likewise for the bioreactors and the air purifier. The entire complex has two independent sets of heat, air, and drain pipes, one below and one above ground. So if one set fails, we'll still have the other. The pond shouldn't run dry if we use it frugally, but if its level drops too low we can drink recycled water. As for food, we'll grow some of it in the hothouse, but even if that fails we'll still have enough canned food to last us a long time."

"And if someone gets sick, I can treat them in that fabulous clinic," added Nicole.

"We're fortunate to have the world's best doctor with us," smiled Larry.

"Perhaps the world's *only* doctor now," Nicole said.

"What if *you* fall sick?" Jessica said.

"I'll try not to," replied her mother, preventing another sharp reaction from Anna.

"Jessica has an amazing way of anticipating my remarks," said Larry. "I was going to talk about what happens if Nicole falls ill. Indeed, about when any of us fall ill. But before that, let's take a look at ourselves. I dragged you all here to be with me in this shelter because I love you. But even otherwise I'd still consider us an ideal team. Do you know why?"

"Because we're cute?" Anna said.

"That's actually icing on the cake," smiled Larry. "But let's pretend you were all ugly as sin. I'd still want you and nobody else here for two reasons. The first has to do with demographics. Small, tightly-knit groups survive best when they aren't too homogenous—a group of just twenty-year-old men, for instance, won't do well in survival situations."

"They'd start fighting from day one," said Anna. "So would a bunch of twenty-year-old women, for that matter."

"We're just five, but between us we have both genders and three generations."

"Not to mention the blood of at least three races," Anna said.

"Exactly. In the days to come that diversity might be valuable in ways we can't anticipate."

Nicole nodded. "There's something in that."

"And your second reason?" Jessica asked.

"It has to do with diversity of a different sort. Each of you brings a unique and essential skill. Nicole's inclusion needs no justification—any of us could fall ill at any time. Anna, we need you because you alone can understand this ecosystem and keep it healthy. Jessica, your computer and mechanical skills are going to be vital when things start to break down, as they inevitably will with time."

"I guess I'm the deadweight here," Elizabeth said ruefully.

"Deadweight?" Larry scoffed. "You might be the most important member of our team."

"Me? I'm no good with plants or machines or computers," said Elizabeth. "I'm not even that much of a cook."

"Your dishes are the only ones I like, Grandma," said Jessica. Elizabeth smiled at her granddaughter and pinched her cheek gently. Jessica couldn't stand much physical contact, but she allowed her grandmother to caress her once in a while. Elizabeth was so warm and gentle that even Jessica, with her touchiness and frayed nerves, found her soothing.

"I'm a pretty fair cook, and so is Anna," said Larry. "It's not your cooking, Elizabeth, but your professional skills that we'll need."

"What skills? The only work I ever did was as a spiritual counselor."

"That's exactly what I'm talking about. You have an incredible ability to help people develop healthy emotions and relationships."

"You are very kind, but what use will that be here?"

Larry got up and took a quick stroll around his couch, almost bumping into the incense bubble which was now emitting fragrances of moonflower and evening primrose. He returned to his seat. "Elizabeth, the biggest danger we face is not some mechanical or supply issue, or even a medical emergency. What I'm really worried about is how well we'll all get along, being confined to this tiny space with only each other for company and a dead planet outside. We might start to get on each other's nerves."

Nicole shook her head. "We've had a couple of scenes, true. But we'll settle down."

"I hope so," said Larry. "But what if one of us goes crazy and tries to wreck the place?"

"Get out of here, Larry!" said Anna. "That can never happen to us." And after a pause she added: "Can it?"

Support for Larry's position came, unexpectedly, from Jessica. "Remember Biosphere?" she said. "By the time it ended its residents were like cats and dogs."

Larry nodded. "That's the kind of thing I mean. I'm not saying it will happen here, but we need to be prepared for it. You, Elizabeth, are our emotional insurance."

"Exactly!" said Anna. "You're always underrating yourself, Grandma."

"Yes, you are," said Jessica. "You're smarter than any of us."

Elizabeth blushed. "You're all so sweet to me. I'm terribly lucky."

A short pause ensued. "All right, it's clear that each of us has a role," said Nicole at length. "But we know so little about this place. How will we be able to help run it?"

Larry cleared his throat. "Okay, let's start with me. I'm your generalist, your jack of all trades. I know a little bit about everything here. I know how to turn things on or off and check if they're working. But if there's a big problem—I don't know how to fix things. On my own, I can't run this place for more than a few months. But we have to keep things running for years, and some things *will* fail."

"Of course we'll help," said Anna. "You've done so much, it's time we all chipped in, right?" She turned to the others, who all nodded. "Even if we screw things up."

Larry smiled. "You'll learn fast, and in no time you'll be telling me how to run this place."

"Don't hold your breath." Anna laughed.

"Very well, let's get started." Larry went over to a console and returned with a layout of the Shell. "Okay, this is what we need to do—each of us needs to master one dome and be familiar with another."

"So we'll have a backup person for each module in case the expert can't do their job?"

"Precisely. Providing what engineers call fault tolerance."

The women studied the plan they had already memorized during their tour. "So who does what?" Jessica asked.

"Jessica, I'd like you to be in charge of Air, with me as your backup. I, in turn, will take charge of Geo, with Anna as backup. Anna, you're in charge of Eco, with your mother under your command. Nicole, you're of course responsible for Health. Elizabeth will be your support. Elizabeth, you're in charge of Food, and Jessica will be your sous-chef."

As he spoke, Larry set up a whiteboard on a stand, drew a floor plan of the Wheel, and wrote their names on the various domes:

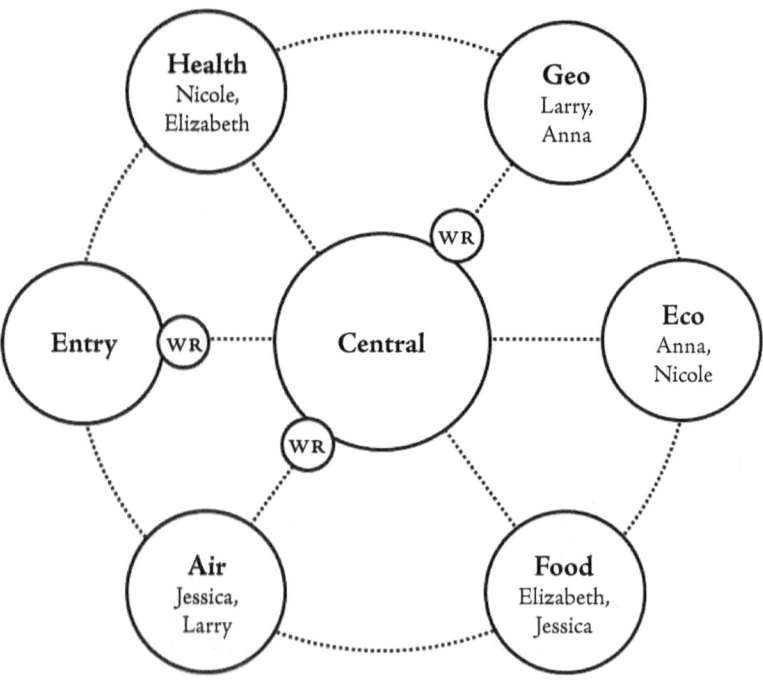

They all gazed at Larry's diagram for a couple of minutes.

"It might make more sense to have Anna or Jessica as my backup," Nicole said, "but I guess they'll be needed elsewhere. Other than that, it seems reasonable." Elizabeth and Anna agreed.

Jessica frowned. "I'd rather back you up in the power plant. Anna's more of a kitchen person."

"Here's my reasoning," responded Larry. "We'll all spend a lot of time in each of our two domes. I've planned it so that each of us will see a different person in our two domes. Since I'm supporting you in Air, I didn't want you supporting me in Power, because then we'd see only each other most of the time. That would limit our interactions with the others."

Jessica bit her lip, but Elizabeth nodded in agreement. "It's probably a good idea to avoid such cliques," she told her granddaughter. "That's something I learned when counseling troubled families. Unless each member of a group has a close and independent relationship with each of the others, there is a risk of us-versus-them mindsets emerging."

"Like what happened in Biosphere," Anna reminded her sister.

Jessica was unswayed. "I want to choose what I do, not have it shoved down my throat." Getting no support from the others, she added: "Can't we at least vote on it?"

Larry sighed. "Jessica, once again you compel me to discuss something that I wanted to avoid or at least put off." He paused and took a deep breath. "The answer to your question is no. Not yet, anyway."

Jessica flushed. "What? That's … that's bloody unfair!"

"I'm sorry. For the moment you don't get to vote on anything."

Jessica turned furiously to the other women. "Did you hear that? We get no say on anything, it seems. And you all just sit there and smile!"

"Jessica, dearest—" Elizabeth began, but Jessica cut in: "This is undemocratic!"

Larry, red in the face himself, took a couple of deep breaths, and spoke with a new steely tone in his voice: "You're assuming that this is a democracy. It isn't. Until you've been here long enough to understand how this place works, you'll have to let me make the decisions. I'll consult you if necessary and listen to your concerns. But I'll make the final call."

Jessica wiped angry tears on her sleeve. "But who appointed you leader? Why can't it be someone else? Grandma, for example?"

Larry looked Jessica straight in the eye and spoke with calm deliberation. "I'm the leader because I designed this place. I made some blunders and I failed to take you all into my confidence. But for the most part my judgment has been sound. You can't deny that. I took the Shroud's threat seriously while most of the world ignored it. I figured out what type of shelter would work the best. Then I hired the world's best scientists, architects, engineers, and workers to build it." He paused for a long breath. "I know this place better than any of you, at least for now. In short, my leadership is the best hope for our survival."

"I wouldn't even dream of questioning your leadership, Larry!" said Anna, frowning at her younger sister. To her, from the day they first met, he could do no wrong. Yet Jessica seemed unable to show any respect or gratitude toward him. Anna wondered if things would have been different if Larry had been a more flawed individual—an alcoholic, say, or a hypochondriac. Perhaps then her sister would have been able to relate to him better.

"Thanks for your support, Anna," said Larry. "To keep this place running, dozens of decisions need to be made daily— how much food or water to consume, how much each module should be heated, and so on. A democracy would imply that we're all equally qualified to make these choices. But we're not. Until you've all had a chance to learn how this facility works, I'm the most qualified. Of course, the situation will change. In time, some of you will surpass me in your knowledge of the systems here. Or I could fall ill. Then I'll gladly hand over the reins."

"But how?" said Jessica. "Each of us will be trapped in our own little bubble. How will we learn about the rest?"

"Good point. We need to have a routine of regular classes, where each of us educates the others. I'll set the ball rolling and tell you a little bit about everything here. As your knowledge of your module grows and exceeds mine, each of you can teach classes as well. In time, we should all develop at least a working knowledge of the entire complex and all its modules. At that point I'll happily share the decision making with you."

Larry paused for a second and continued. "Jessica's question about democracy reminds me of a larger point I want to make. The past few days have been so crazy, and our arrival here has been so stressful, that we may not have had time to realize the extremely unusual situation we're in. As far as we know, there may be nobody left alive but us. And as Jessica pointed out, the world outside is beyond our reach now, perhaps forever, and we're restricted to this relatively tiny space. The normal rules of human society are no longer relevant." Larry paused to let this sink in. "Most of those rules, like freedom, modesty, privacy—they evolved to serve large populations living in large spaces, which is the opposite of our situation here. Here in the Shell, survival takes precedence over almost every other consideration. Just as we had to suspend our feelings of modesty during the shower before we moved in here, we may have to reimagine other norms and principles that we might have taken for granted in the world outside."

Larry took a deep breath and added with slow emphasis: "We'll never do anything evil or hurtful. But if our survival hinges on it, we must be prepared to do what would previously have been distasteful, taboo, or even criminal."

12
Journals

THE REST OF the evening passed without drama. After a relatively cheerful supper, the family gathered back at Central and sat in companionable silence for a while. One by one they began to yawn.

Larry cleared his throat. "Before we retire, I need a small favor."

Anna looked at him quizzically. "What type of favor? Distasteful, taboo, criminal, or all of the above?"

Larry chuckled. "No, no, just a little thing. I hope all of us survive the Shroud and go on to lead happy lives outside. But in case none of us makes it, it would be nice to leave some written record of our existence here."

"You mean, like, keep a diary?" Anna asked.

"I hate diaries." Jessica said. "Waste of time and energy."

Larry looked at her thoughtfully. "If you feel so strongly about it, I won't insist."

Nicole suggested: "What if we didn't write an entry every day, but only on special occasions? Like once a year?" She looked inquiringly at her daughter.

Jessica shrugged her shoulders. "I could live with that."

After some discussion, the family agreed that each would keep a private journal in which they would write entries on just a few occasions—that evening; after completing their first year; and at the end of every fifth year of their Shell existence.

We'll be lucky to reach three entries, Larry thought, but he said nothing except to thank Jessica for her cooperation.

She rolled her eyes. "Good thing the journal's private. You may not like what I write."

Larry's Journal

Today was eventful indeed. Against all odds, we managed to reach the Shell safely. Everything here is working as it's supposed to. I showed the Millers around the Wheel and the Honeycomb. They seem to like the complex, although Jessica had some valid questions. Lunch was a success, but the meeting in the evening didn't go as I'd expected. I was planning to say a few encouraging things, tell them how glad I am and how lucky I feel that they're here with me, and discuss our future here in broad terms. Naïvely, I thought relief and gratitude would prevail, and the meeting would have a more upbeat, celebratory tone, despite the unspeakable tragedy that has been visited on the planet.

As it turned out, I got a lot of push back from Jessica from the get-go. She's highly intelligent and raised some valid concerns. I might have been better off consulting her and the others as I was building the Shell, but it's too late now for that. As she rightly (if harshly) pointed out, I could have tried harder to save more people, including the ones that built the Shell. In a way, I'm lucky I'm an only child with parents who died early—I didn't have any immediate family to worry about. But all my friends, their partners, their kids … it breaks my heart that they're all probably dead. Could I have done more for them? Perhaps. But in my defense, I did speak to a few of them about building a shelter from the approaching calamity. But nobody seemed interested. Even Fred—who knew more about the Shroud than anyone else—rejected the idea as too little, too late. What was I to do? And now that it's all in the past, how should we proceed? Wallow in guilt and despair, or embrace the life that lies ahead?

Then Jessica raised some thorny issues about roles and leadership that I was hoping to address later. Although it caught me off-guard, I think I managed to respond in a thoughtful and respectful manner. Perhaps I sounded dictatorial when I spoke about my role as leader, but I had no choice when she challenged me directly. I'm hoping that all this is just some healthy skepticism on her part, and that she doesn't really question my judgment at every point. That would be highly discordant. I'm hoping for a long, harmonious existence for all of us here.

It's too soon to have a revolt on my hands. I don't even know how I'd deal with it. Even great leaders, including peace lovers like Gandhi and Mandela, were accused of being ruthless with their opponents—maybe that's how they achieved their power and influence. But I love Jessica like my own daughter. How can I be ruthless with someone I love?

Anna's Journal

Oh my God! What an incredible day it's been!! This morning, as I was freezing to death in our basement, I had given up all hope. The sun had vanished forever, and everything around was dead or dying. Saddest of all, we'd seen no sign of Larry—I didn't realize until then how much I cared for him. Even at death's door, his absence grieved me. And then the most marvelous thing happened—a knock on the door, and who should it be but our beloved, peerless Larry himself? At that instant, I knew there was hope. Larry, you are and will always be my hero! Who else but you could rescue your family from a dying planet and whisk them away to safety and comfort?

And what an amazing place this is! I can't even begin to imagine all the brainpower and effort that Larry has put into it. Both the Wheel and the Honeycomb are incredible. I think I love every inch of it, even the stuffy Power dome! But my favorite, of course, is Eco. What a collection of plants! And how sweet of Larry to grow flowers there, all the ones I love! Jessica gave him grief for that, poor guy.

I can't understand why Jessica is so anti-Larry. If it weren't for him, we'd be twice dead already. Perhaps she doesn't really enjoy life and is mad at him for dragging her back from the grave. Sounds crazy, but how else to explain her relentless hostility? And Larry, poor thing, doesn't know how to tackle her—he's tried being nice, respectful, considerate—but she doesn't give an inch. Finally, at the meeting today, he was forced to go against character and put his foot down, and I think it hurt him far more than her. Poor, dear Larry. I hope Jessica doesn't destroy him.

I must seem heartless for dwelling on my own little problems instead of bemoaning the terrible fate that has struck the billions who walked this planet. My only experience of grief was when daddy deserted us; for a year I cried buckets, never smiled, and still choke up at the memory. But the death of billions from the Shroud? I can't feel it yet. Perhaps I'm too numb. I think we have neurological mechanisms that allow us to feel and cope with the loss of a loved one, to mourn for them. But how do you mourn an entire planet?

Nicole's Journal

The world is gone. I don't know what to say. I don't think I have the vocabulary to deal with something of this magnitude. Almost anything I can say to express my horror and grief seems to be incredibly trite and inadequate. Perhaps it's best to not try to express the inexpressible and focus on practical matters.

I should never have doubted Larry—all this time, while I suspected him of losing interest in us or worse, he was toiling on our behalf! He was building and perfecting this place, all for us. The planet outside is dead, but in here, with Larry, I think we have a fighting chance to survive the Shroud. Too bad that Jessica's always needling him, but he loves her, and knows that she too loves him in her own way. I'm sure they'll find a way to get along.

My main concern is keeping everyone healthy. Only problem—I'm a surgeon. Give me a perforated appendix and I know how to fix it. But preventive care isn't something I've provided since my residency years ago. What should I be worrying about? Infectious diseases? Vitamin D deficiency, because natural sunlight is absent? Bone loss? Tooth decay? Eye problems? Too many questions. I hope the computer database will have some answers. Larry says it contains every medical paper ever published!

Minor gripe: Larry, poor guy, doesn't know squat about women's needs. He has provided sanitary pads to last us just six months, whereas he could have got us menstrual cups instead! So once the pads run out, we'll have to improvise. The clothes he got for us are ill-fitting, uncomfortable, and ugly, but we have the ones we came in with (now 100% sterilized and bug-free after their deep-freeze in Entry). And on the positive side the robes he gave us are well-fitting, comfortable, warm, and practical. He seems to have a reasonable supply of them, and shoes too, so we'll manage fine.

The gym in the Health dome looks really nice. I should perhaps start everyone on a regular exercise program. I hope Jessica won't be too resistant, she hates working out. But exercise and fitness are not optional here. How am I going to force her? Perhaps Mum can talk to her. Come to think of it, she too needs to start working out. She's overweight. We don't want her to become diabetic or have a stroke.

Jessica's Journal

Well, we didnt die—yet. Yes, we owe Larry our non-death—that word is more approp for our existence here than *life*. Ill grant that. Anna thinks Im mean & ungrateful bcs I keep challenging him. Excuse me for not sharing her crush on him. Obviously, hes sweated bullets creating this place & taken great risks—mostly unnecessary—to bring us here. So why am I not feeling overjoyed, brimming w/ gratitude, ready to bow down before him as my savior?

Because Im not sure life in this bubble is worth living. Ok, my old life wasnt perfect, but at least I had my museums, libraries, activities. And what to look forward to here? Hours with noisy machinery in the air dome with Larry? Hes nice enough, but bland as beeswax. Hang out in Central w/ Anna? She bores me to distraction. Mums nice, but beyond worrying about my health she doesnt have much to say. The only 1

I like being with is Grandma. Maybe makes sense for me to work with her in Food dome, after all.

Perhaps shdnt have attacked Larry. Hes well-meaning & obviously thinks he has our best interests. But when I myself dont know what my best interests are, how can he?

Contrary to what Anna might think, I dont hate Larry. Might even be a bit fond. But a little of him goes a long way for me. Will try harder to avoid butting heads with him, but hes so stuffy & pompous I cant help myself!

Elizabeth's Journal

How can I ever find words to describe the horror that has befallen our beloved planet Earth? To think of all those billions of innocent beautiful lives snuffed out like candles in a storm! All the love and toil and heartbreak of a thousand generations destroyed in the snap of a celestial finger! My heart brims over with sorrow. Yet, somehow, in the midst of this horror and sorrow, I'm alive and am united with the people I love the most. Deep inside I will continue to weep for my dead planet, but my energies from this day forward I will devote to the welfare of my loved ones.

It's a true miracle that we're all safe and sound. What a blessing it's been that Larry came into our lives! And to think that if it weren't for the Shroud he would never have come to Simpsonville to look for a place to build the Shell—and never met Nicole! He is so much like George—the nobility, the gentleness, the thoughtfulness—but without my poor husband's weakness for food and drink. I lost George far too soon, and dear Nicole, though she won't admit it, never fully recovered from that. And being dumped by her beloved Philip when Anna and Jessica were just children didn't help her at all. It wasn't until Larry came along that I saw her happy smile again.

It's a blessing to be together, all alive, unhurt, and in such pleasant surroundings. But I do worry about how we'll all get along as the weeks, months, and years go by. I already see friction between my granddaughters that I never really noticed before. Poor Jessica, she's always had a hard time with authority, ever since her dear daddy walked out one day and never came back. Although no one could be more different from Philip (charming but deceitful) than Larry (kind, gentle, but strait-laced), I guess she associates them, and at some level distrusts Larry and is unwilling to open herself to his love. Or maybe I have it wrong, and it's because he's so different from her father that she's unable to accept him. Perhaps she's also jealous of her sister's close bond with Larry. She doesn't realize how heartbreaking it was for Anna as well to be abandoned by her father, how fragile she is beneath that surface sprightliness and enthusiasm, and how much she needs Larry's kindness and strength. Maybe one of these days the two girls will have a heart-to-heart talk and realize that they aren't so different from each other after all. It's just that each one deals with her loss differently—Anna by seeking love, Jessica by recoiling from it.

13

Day Two

EVERYONE SLUMBERED LIKE the dead that night, physically exhausted and emotionally drained, overwhelmed by their situation. They slept on the floor, snuggled together on thick Persian carpets and under a large down duvet, each wearing a fur-lined hood in addition to their daytime clothes. The purpose of the sleeping arrangement became clear when Larry turned the heat down and let the temperature drop gradually to minus 10 degrees Celsius. The energy saved, he said, would extend the life of the geothermal well by a year or two. Thanks to the masks, carpets, and duvet, as well as their close proximity to one another inside the tent, the sleepers stayed warm. Anna slept in the middle, snugly ensconced between Larry and Elizabeth, snuggling up to one or the other during the course of the night. Jessica slept on the other side of Elizabeth at one end of the tent, and Nicole slept on the other extremity, her head on Larry's shoulder.

Around 5:00 a.m. the heating came on, and, a little later, gentle artificial sunlight started streaming in. Fresh morning scents of lilac and pine wafted in from the fragrance bowl, and somewhere above them an electronic cardinal began wooing its mate. Larry was the first to wake up, as he often was. He always slept soundly in any circumstance, position, or company—thanks to a combination of hard work, good habits, and a clear conscience, he claimed—but even he had enjoyed deeper-than-normal slumber. He lay still, unwilling to disturb his bedmates, and incapable of disengaging himself from their tight embrace without doing so.

Eventually Nicole stirred, half-awake, and rolled over to the other side. She too was a good sleeper, though she never got enough rest because of her late hours at the hospital. Always on call, her deep early morning slumber after a late-night shift was often interrupted by a beeping pager. (Her medical specialty should have been called *on-call-ogy*, Anna used to say.) Late hours and work pressures were a thing of the past now, she mused. She felt immensely relieved, but her relief was tinged with a feeling of uncertainty about how she would fill the long hours that had suddenly opened up to her. She rolled back, now fully awake, and kissed Larry on his cheek. She had always found it wonderful to wake up next to him. Though her physical desire for him was never as intense and urgent as it had been for Philip—her chemistry with Larry seemed to be based on affection rather than sensuality—her joy in snuggling up to him only got better over time. It augured well for their old age, she thought.

"Time to get up, honey," she whispered, her lips scratching against his stubble.

"Yes," he whispered back, gently brushing stray wisps of her hair off his face. "There's lots to do, and I'm already peckish."

"Me too. Must be something in the air here. Come on, let's get up."

"I'd love to, but what do I do about this boa constrictor?" said Larry, pointing to Anna. She was the poorest sleeper of them all. She woke up at the slightest sounds, and when she did she struggled to fall back asleep. Unpleasant dreams often troubled her. Some of them were so disturbing that she would go and seek comfort in the arms of her grandmother. Only the two of them knew about her problem. Nicole slept too soundly to notice, and Jessica didn't pay much attention to what anyone else did. Whenever Larry was around the house, however, Anna slept better, and her dreams were neutral or pleasant. Now, with Larry right next to her and with Elizabeth's warm, comforting presence on the other side, she slept like a baby for the first time in years.

At that point, as if sensing Larry's wish, Anna released him, rolled over, and coiled herself around her grandmother. Elizabeth too was awake but unable to get up because Jessica was lying on her arm. Now her hopes of getting up soon were further diminished. Nicole grinned at her rueful expression. Larry sprang up, and soon the two of them were snuggled together on a couch, sipping freshly-brewed coffee.

"Let's give them half an hour," said Nicole.

They didn't have to wait that long. Perhaps it was the aroma of the coffee or the loss of one of her sleep-mates, but it took Anna only a few more minutes to open her eyes. Elizabeth then got up, no longer able to lie still, awakening Jessica in the process. Soon they too were sipping coffee.

After a quick wash they followed Larry to the Food dome. Turned on remotely from Central, the oven welcomed them with the warm, yeasty odor of a reheated wholegrain loaf. Breakfast was simple: toast, eggs, fruit, and a drink.

"Delicious," said Elizabeth, after enjoying her first bite of a peach. Jessica devoured a mango with great relish, while the others ate slices of orange and apple. The fruit bowls were emptying fast.

"Glad you like them," said Larry, replying to a compliment about the fruit. "I'm afraid our own fruit will need more time to ripen. Any idea how long, Anna?"

"Hard to tell under these conditions," she replied.

"Take a guess?"

"Well …" Anna put her fork down and stood up. "Let's go and see."

The others followed her to the Eco dome. Anna strode up to the peach tree and tapped on its trunk. "I think this one will bear fruit in, like, four to six weeks." She walked around, examining the other trees. "These citrus trees will need another month or so after that. These two, the mango and avocado, haven't even started flowering, so that's going to be six months at least."

"What are those?" asked Nicole, pointing to a cluster of straight-stemmed plants with large, complex leaves.

"Papayas," said Anna. "They're still young, but I think they're a fast-growing dwarf variety. Give them a year or two. They'll bear so much fruit that we'll be all papaya-ed out."

"So we won't have any fruit shortage?" asked Larry.

"Not once the trees mature," Anna said. "Full marks on your choice of plants, Larry! With such a variety, we should have some fruit or another most of the time. And vegetables too, from what I can see. Between the beans, peppers, tomatoes, and onions, we'll keep our kitchen humming nonstop."

"Wonderful!" said Nicole. "How about bread, Larry?"

"We've more than a thousand loaves in cold storage. Large ones. If we eat one a day, we're good for three years."

"No bread after that?" asked Jessica, raising an eyebrow.

"We'll make our own. We've several tons of flour in storage."

"Won't it go stale?"

"Not in this cold."

"You've got yeast to ferment the dough, right?" asked Anna.

"You bet, and some sourdough starter as well. In fact, we've nearly a hundred varieties of them. And a whole bunch of yogurt cultures too. Hopefully some of them will remain viable."

"You think of everything!" said Anna.

Larry smiled. "I wish! Let me tell you the things I forgot. Fresh eggs and milk, for instance. We've only enough for a few more weeks. We do have loads of powdered stuff, though."

"I'm sure we can manage great with them," Anna said.

"Our stock of fresh fish is limited, too. Only tinned fish after that."

"I've eaten worse."

"And even that was hard to get because the organic food places don't usually carry many animal products."

"Couldn't you find some in the supermarket?" asked Jessica.

"Yes, but I was avoiding the commercial stuff."

"Foolish paranoia!" said Jessica. "Nothing wrong with commercial foods. If there was, we'd all be dying like flies." This was a point of discord with her sister, who wouldn't touch anything that wasn't marked "organic." Evidently, Larry had bought into Anna's philosophy in that matter. "Isn't that right, Mum?"

Nicole nodded. "In the short term, I wouldn't worry. But commercial tinned stuff is often loaded with salt, sugar, preservatives, etc. So in the long-term they might be unhealthy."

"Couldn't we have raised our own livestock?" Jessica said. "Imagine eating fresh eggs, yogurt, and cheese every day!"

"Perhaps it's not easy to keep animals here," suggested Elizabeth.

"The Biospherans did that, didn't they?" Jessica asked her sister.

"Well, they had goats and fish," Anna said. "But they were in sunny Arizona."

"Why can't we do that here?"

"Well, we could've raised a goat or two, maybe. But the fishpond would freeze solid, right?"

Larry nodded. "Unless we diverted some energy to heat it." He turned to Jessica. "I did think about keeping livestock. But I was worried about germs and parasites."

"Zero risk of that," Jessica said. "New Zealand has—had—more sheep than people, and they did just fine!" She looked at her mother for agreement.

Nicole shrugged. "Hard to say. Livestock are generally safe. But this is such a new environment, you can't tell what might happen."

"But what *could* happen?"

"The germs might mutate. A flu virus could jump from a fowl to a goat and mix with another flu virus there. The hybrid could infect us. It's improbable, but not impossible. And some animals carry parasites."

"Ugh!" said Anna. "Once you introduce a parasite like a tapeworm into our ecosystem you'll find it almost impossible to get rid of it. Unless you douse the place with chemicals."

"Oh, let it go," Jessica growled. "I'm outvoted, as always."

"You never cared much for farm animals anyway."

Jessica picked up an apple and opened her mouth to take a bite, then changed her mind and put it back in the bowl. "Farm animals I can take or leave, but it would've been nice to have a puppy."

Jessica loved dogs. In their undemanding and uncritical company, she found a warmth she rarely experienced in human relationships. Almost pathologically revolted by human odors and bodily fluids—and therefore highly uncomfortable with the sleeping arrangement in the Shell—she had no such revulsion for her slobbering, smelly canine friends. She never got tired of romping with them, allowing them to gnaw on her wrists and tear her clothes to shreds. She would emerge from each doggie session with her face aglow and her mood elevated. For the rest of the day, she would be as close to good natured as she could. But she rarely got this opportunity. Her "pet peeve" was that she couldn't have dogs at home—both Nicole and Anna were allergic to them.

"Yes, it would've been really nice," agreed Larry, an animal lover himself. "Perhaps a St. Bernard or two, and a bunch of spaniels."

"Nothing like a litter of puppies frisking around to keep our spirits up," said Elizabeth. "It's a much better remedy for low spirits than any counseling session. Fortunately, people didn't know that, or I'd have been out of a job."

"I love dogs too, though I'm allergic," said Anna. "But our food here is limited, and they'd be competing with us for it."

"We couldn't spare some scraps for a puppy? Are we that selfish?"

Anna clicked her tongue. "Look, this place is designed for our own survival. It's not a Noah's Ark for other species, you know."

Jessica sighed. "Yeah, maybe pets are a luxury."

It was a rare concession, Elizabeth noted. Usually, Jessica stuck to her guns in any argument, unswayed by facts or logic. She gave her granddaughter a swift, pleased glance. *I hope this is a sign of things to come,* she thought.

14

Schedule

WHEN THEY FINISHED breakfast and returned to Central, Larry passed around a printed schedule to everyone.

"This is a rough daily program I've come up with," he said. "Tell me what you think."

6 : wake up
6.30 : gym and shower
8.30 : breakfast
9.30–11.30 : work, session 1
11.30–1.30 : work, session 2
1.30 : lunch
2.30–5 : classes
5–7 : cleaning chores and personal time
7 : dinner
8–10 : family time
10 : sleep

"Looks rather regimented," Nicole said, "but I guess we'll need some routine."

Larry nodded. "Yes. But before finalizing it, I'd like your input."

"Aren't you supposed to be, like, the evil dictator who listens to no one?" Anna teased.

Larry smiled sheepishly. "I didn't say I won't listen to suggestions."

"The work sessions will be in the outer domes, right?" asked Nicole.

"That's right, we'll go to our respective domes. But never alone. None of us should venture outside Central alone."

"For safety?" asked Anna.

"Yes. A lot of thought has gone into the Shell's design, but there are still too many potential risks." He rummaged inside a drawer under the main console and fished out a set of small pen-shaped devices with blinking blue LED tips. "These are communicators," he said. "They work wirelessly within domes and use cables between domes. Carry one of these on you at all times. Click the red button and everyone will hear what you say, until you click it off." He handed the gadgets around. For a few seconds Anna played with hers, clicking it on and off and speaking nonsense words into it until everyone dissolved into giggles.

"Who goes to which work sessions?" asked Jessica.

"I didn't think it through yet. Since we have five teams, we should be able to send a team to each dome for one of the two sessions. This is what I mean," he said and drew the following table on the wall:

	Health	Geo	Eco	Food	Air
	Nicole	Larry	Anna	Elizabeth	Jessica
	Elizabeth	Anna	Nicole	Jessica	Larry
Session 1					
Session 2					

"It won't work!" said Jessica.

"Why not?"

"Logic."

"We have five teams and five domes to work on. Where's the problem?"

"The teams overlap."

"I don't understand."

Jessica rolled her eyes. "Think of it this way. Two sessions, five domes. So one of the sessions should have at least three teams working simultaneously. But each team has two members and there are only five of us."

"Ah, I get it. At any given session, we can't have more than two and a half teams."

Comprehension dawned on the others as well. "Very clever, Jessica!" said Anna. "Beats me how you solve complex logic problems in your head."

"Yes, well done," said Larry. "Looks like I'll have to break the no-single-person rule for myself. Let's say that we do Health and Air in session one, and Geo, Eco, and Food in session two. I'll spend half my Geo time solo, and fetch Anna to join me for the second half. We'll escort Nicole, Anna's Eco partner, to wherever she wants to go."

"I could probably go and help out in the kitchen a bit," said Nicole.

"That won't work, either," Jessica said with a touch of smugness.

"No?"

"No."

"Could you explain?"

"Where would you put Anna in session one? She has to be in either Eco, her major, or Geo, her minor, right? You'll be with me in Air, so she can't join you in Geo, and Mum will be in Health, and can't join Anna in Eco!"

"Got me again!" said Larry. He thought for a moment and drew this new schedule:

	Health	Geo	Eco	Food	Air
Session 1	Nicole Elizabeth Anna				Jessica Larry
			Anna Elizabeth Nicole		
Session 2		Larry	Anna Nicole	Elizabeth Jessica	
		Larry Anna		Elizabeth Jessica Nicole	

"How about this?" he said.

"Cuts our time in Health short, but we won't have much work there," said Nicole. "So works for me."

"Okay with me too," said Anna. "I wasn't planning to become a medical expert, but hey, whatever works."

Everyone turned toward Jessica, half-expecting her to spot yet another flaw, but she merely shrugged and said: "Inelegant, but at least the logic is sound this time."

Elizabeth noted that the schedule didn't put the two sisters together at any time. She wondered if this was a conscious choice on Larry's part or just an accidental fallout of the complicated logic. She debated raising the point but decided to let it go. *Keeping the two girls apart will minimize potential conflicts, at least for now,* she thought.

15

Routine

LARRY'S COMPLICATED SCHEDULE worked surprisingly well. By the second week, life at the Shell settled into a smooth routine. Nicole was pleased to see that everyone took their morning workout seriously. Anna and Larry had always been keen on fitness, so their enthusiastic participation was only to be expected. But neither Jessica nor Elizabeth had previously shown much interest in working out. To her pleasant surprise, they participated willingly, if not eagerly. As time went by, both got trimmer, while the others continued to stay fit. *At least no one will fall sick due to lack of exercise,* Nicole thought.

The work sessions ran smoothly as well. At the Air dome, Jessica initially found the equipment hideously complicated, with its tangle of pipes and gauges, and the manuals practically unreadable. She returned to Central from work each day scowling, with her clothes reeking of lubricant, her face streaked with tears, and her hands chapped and bleeding. But things improved as the days went by. Larry taught her whatever he knew. Building on that, and painstakingly figuring out the purpose of each motor, conduit, or gauge, Jessica soon began to feel more at ease. Larry encouraged her to do the basic maintenance tasks, and within a few months she was more adept at them than he was. Knowing her love of solitude, he stayed out of her way as much as possible and eventually let her do all the maintenance by herself.

Soon, Jessica started to develop a feeling of ownership toward the Air dome. She found the hum of machinery and the smell of lubricant oddly soothing. Her greasy stains and callused hands no longer bothered her. On the contrary, they attested to her growing skill as a mechanic. Machines were wonderful, she felt. Once you learned how they worked, all it took was a squirt of grease or a twist of a wrench to keep them happy. They rewarded your efforts by running smoothly. You didn't have to make conversation with them. They had no feelings to hurt, and they never hurt yours.

At the Eco dome, Anna was equally happy. With her mother and grandmother lending a hand, she accomplished a lot in the hour or two she spent there each day. She couldn't get enough of the trimming and digging and fertilizing and everything else that created the miracle of plant life. After the first few days, traces of soil clung to her fingernails and the musky, peaty smell of the dome that permeated her hair and skin wouldn't go away even when she showered. She didn't care about it, nobody else minded, and Elizabeth thought it lent her an earthy charm that complemented her fragile beauty.

Anna's only complaint was that the work session went by far too quickly. Since she'd never had a chance to work with so many different plants before, she had much to learn. What was the optimal ambient temperature? Citrus and other temperate-zone trees liked it cool and dry, but avocado, mango, and papaya trees preferred tropical conditions. Was there a climate setting they would all be happy with? Larry had been unable to procure bees, so some of the flowering plants would need to be hand-pollinated. Anna had never done that before and knew it wasn't easy to do. The persimmon tree was female, according to the label. How to get it to bear fruit? She'd read of a method, but never tried it before. And there were the bioreactors. In theory, the manure from them should make great fertilizer, but in reality one had to take into account so many other factors— manure composition, plant variety, soil chemistry, and so on. The soil itself would need to be regularly supplemented with vermicompost made from kitchen waste using earthworms, which might need special care to keep going generation after generation.

Figuring all these things out was completely up to her now. "As the only green-thumbed person here, you're in charge," Larry told her. It was thrilling to enjoy such a great responsibility, though sometimes it weighed heavily. To reassure her, Larry pointed out that, at worst, some plants might die, and when this happened she could simply plant new ones. Until the saplings matured, the family would have to fall back on tinned stuff. "It's a minor nuisance, that's all," Larry told her, "so don't lose any sleep over your plants."

The folks at the Health dome had a pleasant time, if not a very productive or eventful one. Elizabeth got a chance to spend time with her daughter, something that had been hard to do after the granddaughters were born. Elizabeth and Nicole had always been on good terms but had drifted apart over the years. It came as a shock to the older woman to realize how much of a stranger her daughter had become.

Nicole's natural reserve had only deepened after her father's death. She had opened up a bit when Philip came into her life—until his subsequent desertion shut her down even further. She had worked even harder at the hospital. She had spent no more time at home than necessary, leaving her mother to raise her daughters. There had never been any tears or emotional outbursts; Nicole wasn't one to wear her emotions on her sleeve. Gradually, Elizabeth had begun to believe that her daughter's emotional wounds had healed. Her belief had only been reinforced when Nicole had fallen in love with Larry and found a new zest for life.

Now, however, their situation was altered. Torn from her hospital work, and in the Health dome, temporarily away from the company of Larry and the girls, Nicole couldn't help revealing her feelings. She remained brisk and matter-of-fact; there wasn't, and would never be, anything touchy-feely about her. Nevertheless, Elizabeth discerned a vulnerable side under her daughter's competent, efficient persona. Evidently the grief of her father's death and the pain of her husband's abandonment still remained; Larry's love had soothed but not healed those wounds. Few could resist Elizabeth's warm, giving, understanding nature—Anna adored her, Larry respected her, and even Jessica, otherwise dour and prickly, never found fault with her. Nicole alone had resisted Elizabeth's warmth; now, however, she too came under its benign influence. Gradually, the two women bonded like never before.

Harmony prevailed in the Food dome as well. Jessica had always found her grandmother's presence soothing. Now she enjoyed working with her to prepare their daily lunch. After wrestling with huge, greasy, noisy machines in the Air dome, the kitchen tasks she previously despised—chopping onions, scouring pots, hovering over a sizzling pan—relaxed her. Elizabeth too valued their time together, but for a different reason—it gave her a chance to observe her granddaughter and gauge her mental state. She often worried about Jessica and her potent mix of emotional confusion, social awkwardness, and odd sensitivities. In Elizabeth's experience, most such people eventually outgrew those traits and led normal lives with careers and families, but a small minority grew more dysfunctional with the passage of time. Elizabeth prayed that Jessica would take the happier path. Their sessions together in the Food dome were reassuring. So far, the girl seemed to be adjusting well to her new environment and even enjoying herself a bit.

It was only at the Geo dome that there was cause for concern. The geothermal well hadn't been Larry's first choice but the one he had ended up with after eliminating alternatives. In designing the Shell, Larry knew that a compact, reliable, and practical heat source was key to surviving the Shroud. He had to rule out coal, oil, and gas—they would need too much storage space, consume too much oxygen, and emit too much carbon dioxide. With the sun out of the picture, solar power was out, and since wind is driven by the sun's heat, that option too was a non-starter. So that left him only nuclear or geothermal as energy options. Some experts he spoke to had recommended nuclear power as a time-tested, safe, and easy-to-install power source. But tailoring existing reactor designs to function within the space, water supply, and other resource limitations of the Shell proved too challenging.

So that left Larry with only one option—geothermal power. With this decision made, he spent months poring over geological maps until he located several sites that had the qualities he was looking for—a strong source of geothermal heat surrounded by solid bedrock, located in an unpopulated area but not too far from an urban center. The site in the Strzelecki desert wouldn't have been his first choice but for his chance encounter with Nicole and her family. And now here they were, he and the Millers, their lives dependent on the 2,500–meter–deep well under his feet.

Things in the Geo dome had gone well so far. All the machinery ran smoothly, and the well seemed to generate enough heat and power for their needs. Larry's concern was for the future. With nuclear energy—or with fossil fuels, for that matter—you could weigh the fuel and calculate exactly how many joules of heat you could generate. Geothermal heat's location deep in the earth's crust meant that only the roughest estimate of it could be made. The geologists on his team reckoned that the well would remain hot for fifteen to twenty-five years. Although the time range compared favorably with the expected duration of the Shroud, its degree of uncertainty was far too high—what if the well failed in fifteen years, but the Shroud persisted for twenty?

There were other questions as well. If the well started cooling off, would it happen gradually or abruptly? How much did it depend on their consumption versus other geological factors? And what impact would the Shroud have on it? How long would the pipes last, and would the heat exchanger buried far below survive the oven-like conditions there? Despite his engineers' assurance that everything was made of the highest-grade titanium-tungsten alloy designed to withstand far higher temperatures, his concerns remained.

Anxious as he was, it was always a relief and a delight when Anna came over to join him, pleased and excited over her horticultural explorations. As he familiarized her with the power plant, he shared some of his concerns with her, but in a casual way so as not to alarm her. He needn't have worried. While she was happy to learn how the plant operated and help with the maintenance chores, long-term engineering concerns didn't interest her—she lived in the moment. Besides, she had too much faith in Larry's ability to worry about them. If the problem could be solved, he would solve it. If it couldn't, there wasn't much use worrying about it, was there?

Although initially dismayed by her blind faith and naïve optimism, Larry soon began to see their value. He could share his concerns with her without any sugarcoating. She listened attentively and even made useful suggestions from her own experience, but in the end didn't dwell on the potential problems. (For instance, she showed Larry how to keep a metallic surface dry by sandblasting it to create a water-repellent texture similar to that of lotus petals.) Some of her cheery optimism rubbed off on him as well. Though he never stopped worrying, his mood lightened when his assistant was around. He and Anna had always gotten along famously; now, in this unlikely setting of hissing pipes, humming machinery, and hellish odors, they grew even closer.

The afternoon classes were a great success as well.

Larry covered fundamental engineering principles such as electricity, magnetism, and fluid mechanics, as well as practical matters relating to the Shell's function. Jessica often found minor flaws in the latter, but overall even she was impressed with the thoroughness and rigor that had gone into the design of their shelter. Nicole taught human biology, pleasantly surprised at how it all came back to her. She had a good grasp of principles, and the minor details she had forgotten were easily recalled by a quick search in the medical database. Her slides were crisp and well organized, and she glided through her material. In school, Larry had never had a biology teacher who could enliven the subject the way Nicole did, and he found her lectures enthralling. Anna taught botany and did it so well that words such as xylem, phloem, and angiosperm were soon part of their everyday conversation.

Jessica lectured on information science with originality and flair. She interleaved concepts of algorithms, networks, and databases with practical computer-programming exercises. Thanks to her efforts, the rest of them were soon much more at home with the vast amount of computing equipment scattered all over the complex. Elizabeth designed her class in psychology as a series of pair and group exercises. She kept theoretical notions to a minimum, encouraging discussion and interaction. She invented an exercise, "Tickle in a Minute," in which each member of a pair got sixty seconds to make their partner laugh or giggle without actually touching them. This never failed to lighten the atmosphere and raise morale. Even Jessica had a funny bone, it turned out. She couldn't resist a certain type of black humor in which the teller wryly admits their naïvety or foibles. Larry's tale of the Chinese desalinator company made her crack up with laughter.

After class, Elizabeth and Jessica usually went downstairs—one to rest and meditate, the other to read. Nicole and Larry often went to one of their rooms to enjoy some private time together. Anna elected to stay upstairs and listen to music or read a bit. Occasionally, they would all use the two hours between class and dinner to clean the Central dome and the hex underneath. This didn't have to happen often—being isolated from the world outside, they had very little dust or dirt to worry about.

Dinner was a relaxed, companionable affair, with everyone pitching in to prepare the food and clean up afterwards. It offered an excellent opportunity to exchange pleasantries and reminisce about old times. The meal was usually done by 8:30 p.m., which gave the family an hour or two at Central before bed. They sat together in the living space and chatted, played games, or watched one of the thousands of films and documentaries in the database.

By 10:00 p.m. they would be yawning, exhausted from their work, teaching, learning, and chores. With no noise or light to bother them, snuggled tight against the cool air, sleep came easily. Even Anna's dreams were pleasant.

16

First Anniversary

ON THE ANNIVERSARY of their arrival, the family held a thanksgiving celebration at Central. Soft music and subtle scents filled the air. Larry produced a bottle of Dom Perignon and filled everyone's glass.

Nicole, looking rather self-conscious, cleared her throat. "Honey."

"Yes?"

"I'm a matter-of-fact person. I don't speak fancy words. But I've been wanting to tell you this—you're wonderful. You've created this marvelous oasis and shared it with us. I'll never find the words to thank you. All I can say is," she raised her glass, "good health to you, forever my hero and my love."

Seeing Larry color, look down, and fidget, Anna told him: "You know, maybe one day you'll learn to take a compliment without blushing."

Larry laughed and then grew serious. "Dear Jessica, Anna, Elizabeth, and Nicole," he said. "What can I say in response to that most undeserved praise? Here's good health to you, the Millers, the most wonderful family in the world. Without you, this place wouldn't exist. Even if it did, it wouldn't be worth living in."

Many hugs and kisses later, the family sat down in a close circle. Everyone sipped their champagne for a few moments, savoring the moment.

Elizabeth placed her empty glass on the tray and coughed gently. "Larry, can I ask you something?"

"Anytime and always, my dear."

"You've done wonders in building this place, but I can't help wondering—might there be other shelters elsewhere? With other survivors?"

This question had been at the back of everyone's mind once the excitement and novelty of the first few days had receded. By tacit agreement, however, they had never articulated it until now. The implications were too overwhelming. What if they were the only humans—perhaps even the only land animals—left on Earth? The question became increasingly pressing as their radio system, perpetually scanning the airwaves, failed to pick up any signal.

Elizabeth had sensed this, and in her considerate manner had spared Larry the discomfort of raising the issue. Larry's strength of character was obvious, but Elizabeth had begun to glimpse another side of him—an extreme reluctance to do or say anything that might upset or worry them. An instance of this had been his failure to tell them about the Shell for fear of disappointing them in case it didn't work out. But even in everyday interactions the tendency manifested itself. A few days before, she had accidentally put salt instead of sugar in his coffee, and he had drunk most of it without complaint. It was only when Nicole took a sip from his cup and spat it out did Elizabeth realize her error.

The trait wasn't quite a weakness, maybe just a *softness*, but nevertheless it meant that he couldn't always be a strong leader. Although he was both tough and loving, he was incapable of the "tough love" that a leader sometimes has to employ in difficult situations. He was overprotective and overconsiderate; sometimes he needed a little nudge from someone less squeamish.

Larry glanced at a thermometer that showed the temperature outside the Shell. In their first few days inside the reading had kept dropping, and then stabilized at minus 127 degrees. The Entry hex had highly insulating "spacesuits" that could be worn if the heating failed, but such apparel wouldn't keep them alive longer than an hour or two outside. Indeed, they would be much worse off than astronauts, whose bodies lose heat only through the slow process of radiation, whereas they would cool off much faster due to conduction and convection via air molecules.

"Can I speak frankly?" Larry said.

"You have to," replied Nicole.

"I think we may be the only people left in Australia."

Silence prevailed for a few seconds while the family digested this expected yet unwelcome opinion.

Anna sighed. "I feared that, but I was hoping, you know, that ..."

"What makes you so sure?" Jessica asked Larry.

"If others were building cold shelters in this part of the world, I would've heard of them."

"Even if they kept it under wraps like you?"

"Even then."

"But we do have nuclear shelters, don't we? Hundreds of 'em."

Larry shook his head. "Those were designed for impact resistance and radiation shielding, not temperature insulation. And they wouldn't have an energy source like our geo well. How could their residents deal with this much cold for this long?"

"You think they'll all be dead?"

"I'm afraid so. Long dead."

"Ouch," said Anna, and after a pause: "I was hoping at least some of our leaders and military types would've managed to build a real shelter."

"They built one in the US." said Jessica. "In Virginia."

"You mean the one in Cheyenne Mountain?" Larry said.

Jessica nodded. "Wasn't that a nuclear bunker?"

"Yes, it was. One of the biggest and best. They probably had a nuclear reactor or two as well. While I was looking for ideas that's the first place I wanted to check out, but they wouldn't let me in."

"So there might be survivors there?"

"Possibly. Maybe a large number of them."

"How would they decide who to admit?" Nicole asked.

"I suspect it would be the ones with clout that got in. You know, the President and other political leaders, some military brass, corporate leaders, billionaires, and perhaps a few celebrities as well. Privileged folks."

"Bad recipe for long-term survival," said Jessica.

"Yes. I'm only guessing here, of course, but I suspect they would have been driven by short-term thinking. They would've been better off dumping all the bigwigs and admitting only scientists, engineers, doctors, social workers, and the like."

"And taking in a good number of young people as well," Anna added. "You know, folks who can do real work and are willing to learn."

"Instead, they probably got a group of rich people with huge egos," said Nicole.

"Good luck getting VIPs and movie stars to clear the drains or fix the wiring," said Jessica.

Anna snorted. "If they make their beds and clean their loos, you can count yourself lucky."

"I hope we are wrong. Otherwise it doesn't sound good for America," said Nicole.

"No, it doesn't," said Larry. "If there are any survivors, I wonder what state they'll be in." He turned to Elizabeth. "Maybe you have some thoughts?"

Elizabeth looked self-conscious. "Oh dear!" she said. "I don't know. A crisis can bring out the best or worst in people. It depends so much on the specific situation. But in this case, based on what you said, I'd fear the worst."

"They might be, like, tearing each other apart?" Anna said.

"I hope to God they're not," said Elizabeth. "But who can say? People in bleak survival situations might revert to primal behavior."

"Like *Lord of the Flies?*"

"And they had tons of weaponry," said Jessica. "Big guns + big egos = big disaster."

"How about the Indians or Chinese?" Nicole asked.

Larry shrugged. "According to my relatives in India, their leaders did nothing, just denied, bickered, and vacillated. Since they didn't even have bunkers or bomb shelters to start with, I don't rate their chances too highly. But then again, they flew a spacecraft to Mars for the cost of a house in Sydney. You can never tell with them."

"And the Chinese?"

"They could certainly have managed to build something, given their discipline and resources. But they too were slow to react. So great potential, but late start. I would rate their chances of survival as better than the Indians, but worse than the Americans. Same with the Russians."

"Africa? South America?"

"Low chances."

"So that leaves us with western Europe, mainly?"

"Right. I think France and Germany were trying to build something at the last minute, just weeks before the Shroud. They were throwing everything they had at it and might have pulled it off. I'll rate that possibility at ten percent."

"How about Scandinavians?" said Jessica. "They were at the cutting edge of everything. If anyone could have done it, it would be them."

"I think so too," replied Larry. "They're our best hope. They're used to very cold temperatures and spent decades perfecting bomb shelters, living in the shadow of the Soviet Union. More importantly, their culture is—was—less dominated by politics than most others. Their press was far more independent than in the US, and some of their journalists paid attention to the Shroud before their American colleagues. And their astronomers were still respected."

Larry's choice of the past tense cast a chill over everyone. Even after a year into the Shroud, their minds had not become inured to the grim reality outside; it invaded their consciousness in myriad subtle ways, tingeing even the most pleasant moments with existential dread.

Nicole pulled herself together. "So there's a good chance that some of them have made it?"

"I'd say fifty-fifty. As far as I could tell in those chaotic days before the Shroud, their societies were among the last to collapse. And didn't you tell me, Jessica, that you picked up a radio transmission that sounded like Turkish, a few hours before you came to the Shell? I once met an exchange student from Turkey who told me Finnish sounded similar to her native tongue."

"So it might have been from Finland?"

"Yes. It was long ago, but do you recall any words?"

Jessica's memory was a constant source of amazement and exasperation to her family. She could never remember routine, mundane stuff—she ignored appointments, mislaid things, and missed exams, all through sheer forgetfulness. But her memory for facts, figures, sounds, and sights was uncanny. The quirkier the fact, the better and longer she would remember it.

"I remember it said 'to land beyond' over and over. Also, something that sounded like 'Jakarta.' I wondered if it came from Indonesia."

"To land beyond?"

"Yeah."

"Hmm … could it have been *tulen pian?*"

"Maybe. Why, does that mean something?"

"It means 'come quickly.'"

"And 'Jakarta'?"

"I'm not sure about that one. The closest Finnish word I know is *kartta*, meaning 'map.'"

"Hmm … perhaps they were directing survivors to a certain map location?"

"Yes, perhaps. Just speculation, of course."

"Perhaps the Scandinavians pooled their resources to build, like, a gigantic shelter," said Anna. "Wouldn't that be amazing?"

"Let's hope they did," said Nicole. "When we leave this place, it'll be nice to have some other humans to connect with. Even if they're on the other side of the planet."

"Indeed!" Larry nodded and smiled, though he couldn't help mentally rephrasing Nicole's words: *If* we leave this place.

17

Journals

Larry's Journal

As HUMAN BEINGS, our capacity to adjust to any situation is incredible. Take the five of us here, leading lives that seem almost normal. Our private thoughts might dwell on the unspeakable horror of the Shroud, but we don't talk about it. Instead, we discuss everyday matters, deal with practical issues, eat, sleep, even laugh, play, and sing.

Outside, the outlook is as grim as ever—not even the slightest glimmer of light or a gust of warm air. The exterior thermometer still shows minus 127, and the light meter reads zero. And there's no signal on the radio.

But inside, things have gone much better than expected. We've managed to stay alive and healthy for an entire year. We've suffered only minor glitches in the equipment. More importantly, we've all been smoothly settling into our roles here. The Millers and I were a family, and now we're a team as well. If I were religious, I would be sending a prayer of thanks to God. But since I've a rational mind, I would also have to condemn Him for wrapping us in the Shroud in the first place. Perhaps it's best that I'm not a believer. Anger and gratitude are hard to reconcile.

I think, instead, I would like to record my appreciation toward my team members.

Nicole, after all the years she spent in a busy surgical ward, must find it hard to adjust to the total lack of professional challenge or stimulation here. But she gives no sign of frustration or regret. She's been as wonderful as ever—supportive in public and affectionate in private. I haven't figured out what she sees in me, as all her previous relationships seem to have been with extroverted, charismatic, "party animal" types. Compared to them, I must appear dull and stodgy. Perhaps she sees me more as a father figure? Whatever it is, I'm not complaining. I used to worry that she'd get bored with me, but that hasn't happened yet. Perhaps being the only man left on the continent has preserved my appeal!

Anna has been as sweet, lively, and delightful as ever. I'm so glad I took the trouble to set up her greenhouse. Even though, as Jessica pointed out, having all those flowering perennials is a luxury, Anna's joy in her botanical friends makes it all worthwhile. And she's been such an unexpected asset in Geo. She's perhaps the least mechanically minded of us all, and my choice of her as my assistant was perhaps more for the pleasure of her company than her skills. But she's been extremely willing to help out with all the tedious maintenance tasks. And when I want to talk about some of my energy worries, she's a great listener.

Jessica has been a great asset as well. She was a natural fit in Air, so her enthusiasm and competence there came as no surprise. What has come as a pleasant surprise, or perhaps just a relief, is that she no longer seems to compare our existence here unfavorably to the pre-Shroud life. She seems less prone to criticizing things just for the sake of being critical. Now, when she points out flaws, it seems to be more constructively motivated. That I can live with. Her intelligence will prove invaluable if (when?) things start to fail. I used to think of her as clumsy and uncoordinated. Either I was wrong, or she has outgrown that phase and is turning into a young woman of dark good looks and sultry charm. It's tragic that two such attractive girls should blush unseen in the Shell.

And Elizabeth ... how can I praise her enough? She's such a wonderfully calming and reassuring influence on all of us. She must have anxieties like the rest of us, but that never stops her from looking after others. And she doesn't have to *do* much; her smiling, warm, gentle, lovely presence is enough to hold us together and keep us sane. And she seems to have grown younger and sprightlier during the past year. This morning when she emerged from the shower with her face aglow, I could have taken her for a forty-year-old. And the other day in the kitchen, as she offered me the Shell-shaped cake she baked for my birthday, her cheeks blushing from the oven's heat and her eyes dancing with mischief, she seemed like Jessica's older sister. She's too modest to admit it, but her influence is more vital than anything I do with my machines and systems and work schedules. My only regret is that I don't get to spend any time with her alone. When I think of how many things could go wrong here, and how even some little things could blow this place wide open to the elements, I'm terrified. I could use some of her calming influence! I some-times envy Anna and Jessica for being able to snuggle up to her at night. It would be so nice to drop all my adult worries and be a child again in her arms ...

Anna's Journal

A year ago, before Larry showed up in our backyard, I couldn't have imagined that I'd now be sitting in a warm, pleasant room, sipping coffee and scribbling this entry. I'm as optimistic as they come, but not even I could hold on to any hope. Beyond a certain point, optimism is just stupidity. But that point hadn't come then, as events proved.

What can I say about the past year? I can describe it only in such extreme and contradictory terms—strange and disorienting at first, yet now familiar and comfortable. Terrible, yet wonderful. Incredibly sad, yet unbelievably joyful. Billions have perished, but we're alive and well. It's colder than Mars outside, but snug as a bakery kitchen in here. It's a barren wasteland outside, but the Eco dome is a veritable jungle of all kinds of marvelous plants. How glad I am that I took all those classes in botany and ecology and went on those field trips, and how I wish I'd spent even more time on them and less on partying! Almost everything I learned has come in useful, and the computer database has helped me plug some of the huge gaps in my knowledge.

As we had expected, we ran out of store-bought fruit in two weeks after moving in and had to wait until July for the peaches. But the fruit was well worth the wait. They looked rather washed out, but my, were they delicious!!! And I'm not even as great a peach fan as Jess, who was obviously delighted when she took her first bite. The tree should keep us in fruit for several years, but I've saved some seeds in case something happens to it. And then came the tropical delights—the bananas and mangoes. The bananas were only okay—better for baking—but the dwarf Alphonso mangoes, a fast-growing hybrid variety, were out of this world. If it wasn't for Larry's

Indian roots we would never have heard of this fruit. In the old days we were content to eat the local Honey Gold or Pearl varieties. The difference is night and day. Trust the Asians to know what's good to eat! (I guess that's not much comfort for a group of people that has probably vanished from the face of the planet.) I can't wait for the avocado, but it's still a young tree. Give it a year or three.

Only one minor gripe—one would think a guy with Larry's breadth of knowledge would have heard of hydroponics, but no, he hasn't made any provision for growing plants without soil. But I'll rig something up in the corner of Eco and see if it can grow something for our daily salad.

Toward the end of the year we started running low on fertilizer. There's still enough left for a few more months, but I'm going to start experimenting with manure from the bioconverters, just in case. The first batch of manure came out in November, and I ran some basic chem panels on them. They seem alright, but I need to be cautious. Perhaps I'll try it on the rose bush first. I love that plant but it *is* a luxury, and if I have to kill something by accident let it be that and not a fruit-bearing tree. That shows how pragmatic I can be, contrary to what Jessica might think. It's just that I'd be pragmatic only as a last resort!

Talking of my sister, it's funny how little interaction I've had with her given that we all live in one small space and are perhaps the only two girls left on this continent. She seems to be quieter, less on edge. Perhaps she's finding that life here isn't too bad. I hope she's getting along well with Larry. She doesn't realize it, but she needs him just as much as the rest of us. And surely he and the rest of us need her as well.

Nicole's Journal

Putting my thoughts down is a new experience. I never did it in my pre-Shell days. There was no time! Having so much leisure continues to be a novel sensation, even after a year. It's making me think about things that never entered my mind before. Pre-Shell, I thought only about my job or home. I never had time for what Mum calls "existential questions." She, of course, with her background in philosophy and psychology and her interest in spiritual matters, has always pondered such questions, and is at peace with herself despite that. Lacking her sense of peace, I find my thoughts disturbing. My basic question is about what it means to be alive. What's life's purpose? In the old days, if the topic ever came up, my response would have been brief and simple—my purpose is to give my patients the best possible care, while I raise my daughters and then help them raise their kids. But my patients are gone. The girls are growing into adulthood but are unlikely to become mothers. I guess I had implicitly believed in my place as one strand in the web of life, but now that we might all be extinct really soon, what should I live for? Larry, with his love for me, can't see how I could even entertain that question. Nevertheless, I'd like some kind of answer.

That apart, I've been having as great a time as possible under these circumstances. Larry will never allow me to utter a word of praise when I'm talking to him, so here's my opportunity—Larry, you've made life possible for me, and you've made it worth living in a hundred ways. Yes, I do sometimes question the value of an existence that, in Jessica's words, is a "spatiotemporal dead-end." But if life has any value at all, much of the credit goes to you. I'm glad I have the opportunity to record it here because I don't know what will happen to me in the years to come. Will I become sad, withdrawn, angry, or crazy? If so, it will be interesting to look back and read what I wrote before my nature changed.

Coming to more practical matters, there hasn't been much for me to do, work-wise. The irony is that I'll be most useful when people get sick, which of course I don't wish for, so I have to hope to be useless, which gets me back to questioning life's purpose. But here I am, philosophizing again, when I said I'd be practical. As I wrote earlier, the most practical and useful thing I can do (when things are going well) is to ensure everyone stays fit. The workout routine I concocted—combining yoga, Pilates, aerobics, and weights—has worked really well. Larry and Anna seem to enjoy it, while Jessica does it without complaining. The one I'm worried about is Mum. Though she has become stronger than before, she still seems to get breathless so quickly, and the other day she almost fainted after carrying a pail of water across the kitchen. I guess I should have paid more attention to her health these past years. Both her mother and grandmother died in their fifties from strokes, and she may have inherited that genetic tendency. And now I can't do an angiogram to see if she has any blocked arteries, and even if she has, I can't do much about it. Larry has built an amazingly well-equipped clinic, but I can hardly expect even him to provide a fully functional operating room and a platoon of nurses!

It's ironic that I've been so preoccupied in taking care of my hospital patients that I've managed to ignore my own family's health. It's doubly ironic that, but for the Shroud, I'd never have realized this until it was too late.

Jessica's Journal

1st Year of the Shell—& the Shroud—ends, & were still alive & thriving, sort of. I hand it to Larry, hes done a decent job in building this place. Nevertheless, Id rather not be imprisoned in a synthetic bubble on a dead planet, protected from the vicious cold outside only by heat from a dodgy geothermal well. Food is monotonous, confinement is depressing, & silence is deathly. What I wdnt give to hear traffic on a busy street! Larry has simulated a natural-seeming environment at Central, but fake sun, fan-blown breeze, & digital bird sounds only remind me of what weve lost.

Thats perhaps why I enjoy the Air dome. At least there Im *doing* something! Air exchangers & purifiers seem to be working so far, & Im getting to know them really well. Each machine has its own personality, something Larry doesnt get. His style is to follow the instructions in the manual to the letter, but thats not how you get best perf. I showed him how we cd cut the power consumption by a third simply by increasing valve pressure by 10% over the manufacturer-specified value. Opened his eyes. Ill say this much—when hes wrong, which is more often than hed like, he has no problem admitting. If he was one of those idiots who dont listen, Id be really worried about future.

Future … thats now a taboo word. Better to think of "extended present," focus on imm issues we can solve rather than on things outside our control.

Finally, Ive to admit that social aspects of being imprisoned in hermetically sealed space w/ only my family for company havent been all that bad. As long as I do my morning work-out, Mum leaves me alone. Shes quieter & more thoughtful than Ive ever seen her, but who but an incurable optimist wdnt be depressed? Talking of incurable optimists, I dont get to see much of Anna. She seems as cheerful as ever—must be enjoying herself w/ all those manures & soils—good for her. In the old days she wd annoy me w/ her pep talks, trying to cure me of what she called "negative thinking." Fortunately, shes stopped doing that, & on those rare occasions when we are together just the two of us, she doesnt seem to have much to say beyond polite small talk. She pretty much lets me be. Thats what I always wanted, & so shd be pleased, but it somehow leaves me w/ slightly hollow feeling. Perhaps I miss her but am not sure how that cd be. Never missed her company before.

Grandmas as wonderful as ever. Shes the one bright spot here. Id go crazy if she werent around.

Elizabeth's Journal

What an incredible year it's been. I can safely say that no other human beings in history could have experienced anything similar. No, only in the space colonies of science fiction could a comparable situation exist. We're all still alive and well, against all odds. What a blessing!

My understanding of practical matters is rudimentary, but I get the sense that the Shell is living up to what Larry expected. I've never taken much interest in equipment and architecture and stuff like that, but I'm now realizing how much thought and genius goes into all of that. To make the air breathable, to keep the water clean, to handle our wastes—how complex all of that must be! In the past, I always took such things for granted, leaving it to the practical folks to work things out. Psychology, philosophy, spirituality—that, and some child nurturing, was the sum total of my interests. I'm beginning to feel that I should not have neglected life's practical side—studying things, making things, making things work. The other day, I ran into a minor glitch in the kitchen—the garbage disposal wouldn't work. Something had got stuck in it somewhere, that's all I could tell. It took Jessica all of 30 seconds to unscrew a cover, remove the offending object (a bit of onion peel), and get the unit working again. What if I had a more serious mechanical emergency, such as a burst pipe or a grease fire, and I couldn't get hold of Jessica or anyone else easily?

Although I've admired scientists, engineers, doctors, and all the practical people who can create and fix things, I always used to think that by spending all their time and effort in the "real world" and not developing their inner lives or pondering life's ultimate meaning, they were missing out on something vital. Perhaps they were. But then again, perhaps I was missing something equally vital—life's practical side. Larry—dear, sweet Larry—will insist that I'm the most valuable person in the universe. Has he ever said anything but the kindest words to anyone here? But I'm wondering if I wouldn't be of more use if I were a plumber or an electrician, not a psychologist. After all, physical survival is a precondition for psychological health, not the other way around.

Talking of psychological health, the news, overall, is good, given our very unusual conditions. Jessica seems reasonably contented. She isn't (and might never be) a "happy camper" here, but she doesn't seem to have any major complaints so far. She seems to like working with her machines and gets to spend some exclusive time with her mother and me in the kitchen. I was the most worried about her when we first moved in, but she seems to be coping well enough.

Anna seems to be doing okay too, but I could never really tell what she's feeling deep down. She's always been an odd mix of child and adult. When she's teaching us or pulling Larry's leg, she seems to be her mother's twin, perky and confident, but when she has her nightmares—so rarely now, thank God—I can feel her trembling like a baby. It's hard for me to say if being in the Shell is helping or harming her. She obviously loves her plants and cherishes time alone with Larry. But she used to be such a social creature, and she must certainly be missing her parties and cafes and music lessons. I'm so glad that Larry gets us all to sleep under one blanket, literally and figuratively. I wouldn't be comfortable if Anna were sleeping by herself in a separate room, with nobody to turn to if her mind started playing its tricks on her. I think as long as she feels safe and protected, and she keeps busy with her plants and leans on Larry's gentle strength, she should be fine.

So the girls are okay for now. I'm not sure what to make of the adults, though. Larry has been as calm and reliable as ever, but he must be under a lot of pressure. He hinted to me the other day that though things are going well now, the situation could "turn on a dime" if any of the key systems began to fail. He immediately backtracked and told me that such a contingency was highly improbable. But, for an instant, he let down his guard, and I could see the weight he was carrying on his shoulders. I glimpsed the worry in his eyes. I wish I could get him to open up to me. Even though I'm the least practical person on the planet, I think it would comfort him to share his anxieties. Perhaps I can convince him that the burden of our survival is not for him alone to bear, but for all of us to share.

Nicole, my dear, sweet child. I've never been this close to her before, and yet I'm only beginning to understand her. Deprived of her personal "Shell"—her work and her busy routine—she's far more wounded and vulnerable than I'd imagined. And yet I can see some signs of healing as well, thanks no doubt to the precious gift of Larry's boundless love. Whenever he's around, she smiles. But at other times, she seems strangely troubled, and her concerns don't seem tied to present-day worries. Indeed, whenever we experience a health-related problem—we had a couple of minor emergencies this year, I twisted my ankle and Anna cut herself with the garden shears and needed two stitches—she seemed the old Nicole, practical and matter-of-fact. It's only during the quieter moments that her disquiet seems to emerge.

18

Year Five

LOOKING BACK, LARRY would think of the first five years in the Shell as the Steady State period, an engineering term for an extended period of stability following a brief chaotic phase that occurs when a system is switched on.

Many of the bugs in the Shell had been worked out. The air flow in the initial days was erratic, and at times it got stuffy inside Central. Larry and Jessica spent several days trying to diagnose the problem, finally narrowing it down to a defective valve that wasn't letting stale air back into the purifier. Once diagnosed, the problem was easy to fix. Something similar happened to the heating as well, with temperatures occasionally oscillating inexplicably between uncomfortably cold and wastefully warm. Here, lacking Jessica's help, Larry was to some extent on his own as far as diagnostics were concerned. Fresh from his Air dome repairs, Larry initially checked the valves, but they all seemed to work fine. The motors ran smoothly. The ducts and pipes ran clear with no leaks.

"What do you think the problem is?" he asked his assistant. Though Anna lacked her sister's ability to break a

complex system down into components that could be indi-
vidually analyzed, she had a fresh, direct mind, and was sometimes able to go to the heart of a problem in a holistic way.
Despite her naïve understanding of mechanical systems, she
often helped Larry think laterally and approach a problem
from a different angle.

"Can I ask a stupid question first?" Anna put down a coil
she had been rewinding and wiped her hands with a rag.

"There are no stupid questions, only stupid habitat
designers," Larry smiled.

"If you're stupid, what does that make me?" Anna said
with a toss of her head. "Anyway, my question was—how do
you set the temperature?"

Larry pointed to a panel with several knobs and sliders.
"Do you see the control here for the thermostat? We can set
it to any value between plus or minus 45 degrees."

Anna nodded. "But we mostly keep it at 20 degrees or so?"

"Right. It's linked to a thermometer in Central."

"What happens if Central warms up to, say, 25 degrees?"

"The thermostat would shut off the flow of heat to Central
until it fell below 20 degrees."

"How quickly does that happen?"

"Instantaneously. As is the switching back on."

"I see." Anna scratched her nose with a ruler and thought
for a few seconds. "Okay, the thermostat reacts fast, but how
long does it take to cool off or warm up again?"

Larry reflected for a moment. "Hmm ... I think you might
be on to something." He doodled a graph on a notepad
and showed it to Anna. "Look! There will be a delay in the
system due to thermal inertia. So when the heat is shut off at

25 degrees, the room will cool down to 20, and keep cooling further even after the heat comes back on."

"That might be causing the oscillations?"

"Yes. I should've thought of it before." His grimace turned into a smile when he saw Anna's pleasure at having been of help. He wiped away a spot of grease on her forehead with his sleeve and told her: "What would I do without you?"

Larry reprogrammed the thermostat to anticipate the ambient temperature instead of reacting to it, and that fixed the oscillation problem. It took nearly a year to work out the rest of the kinks in the system, but by the middle of Year Two things ran quite smoothly. The climate inside the Shell now remained stable. The heating and air quality systems worked seamlessly to maintain Central at a comfortable 20 degrees. The air never felt stale. Though the relative humidity varied between thirty and forty percent, it never got too dry or too muggy.

The food situation underwent major changes but remained comfortable. As Larry had foreseen, their supply of fresh eggs, milk, and fish ran out by the end of the first year, and they had to switch to powdered eggs, condensed milk, and tinned fish. The Shellmates found the substitutes a little hard to swallow initially, but soon adjusted to them.

"We just need to recalibrate our taste buds," said Jessica.

The end of their bread supply—they ate their last loaf on May 16 of Year Four—hit them harder. Their own attempts at breadmaking were only moderately successful. The end results were palatable but couldn't compare with the delicious gourmet loaves that Larry had provided.

"Perhaps you should have stocked up with supermarket loaves instead," Anna joked. "Then our homemade bread wouldn't seem so bad in comparison."

The bright spot was in the horticulture department. Anna's manure and hydroponics experiments had proved successful, and they had a steady supply of fresh produce to supplement the dry goods and tinned foods that formed the bulk of their diet. Their Stayman Winesap now yielded excellent fruit—sweet, tart, juicy, and crisp—but the apple of Anna's eye was the avocado, which began yielding fruit in its third year. Plump, smooth, and delicious, the emerald-fleshed produce of the avocado tree was so abundant that they soon had more than enough for their needs, and Elizabeth began freezing the surplus for a future avocado-less day.

Nicole continued giving her periodic health exams and was relieved to observe that no one showed signs of suffering from their prolonged stay in the Shell's artificial environment. Their bone and muscle masses remained stable, while their heart rates and lung capacities showed improvement. Jessica, exercising regularly and eating sensibly for the first time in her life, seemed to be bursting with health, her pudginess gone and her complexion now clear and smooth. Anna seemed as fit as she used to be. Deprived of his rock climbing and surfboarding, Larry was no longer as athletic as before, but he was still fitter and stronger than most men would be at his age.

Again, the one who caused Nicole the most concern was her mother. While Elizabeth, like Jessica, seemed leaner and fitter than before, she didn't have age on her side. She continued to fare poorly on the cardio stress tests, but without extensive diagnostics it was hard to identify the cause. Nicole reproached herself for not having had her tested years ago. To improve Elizabeth's blood lipid profile, Nicole prescribed her a newly approved medication that was—miraculously, it seemed—among the drugs in the clinic's stocks. Perhaps if she had put her mother on statins years ago, Nicole thought, her arteries would have remained clear. She felt guilty about her negligence, but there was nothing to do now except to monitor her carefully and make sure she got the best possible diet, the right kind of exercise, and plenty of rest. She shared her fears with Elizabeth and Larry, but if she expected a word of reproach from them she was disappointed. Elizabeth, used to giving rather than receiving, was always touchingly grateful for even the slightest attention shown to her. Overwhelmed by everything her family did for her wellbeing, she was shocked that Nicole would entertain even the slightest feeling of guilt on her behalf. And Larry, of course, who could never see Nicole as anything but the sincerest of women, laughed away her self-reproach.

"With the benefit of hindsight, we become aware of the thousands of errors in our lives," he said. "We can't go around blaming ourselves for all that." Nicole was comforted by their support, but her nagging guilt never went away completely.

Larry's work schedule enjoyed great success. The girls soon mastered the workings of their own domes, and both were happy to be given a share of the responsibility of their survival and eager to show themselves useful. Each of the five teams continued to work harmoniously. Larry had toyed with the idea of a reshuffle as part of his plan for all of them to develop some degree of all-round competence, but now he hesitated. Everyone was in a nice groove, and a major change in dome assignments would be disruptive. He consulted Elizabeth. "Perhaps we should hold off a bit," she suggested, and Larry agreed.

The afternoon classes were a mixed bag. Larry's talks on Shell design had been very popular, but by the end of the second year he had exhausted that topic. He continued lecturing on engineering topics that were of interest only to Jessica, though Anna and Nicole made a game effort to keep up. Nicole's medical lectures were popular as well, but there was only so much she could tell them about the human body in a classroom—a biology lab would have made such a difference! She could demonstrate the chemistry of body fluids using equipment from the clinic, but it was impossible to make anatomy interesting without animals or cadavers to dissect.

Her daughters were luckier in this regard. Anna was able to explain the principles of botany using specimens from the Eco dome, showing her students how seeds, pollen grains, and other plant parts looked under the microscope. This made it easier for them to visualize the intricate docking of the pollen with the stigma and its subsequent journey down the pollen tube to the flower's ovary. They were no longer mystified by the complex biology that magically transforms a dry, hard seed into a living plant. Jessica was in an even better position to teach her subjects—all she needed was a computer, and Larry had equipped Central with the best available. Soon, everyone at the Shell was not only a competent programmer but could understand some of the complex algorithms that regulated their living environment.

By the fourth year, however, even the girls had exhausted their repertoire. Elizabeth continued to hold an occasional workshop focused on laughter, mindfulness, or communication, but she didn't feel the need to do it every day. Her main concern had been to maintain harmony, and that battle was now won.

The need for instruction in practical matters now felt less important. The family decided to focus their teaching on culture instead. Every week, one of the five assigned the others a book or film that they liked and led a discussion on it. Nicole taught the girls the basic steps of tango. Larry proved to be a waltzer of some ability, and he helped the others master the basics of that classic dance form. Anna taught the others how to play simple tunes on a piano that was cleverly hidden behind one of the large computer panels. To remind themselves of the lost human civilization, they told each other stories of the people and customs they had seen and experienced. Elizabeth gave lessons in Maori, as did Larry in Tamil and Nicole in French. The students had great fun trying to master new and unfamiliar sounds in each language, in particular the *zh* and *L* consonants in Tamil, the *r* and *œ* in French, and the *wh* in Maori. The language lessons were popular—actually, too popular, as the girls began to adopt so many non-English words that their language threatened to turn into a patois.

"Combien de wai irukku in the pot?" ["How much water is there in the pot?"]

"Pot est kali." ["Pot is empty."]

The elders grew worried. "What if we leave this place someday and nobody understands us?" Nicole said. The family then adopted a policy of speaking a different language during breakfast each day, but without any mixing of tongues.

Aside from the culture lessons, the afternoon classes evolved into a self-study period, with each member busy with their own interests. Occasionally, one of them would seek input from another or from the group, and an animated discussion would break out. But more often companionable silence prevailed.

So life went on in the Shell, year after year. Everyone did their share, and other than an occasional flash of temper from Jessica—which seemed now more out of habit than from any real vexation, subsiding almost as quickly as it started—there was rarely any discord. Even though they didn't speak to each other as much as before, their need for each other's physical company grew stronger. Even Jessica preferred to remain upstairs during her private time. Everyone seemed to feel solace in the family. Although necessity forced them to work in separate teams, they exercised, ate, studied, played, and slept together.

The comforting presence of one another became their best defense against the terrifying reality outside.

19

Fifth Anniversary

O N THEIR FIFTH anniversary, the five held a special celebration. They gathered at Central after dinner, with subdued but raucous Bhangra music wafting from the sound system accompanied by scents of patchouli and honeysuckle from the incense bowl. Larry produced another excellent bottle of champagne from a source that even Jessica's shrewd eyes had failed to locate.

"Awesome bubbly!" Anna said. "Can you believe it? Five years in storage and it's, like, the freshest and fizziest champagne ever."

Everyone sipped their drink in silent enjoyment for several minutes. "Mmm ... this is nice," said Nicole.

"Full marks for understatement," said Jessica.

"I think we exhausted our superlatives long ago," said Elizabeth.

Anna refilled everyone's glass. "Feels like I'm living in a dream," she said. "Maybe I'll wake up one day to the sounds of, you know, traffic outside and Mrs. Rack's collie barking next door."

Jessica laughed. "Or maybe that was the dream and this is the reality."

"It feels unreal to be alive," Nicole said.

Silence prevailed for a minute. "It does feel unreal that we made it this far," Larry said at last.

"You didn't expect us to?"

"To be honest, no. The Shell is like a space station—so many things have to work properly for it to be livable. I'm amazed they have."

Elizabeth put her glass down and placed an arm around each of her granddaughters. "I've said *miracle* too many times, but I'm going to say it again. Any life is miraculous, but being alive now feels especially so." After a pause, she added: "I hate to ask, but how much longer will we be able to carry on like this?"

Elizabeth had once again given Larry the opening he was looking for. His sense of delicacy and fear of spoiling a golden moment had prevented him from bringing up the issue on his own.

"I'm glad you asked." He stood up, paced a step or two, and sat down again. "This is a conversation we should have had long ago, years ago, but somehow the moment never felt right. Things were working fine, and I didn't want to strike a … negative note." Larry looked around and got sympathetic nods from the women; until now, they too had preferred to dwell in the present. "Thanks to our joint efforts, nothing major has gone wrong. The system design has proved robust."

"So far, so good?" Nicole asked.

"Right."

"But looking ahead?"

"Looking ahead, there are three main areas of concern. One—something vital could break down and be hard to repair. Of course, that 'something vital' includes not just equipment but all of us as well. By maintaining ourselves and our equipment in good condition, we can reduce that risk. I used to fear that the confinement might drive us crazy, make us go around wrecking things or something." Gesturing toward Elizabeth, he added: "But thanks in large part to our resident Lama's benign influence, that danger seems remote."

"I did nothing," Elizabeth said, blushing.

"You don't have to *do* anything," said Anna. "Your being here is enough."

"My sister's right for once," said Jessica, and Anna stuck her tongue out at her. "You stop us from being mean to each other, Grandma."

"We're lucky to have you," Nicole said.

"Absolutely," said Larry. "Moving on to concern number two—we could run low on food or water. If that happens … well, we don't waste much here, but we could try to be even more frugal. Beyond that, we could also reduce our food intake a bit, couldn't we?"

Nicole nodded. "We certainly can. We're now averaging about 2,100 calories a day each. We could cut that down to 1,800 or, in an emergency, all the way down to 1,200."

"With no adverse health effects?" asked Larry.

"None apart from becoming leaner and hungrier. We could trim our morning workout to compensate for the lower energy intake. Since we'd be sweating less, we'd also get less thirsty."

"Mild hibernation?" asked Jessica.

"Yes, something like that. Within a range, we can eat and exercise more, or eat and exercise less, while staying healthy."

"The third concern," Larry continued, "is running low on energy. This is hard to predict, but I'm hoping that we can see it coming well in advance and cut down on our heating needs. We could, for instance, shift the stuff in the Health dome to the basement of Central. That's not optimal, but we could then save energy by turning off all heat to the Health dome. We could also turn down the temperature in Central a tad and put on an extra layer of clothing."

"Sounds even more like hibernation," said Jessica.

"Unfortunately, yes. Anyway, those are my three concerns."

"You've missed the most important one," said Jessica.

"Did I? Which one?"

"Something else could happen. Something unforeseen."

Anna made a face. "Ugh, I don't like the sound of that."

"Denial won't help," said Jessica. Unlike Larry, she always spoke her mind bluntly and never tried to soften the impact of her words. "There could be some crisis we haven't prepared for. Then everything will fall apart like that." She snapped her fingers.

"Good Lord!" said Anna. "Don't be such a doomsayer."

But Jessica went on. "It's just like what Mum told us about the human body—once the heart fails, the lungs collect fluid, the liver stiffens, the kidneys shut down. Everything goes kaput."

Nicole gave a quick, troubled glance at Elizabeth. Jessica had unintentionally hit on Nicole's worry about her mother's condition. That was exactly the kind of cascade of failures that ER teams tried to prevent but was much harder to do with the Shell's limited facilities. Elizabeth, however, looked as tranquil as ever. If her health worried her, it didn't show.

But Jessica wasn't done. "Know what destroyed past civilizations? Things they didn't expect. Take the Easter Islanders and the Indus Valley people. They flourished until ecological collapse and other factors wiped them out. Take the Romans. All their might was useless when the Goths appeared. Then the Mayans and Incans, who were helpless when the Spanish landed with Old World weapons and diseases. And then the Okhotsk people in the Kurils. They were nice and happy as long as tribes in bigger islands supplied tools and weapons; when those people moved away, the Okhotsk went extinct." She paused for effect and then concluded: "And the human race itself has been wiped out because the Shroud caught us unprepared."

The others looked at one another uncomfortably. "That's a fascinating lecture, but what's your point?" Anna asked her sister. Jessica just shrugged her shoulders. She had said what she thought and couldn't be bothered to justify it. She scorned Anna's principle of not saying anything pessimistic unless it led to positive action.

"Is there anything we can do to prepare for such situations?" asked Elizabeth.

"Nope," Jessica broke in as Larry was about to answer. "We can't prepare, since we don't know what's going to hit us. We might anticipate some disaster and plan for it, but we might be completely off target. Remember all the effort to fight global warming just before the Shroud appeared? Remember Larry's satellite network?"

The other women cast a troubled look at Larry, who sighed. "It seemed like a good idea then."

"But it solved the wrong problem," Jessica said, and Larry nodded wryly.

"You make it sound so hopeless, dear! Surely we can do *something?*" Elizabeth turned to Larry for support.

Larry cleared his throat. "Jessica is right in that we can't prepare for a specific unknown crisis. But that doesn't mean we're helpless. No, I think the best preparation is what we're all doing everyday—staying healthy, informed, and vigilant. And functioning harmoniously as a team."

"Then we hope for the best, right?" asked Anna.

"Absolutely. And we have plenty of reason for hope. Because if ever there was a team of people ideally suited to survive any crisis, it's us."

Elizabeth stood up. "And on that note, I'd like to propose a multiple toast." She picked up the champagne bottle and doled out the last of it. "Firstly, to the Shell, our protector, for keeping us safe and comfortable. Then to all of us, for staying loving and united despite all the challenges we've had to endure. Next, to our planet Earth, hoping that one day in the not-too-distant future it can shrug off its Shroud and resume its life-nurturing ways." She waited for everyone to drink before continuing on a softer note: "And finally, I'd like to propose a toast to myself." She paused as everyone looked at her in surprise and expectation. "Here's to hoping I can remain alive long enough to see you all leading normal, happy lives outside."

Tears flowed freely after that. Nicole sobbed her heart out as all the anxiety about her mother's health finally found expression. The girls, who had always taken their Grandma as a constant fixture in their lives, broke down in tears as well. Larry, whose affection for her knew no bounds, wept silently.

Everyone huddled very close that night as they slept. They had never needed each other more.

20

Journals

Larry's Journal

FIVE YEARS IN the Shell … now that's a milestone we're lucky to reach. I couldn't say it aloud, but I really didn't think we would make it beyond a year or two, at least not without major crises. And yet we have. For something that had never been tested before, something that was nothing but a prototype, the Shell has succeeded beyond all expectations. And my fellow Shellmates have been beyond terrific—I don't want to start praising them or I'll never stop. Suffice it to say that each of them, in her unique way, has helped change what would be a nightmare situation into one that's not just bearable, but actually joyous and wonderful. If it weren't for the grim reality outside, I'd be jumping with delight.

So I guess I have much to be grateful for. But my anxiety has only been growing. I tried to put a brave face on it during our quinquennial celebration, but I'm not at all easy in my mind about our future. The first three areas of concern— food/water, equipment/health, and energy—are more worrisome than I made them out to be. Food/water shortages I think we can handle in the short or medium term, since we have a good inventory of what we have and can pace ourselves. But a crisis related to one or both of the other two could hit us without warning, and I'm not sure how well we'd cope. The health situation seems to be under control and we have back-ups in case of equipment failure, so even that is a lesser worry. The energy situation is the real concern. The well is as hot as ever, but I'm worried that it could suddenly start to cool. Things would get really bleak then. Perhaps we should start work on our plan B—heating with diesel.

But worrisome though these scenarios are, they can't fully explain my dread, as that's what it really is. I hinted at un-known dangers that may be around us. I can't put my finger on any, though. Everything is going great really, and I'm as happy as I could ever hope to be under these circumstances. But I have this sense of impending calamity that I'm unable to shake off. I hope I'm just being paranoid—but I never used to be.

As far as the outside is concerned, we used to be so anxious during our first few months, constantly monitoring the exterior light and temperature gauges and checking for radio transmissions. But now we've almost stopped caring. So much so that, when the gauges went kaput a year or two ago, we didn't bother fixing them. At that time, it was still minus 127 degrees and pitch dark, and I'm pretty sure that's exactly what it is now. The radio too has gone on the blink. It's almost as if the gods want to shield us from the grim external reality.

In this comfortable yet precarious existence, the Millers have been marvelous companions. I've always been very close to Anna and Elizabeth, and now I can add Jessica to that list. She and I don't rub each other the wrong way like in the old days. We lock horns once in a while, as she's far too intelligent to let anything dubious from me go unchallenged, but now it's all done without rancor. On the flip side, I have to reconcile myself to the fact that Nicole and I are no longer an "item." Had I written my diary last year, I'd have noted that sometime during Years Three and Four our relationship petered out and we became just friends. I'm not sure why this happened, but it somehow felt like a natural progression. We don't have enough in common to be lovers, I guess. Nevertheless, I'm sure that each of us will always remain a caring friend and companion to the other. I continue to admire and respect her, and I think she feels the same.

Having broken up with my fiancée, I would normally have got into an intimate relationship with someone else in due course. But nothing is normal in the Shell. I continue to remain *single*, if that word has any meaning here. One might wonder why the constant presence of two very attractive girls doesn't create temptation for me, but Anna and Jessica are the closest I'll ever come to having daughters of my own. What I feel toward them is not lust but love, deep, pure, intense love. And I think the feeling is mutual.

And what to say of Elizabeth? My regard for her grows with each day, but so does my concern. That heartbreaking speech of hers! Was it just a spur-of-the-moment thing, or was it driven by some deep sense of impending mortality? I hope it's not the latter, because existence without her is unthinkable.

Anna's Journal

I'm finding these entries hard to write, even though this is only my third. There's so little to talk about, yet so much!

In pre-Shell days I wrote about birthday parties and movies
and friends and stuff like that. Now all that is gone. Oddly, I
don't miss any of it so much. I don't even miss my teachers,
my friends, or my relatives too much, except now and then
when something triggers a memory and makes me suddenly
realize what I've lost and for a while I weep like a child. But
the feeling doesn't last and I find myself going back to my
work and my life here as if the rest of the world never existed.
And the others here seem to feel the same way. The world
has narrowed to just the Shell and the five of us inside it.
Yet in so many ways even the dullest moment of my life here
is much more remarkable than the most exciting one in the
old days. Just to think of our survival, moment to moment,
against such incredible odds is mindboggling.

The Eco dome continues to be a constant delight. My
initial nervousness about being given the sole responsibility
for it is gone, and I feel confident about what I do there. I'm
particularly proud of the way I handled the manure issue,
introducing it very cautiously and looking out for positive
or adverse reactions. That's how I found that all the plants
except the tropical fruit trees thrive on it. For the latter, I
will keep using chemical fertilizer. It won't last very long, but
I'll try to stretch it out as much as I can. It's such a delight
to bring a basket of fresh produce to the table each day and
watch everyone's faces light up!

I'll never make it as an engineer, but I can't believe how
comfortable I am around machines now thanks to my stints
at the Geo dome. I think I'm actually of some use to Larry
there. Poor guy—he worries so much about us. Too much.
Sure, the well could run cold one day, as he fears, but why
worry about that now? Besides, that might never happen.

It's so great that he confides his fears in me. His trust means worlds to me.

Nicole's Journal

Five years after the Shroud. I've never been good with words and have none to describe our situation here. Was there ever a group of humans whose existence was compounded of such extremes? Death and dark and cold and horror outside—love and life and comfort inside. Perhaps Anna, with her gift of the gab, or Jessica, with her odd but spot-on phrases, can describe how it is to exist in a little oasis of life surrounded by a cold, dark, strange landscape, but I can't do justice to it.

Talking of the Shroud, what does it all mean? Normally I'm the most practical person imaginable and have little interest in matters outside my immediate sphere. But the Shroud is a reality, not an abstraction. Its existence demands some kind of explanation. I keep coming back to the same questions about the meaning of everything—if the entire human race could be snuffed out so easily, what's the point of existence? It's ironic that in the old days I never believed in a creator, and if anyone had asked, I would have said that life was simply a biochemical accident. But now that almost everything's been destroyed, I'm no longer satisfied with that explanation. Paradoxically, the destruction makes me more inclined to accept the idea of creation.

I talked to both Larry and Mum about this issue, and their responses were typical. Mum says that the Shroud has overturned her Buddhist worldview, in which lower life forms, including humans, keep evolving until they attain the supreme state of perfection and merge with the Infinite. She says Buddhist theory can't explain the Shroud, but she continues to believe in the immortal soul that persists beyond the death of the physical body. So the fact that the human race was virtually wiped out doesn't mean the end of existence, just the end of our bodies. Perhaps the souls will continue to evolve in some other way without physical existence. Her ideas are interesting but, in the end, resolve nothing.

Larry agrees that the Shroud raises fundamental questions about our place in the universe, but he prefers to focus on immediate concerns. He's always been even more practical and down-to-earth than me and has never had much interest in philosophy or spirituality and stuff like that. Oddly, though, he has tremendous admiration for Mum, despite her spiritual beliefs. Perhaps it's *because* of them that he's drawn to her, sensing she has something to offer that he needs? If so, I don't think he's conscious of it, nor is he ready to open up and sit with her for an Om chanting session. It would be so good for him if he did, though. Perhaps he would worry less about our safety and be more willing to accept whatever happens.

Not that I'm pondering these issues all the time. I try to keep myself busy. It's not the same "busy" of my hospital days, when I worked round the clock to save lives, but it feels just as important, if not more so. Mum's still a big worry. She's growing stronger and stronger, yet she's still vulnerable to spells of breathlessness and feels dizzy after any sudden exertion.

I realize that until the Shroud I was never really a member of my family—just a provider and occasional caretaker. But now I'm much more—a daughter to my mother and a mother to my daughters. It's a pity that the Shroud had to wipe out the planet before I realized how much my family meant to me.

My relationship with Larry too has evolved. He's turned from a lover into a dear friend. We started off as romantic partners, but as time went by our mutual passion began to subside, and about a year or two ago it went out altogether, leaving in its wake something perhaps even more valuable— deep affection. I think we care for each other more than ever, but in a different way from our romantic passion of old. We're like brother and sister. It's no loss to me. I've always wanted a brother, and could there be a better one than Larry?

Jessica's Journal

Five years gone, & weve settled into a groove. Work is still fun, though routine. Ive learned as much about the air system as there is to know. Hope Larry will move us around a bit—will be nice to work at Geo. He hides it, but hes really worried about it. I cd be of some use there. Anna, poor thing, is eager to please, but not the obvious choice for it. Though she amazes me w/ how much practical skill shes picked up. She still mixes up ohms & farads, or volts & amps, but she can now take a motor apart, replace the coil, & put it back together. Now thats a surprise. All that on top of her exploits in the greenhouse. Shes not such a flake as I thought. Perhaps I shd go there sometime & see what she does w/ her plants. That will give me a chance to spend some time w/ her as well. Perhaps if we spent more time together shed stop acting as if shes walking on eggshells when Im around. I might even be of some use there ... the idea of handling manure is repugnant, but perhaps I can get used to it, as one gets used to anything, including living inside a tiny insulated bubble on a cryogenic planet.

Other surprises. A big one is that Larry doesnt annoy me anymore. Once you give up hoping for something quirky or original or unexpected from him, he isnt too bad. He has the great ability to leave you alone. But perhaps I dont want to be left alone so much—now thats a surprise for you! Wish I cd hang out w/ him, be pally, like Anna. Wish I had her gift for prattle. I can see how much he enjoys it. Perhaps I can try to strike up a conversation on some neutral topic—nothing Shell or survival-related, or hell get into his anxious carrying the world on his shoulders mode. Perhaps books or movies? He doesnt like anything edgy or twisted, Ill bet, based on what Ive learned about him & based on his collection here. So definitely not the *Hostel* movies or any Neal Stephenson books. No, probably something like Dickens or Thackeray or Maugham or Wodehouse or Shaw. A bit dull, that stuff, & really, really dated, but not all of its bad. Perhaps talk to him about *Vanity Fair* or *Pygmalion*, that cd be a starting point.

Another surprise is Mum. Or perhaps I shd say *puzzle* rather than *surprise*. Ive never seen her so openly affectionate. She, who never gave me or Anna time of day, now hugs & kisses us at every opportunity! This place has done crazy things to all of us, but her transformation from full-time pro to loving mum is still puzzling. Its very touching, but theres something odd & confused about it, perhaps even desperate. I guess she thinks a lot about the outside, & that makes her fearful. But its not fear of the perils outside that I sense in her—its something more fundamental. In a way its too bad weve all enjoyed great health so far. A couple of patients on her hands wd help take her mind off other stuff. Perhaps I shd fake an illness. No, that wdnt work. She wd see through it in an instant. Im too bad an actor, & shes too good a doctor.

Grandma, shes the one whos remained constant. Yet she too caught us all by surprise, except perhaps Mum, when she gave toast yesterday. Was that a generic comment about hoping to be alive when we got out, or does she really think she hasnt got long to live? I cant ask her directly. Ill ask Mum. I desperately hope it was just a remark. Larry said she might be the most important member here. I think shes already proved that. Shes the glue that holds us together. Its not anything she does thats special. But if were all feeling better & acting nicer, its largely due to her presence. If not for her, Id be snapping at everyone left & right, Anna wd be starting at every noise, Mum wd be running around like a headless chicken, and Larry wd be alphaing us all the time. She softens everything. W/o her wed all fall apart, incl. Larry.

Elizabeth's Journal

What can I say? My heart is too full for words. Five years from the day we walked into the Shell we're still alive. It's miraculous. How many times have I used that word? Yet with each passing day, the word justifies itself even more.

Yesterday's celebration. I wasn't really planning to talk about my mortality, but it just came out. Sometimes you simply can't hide the truth from the people you love, and perhaps you mustn't. Nicole, poor, dear child, has been trying to hide the truth from me, but you don't become a spiritual counselor without developing a nose for the white lie. She thinks I don't have much longer to go and she doesn't want me to know it. But she needn't have worried, I knew it long before she did, before we even came to this place. Since then, my awareness of my impending demise has only been growing. My meditation sessions have been getting more and more intense and profound. Whereas in the past it took me a good half-hour to quell my thoughts and get into a meditative state, now I get into a trance almost instantly. And my trance seems to be getting deeper, and I feel increasingly in touch with some blissful part of me that I could only occasionally sense in the past. And even when I'm doing my other activities, that feeling, that connection, never goes away entirely, like it used to in the past.

It takes me back to my time with Lama Amoli in Nepal. Usually alert, engaged, and animated, one day she started to slowly withdraw into some special place where we couldn't follow. Three years later and she was no longer with us, gone to her Samadhi at the age of forty-eight. I can see some of that happening in me now. I hope I can slow it down enough to see everyone safe and sound in the world outside, no longer cowering under the Shroud.

I never gave it much credence when my family members said how much they needed me, but now, at the risk of sounding arrogant, I must say that I've started thinking so too. Even though everything has gone smoothly so far in the Shell, the psychological stress of life in this highly artificial setting is severe. Although we go about our daily tasks as if nothing is wrong, deep down we are only too aware of the horror that lies outside. So anything that I can do to reassure people and keep them sane and happy and laughing is of value. I think I'm of use to Nicole—by getting her to worry about my health, I keep her from asking herself too many disturbing questions.

My sweet little granddaughters need me more than ever, although my earlier fear—that this strange environment, with only three older people and each other for company, with no other role models, might make them grow up strange and confused—has proved utterly baseless. They were innocent, awkward teenagers when they walked in here, now they've blossomed into charming and wonderful women. Too bad there aren't any young men around to admire them. How tragic it is for them to grow up never knowing the joys of romance and relationships! The only man here is Larry, who is as loving and wonderful as a man can be—even Jessica now likes him without reservation. Too bad we don't practice polygamy, or else I could have persuaded Larry to add all of us to his harem! We'd each of us drive him crazy in our own way, and he'd only love us the more for it. Perhaps that's what he needs to divert his mind from his worries. I know I'm being naughty here, but old women have their fantasies too! Besides, he reminds me so much of George.

21
Valves

GIVEN THEIR BIZARRE situation and grim outlook, the Shellmates enjoyed the first few years much more than they could have anticipated. They lived in comfort. Within the constraints of their dwelling, they lacked almost nothing. They ate well, they enjoyed their work, they had games and books and films to relieve the monotony of their existence. Given the choice, they would no doubt have preferred a normal life outside. But bereft of that possibility, they would have been happy to live in the Steady State indefinitely.

Unfortunately, those pleasant conditions didn't last.

The first sign of trouble came in the "autumn" of Year Six. The seasons of course meant nothing anymore. Outside the Shell it was just as cold and dark in peak summer as in midwinter. The temperature appeared stable at minus 127 degrees—whether in reality or due to a broken gauge, they couldn't tell—and it stayed pitch black, without a ray of sunshine to relieve the endless night. Only in the Eco dome did the artificial climate vary during the year to accommodate the natural growing cycles of plants from across the world. Else-where in the Shell seasonal conditions remained constant. The time of day meant nothing either, with only changes in the temperature and light settings to distinguish day from night. Nevertheless, the Shellmates adhered to pre-Shroud calendar and clock conventions, with the Australian autumn going from March through May.

The trouble started on March 25 during the morning shift at the Air dome. Jessica, looking up from a pressure gauge she had been examining, beckoned Larry.

"Didn't we replace this valve just a few weeks ago?" She tapped on an air intake pipe connected to the gauge, which started beeping at that moment.

"Yes, we did," said Larry. "In fact, we replaced it twice within the past year. Is it acting up again?"

"It's stuck closed, so intake pressure is down."

Larry frowned. "What's the reading?"

"Should be 2.5 atmospheres but reads 1.2. Way below spec."

"Hmm, that's not good. It means the air isn't getting scrubbed."

"Notice anything this morning?"

"No. Did you?"

"The air in Central felt stale."

Larry's brow creased with worry. "Then we have a problem. You and Anna have a much better sense of the environment than us older folks. If you thought the air was stuffy, it's prob-ably going to get worse very soon."

Larry's communicator buzzed. He spoke for a few seconds, and then hung up, biting his lip. "It's already happening. That was your mum from the clinic. They found it stuffy in there and have gone off to see if it's the same story at Central. In any case, it looks like we've got to replace the valve at once."

"Aren't we running low on valves?"

Larry was about to respond when his communicator buzzed again. The air in Central was also stuffy, it seemed.

"And this is why," Jessica said, beckoning Larry to a console that showed air quality parameters. "Carbon dioxide should be under 500 ppm, but it seems to have gone above 2,400. We can blame the valve for that."

"But how did this happen so quickly? We were okay last night. Even you and Anna didn't seem to notice anything amiss."

"Could've happened while we slept. We wouldn't have felt it then."

"Whatever happened, we've got to fix it immediately."

At that moment another pressure gauge started to beep. This was on one of the exhaust pipes.

"Hello, another valve's died," Jessica said and, after a quick check, added: "It's also stuck closed."

Larry rushed over to join her, and together they looked at the gauges for the various exhaust pipes. Several were now in the red zone, though none were beeping yet. They raced back and looked at the remaining intake gauges. Many were showing red.

"It must be a cascading effect," said Larry. "One valve fails, and it creates additional load on the remaining ones, causing them to fail in turn. I suspect many if not most of our valves are getting ready to fail." Larry took a deep breath. "Nothing to do but to check each one and replace as many bad ones as we can before we get more failures."

"But we don't have that many valves in stock!"

Larry made a quick decision. "We'll have to take the valves from the spare pump."

Jessica stared at him. "Are you serious? That will kill the spare pump. Then if the main one fails we'll have no backup."

"True," said Larry grimly, "but we have no choice."

"Can't we shut the air system down until we figure out what the hell's going on?"

"How? The air is already stuffy, and with the purifier off it will quickly become unbreathable. Unless we switch to the spare, which we can't because we need to steal its valves. All we can do is run the main pump at its lowest setting."

Jessica needed no further persuasion, and the two of them raced against time to replace the valves. They were only half-way done by lunchtime but couldn't afford to take a break. So far their luck had held, and no other valves had failed. But it was just a matter of time. It took them until 3:00 p.m. to replace all the malfunctioning valves and switch the air pump back to full power. Fortunately, no others failed in the interim, and the situation was stabilized. But they were now out of spare valves and had lost their backup pump.

By the end of dinner the air felt fresh again, but the mood at Central was gloomy. Larry let Jessica explain the situation. Her knowledge of the air system now surpassed his, and it was a huge relief to share the responsibility with her.

"As you learned during lectures, the purifier freshens stale air by scrubbing carbon dioxide from it," she said. "It relies on a set of high-tech valves that regulate inflow and outflow. The valves are supposed to last forever but have been failing left and right. We don't know why—maybe it's thermal stress, metal fatigue, or something else. No clue. The problem is, one failed valve stresses the others."

"And causes them to fail, too?" Anna asked.

"Right. But until now, it's been one at a time, and we managed to fix the problem before it got out of hand."

"And now?"

"One valve must've died last night while we slept. Since we didn't replace it, others started failing one after the other, faster and faster. Once they fail we can't repair them, only replace. Which is what we did. Like crazy."

"We replaced nearly forty valves today," Larry added. "Virtually all of them."

"So you managed to save the day!" said Elizabeth. "You're both wonderful."

"What's worrying you then?" Nicole asked.

"We used up all our spares." Jessica paused, waiting for the news to sink in. "And when the next valve fails, it's curtains for the air purifier."

Elizabeth exchanged wide-eyed looks with Nicole and Anna.

"Jesus! What do we do then?" cried Anna, turning to Larry. "Couldn't we just, like, punch a hole in the wall and let in fresh air from outside?"

"We could, but the air outside is at minus 127 degrees. It'll take way too much energy to heat it."

"Surely there must be something we can do?" Anna looked from Larry to Jessica. "We can't just fold our hands and pray another valve doesn't fail!"

Larry pressed Anna's hands. "There is something *you* can do."

"But what?"

"Remember the chlorella panels? They might be our only hope now."

"And they better work," said Jessica, "or else we'll choke or freeze when the next valve fails."

Anna stared at her and then at Larry, her mouth open. "You must be kidding! The algae might not even be viable after so many years in cold storage. Even if they are, they'll need, like, months to grow."

"I know," said Larry. "I didn't expect the air purifier to fall apart so quickly. I thought we'd have a year at least to work on alternatives. I was wrong. Now we have just weeks, not months."

"Are you serious? You want me to raise the chlorella from the dead in a few weeks?"

"Yes. Can you do it?"

"How can I know?" Anna gave a short, incredulous laugh. "It's not as simple as, you know, planting a seed and letting it germinate."

Larry shook his head apologetically. "I'm sorry to put you on the spot. But it's all in your hands now."

Anna said nothing for a moment and then sighed. "Okay, I'll try. But I'll need to work around the clock on it."

Larry nodded. "Yes, I thought of that. Let's change our schedule and drop the nobody-goes-anywhere-alone rule. From now on, I suggest you spend as much time in Eco as you need. Anyone who's not busy with other stuff will come and help you."

"Thanks," Anna said. "I'm going to need all the moral support I can get."

Larry paused, and after some deliberation, said: "There's one more issue I want to draw your attention to. Nothing major, nothing at all like the air problem, but nevertheless something that you should know. We seem to be running a tad low on energy as well. The—"

"What!" Anna broke in. "And you told me nothing while I was working with you?"

"I should've told you. Forgive me."

"Don't be silly, I didn't mean to accuse you. But what's causing the problem?"

"For some reason, the well has been producing less heat in recent months. I think it's due to geological factors, not our energy use."

"How come we didn't feel any difference?" Nicole asked.

"Well, the system compensates for the diminished heat output by increasing the rate of fluid flow. So the energy available to us has remained constant."

"Then what's the problem?" said Nicole.

"I think I can answer that," said Anna. "When we increase fluid flow we extract heat faster. That reduces the useful life-time of the well."

There were more worried looks.

"So we might consider cutting down on our energy use a bit," Larry suggested.

After a chorus of groans, there was a long pause until Jessica broke it. "There's a silver lining to all this," she said. Everyone looked at her in surprise—they'd expected her to paint the worst-case scenario, not point out the bright side. "If the air purifier fails, we could seal off the Air dome. That would save a ton of energy!"

Larry smiled. Over the years, he had learned to appreciate Jessica's dark humor. But the others didn't look reassured.

"Well, that's one way of looking at it," said Anna.

They talked about it some more but concluded that they could do nothing about the air problem except hope that Anna's chlorella panels kicked in before the purifier broke down. "We could try breathing less," Jessica said, winking at Larry. Anna and Nicole grimaced, but Elizabeth said, "Many a true word is spoken in jest," and promised to teach them a breathing exercise used by yogis to slow down their respiration.

For the energy problem, they agreed to institute some conservation measures. They would turn all the thermostats down by two degrees, shower on alternate days and for shorter durations, wash their clothes less frequently, and use fewer dishes every day. To adjust to the cooler temperatures, they would wear an extra layer of clothing.

"Don't say the H-word, Jessica," said Larry in a mock-warning tone.

"I'll never mention hibernation again," promised Jessica. Her hibernation references had become a running joke between them.

"But you just mentioned it," said Anna.

"Mentioned what?" asked her sister innocently.

"The H-word," said Anna, refusing to be trapped.

"You silly young things," chided their grandmother affectionately. The tension ebbed as the girls dissolved into giggles. Of late, they were often seen sharing a private joke, something they had never done before. As teenagers, they'd had very little in common, but as young women they shared an unspoken *complicité*. Jessica occasionally excused herself from Air or Health to help her sister in the Eco dome; if she disliked handling soil or manure, she didn't complain about it.

"As long as we can laugh, there's hope for us," smiled Elizabeth.

22
Chlorella

THE ENERGY-USE RESTRICTIONS went into effect without causing too much inconvenience or discomfort. The chillier air made them a little lazy, but it also gave them an excuse to snuggle up even more than usual. The reduced showering schedule bothered the girls the most. After some discussion it was agreed to let them shower every day, while the others reduced their frequency to every third day to compensate. Elizabeth initially struggled to manage the kitchen on a lower energy budget. Soon, however, she figured out simple tricks to achieve her goal, such as cooking with closed containers or heating water in the oven while baking.

"Energy's overrated," Jessica said.

Nevertheless, the next three months were an anxious period. With the threat of air-purifier failure looming over them, they followed Anna's chlorella work with anxious eyes. Early signs from this endeavor were unpromising. Anna's initial set of six test panels, each with a different feeding mix, remained obstinately inert even after two weeks. She then experimented with different temperatures and humidity levels, but to no avail.

"Why the hell isn't it waking up?" Jessica asked, flicking one of the lifeless panels.

"I'm not sure." Anna rubbed her eyes, red from long hours of work. "I suspect chlorella might be super-sensitive to growing conditions. You know, feeding mixture, temperature, humidity, light exposure—one or more of those factors."

"Maybe you just need to find the right combo."

"Maybe. Obviously, I haven't found it yet." Anna groaned in frustration. "God! I want to take these goddamn panels and smash the crap out of them." Then her voice changed. "I'm beginning to think I'm no good at this." A teardrop emerged from her left eye and coursed down her cheek.

"Don't be an idiot." Jessica spoke sharply but wiped her sister's tears gently with a handkerchief. "Here's an idea— what if we all pitched in?"

Anna sniffed. "How? Aren't you already doing everything you can?"

"It could be more systematic. We can break the panels into smaller pieces. Each of us could work with a dozen pieces and vary a different factor across them."

While Anna was mulling over her sister's idea, Larry jumped in. "That's brilliant. It's a much better way to sample the combinatorial space."

"Makes sense," said Nicole. "Instead of making Anna do everything, we'll all help."

Though skeptical, Anna put the plan into effect at once. She allocated to each of her assistants a different dimension to explore. Larry would try a different humidity level on each of his panels while keeping the other parameters fixed, while Jessica would vary only the feeding mixture, and so on. Anna's skepticism seemed well-founded—four weeks later, her sister's strategy had nothing to show for it. Not a single panel had come to life. By the middle of the third month, a pall of gloom fell over everyone. *It's hopeless*, Larry thought. *We're going to die, and it's entirely my fault.*

On the positive side, the air purifier continued to run perfectly, as if to make up for its earlier valve-wrecking tantrum. But, as Jessica reminded them, the purifier had worked perfectly in the past—until it failed. Unless the chlorella started growing, and fast, they were one valve away from breathing bottled air. As an emergency measure, Larry and Jessica moved some oxygen cylinders from Health to Central, ready to be opened at a moment's notice. If the worst happened, the family would at least get a few extra hours of respiration.

One morning toward the end of June in Year Six, as Larry and Jessica were morosely performing routine maintenance on the air system, Anna called them from Eco.

"Hey guys, when you have a moment I want to show you something here," she said. She spoke calmly, but the unnatural deliberation in her voice betrayed her excitement. Larry and Jessica rushed over to Eco, their hands still greasy, their gauges and pipes forgotten. They found the rest of the group peering at one of the panels. Anna was talking in an excited voice.

"Oh, there you are, you two air-heads!" she sang out. "Come and take a look."

The Eco dome was now chock-full of panels, and they all looked uniformly gray. All except one. Near the center of this panel, amidst a drab expanse, was a greenish stain about two inches in diameter.

"Guess what that is?" she asked.

"Is that your famous chlorella?" Jessica asked, grabbing her sister's arm in excitement, her customary pose of dour nonchalance forgotten.

"Yes, ladies and Larry, we have live growth!" said Anna. "It doesn't look like much, but give it another two weeks and we'll see."

"How did you pull it off?"

"I did something I should have tried long ago—I looked at all our failed panels under the microscope. It turned out that not all the failures were equal—some of them had come pretty close to success. So that told me what parameters to tweak. Using the best failures as a starting point, I tried like a hundred feeding mixes until I found one that worked."

"Bravo! So you found the right growing conditions?"

"No, *we* did."

"Great work, Anna!" exclaimed Larry, hugging her.

"You did it!" cried Nicole. Everyone beamed in delight. This was the first bit of good news they'd had in a while.

Now that they knew the exact conditions under which the chlorella would grow, Anna and her assistants worked around the clock to replicate the conditions for their entire stock of panels. The alga grew painfully slowly at first, creeping across the panels like a snail in slow motion. Adjusting the light frequency to the bluish side of the spectrum seemed to accelerate the growth slightly. Minor changes to the feeding mix also seemed to make things go faster, though not by much. Emotions in the family alternated between jubilation and despondency. Then, exactly 29 days after Anna's initial success, some sort of positive feedback seemed to occur. The organism started growing faster and faster, and by the end of the sixth week it completely covered the panels. Carbon dioxide levels in the Shell fell below 300 ppm for the first time ever.

On July 31 the family held a celebration in Anna's honor. Jessica baked her a cake in the shape of a chlorella panel. Elizabeth and Nicole told anecdotes about how, even as a child, Anna could get the stubbornest seed to sprout and the frailest sapling to thrive. Larry proposed a toast to her as "the savior of our breath." It was Anna's proudest hour.

Her achievement turned out to be timely. At 11.37 p.m. on August 6 of Year Six, an intake valve failed. Others followed in rapid succession. By 6:00 a.m. the following morning the purifier was dead.

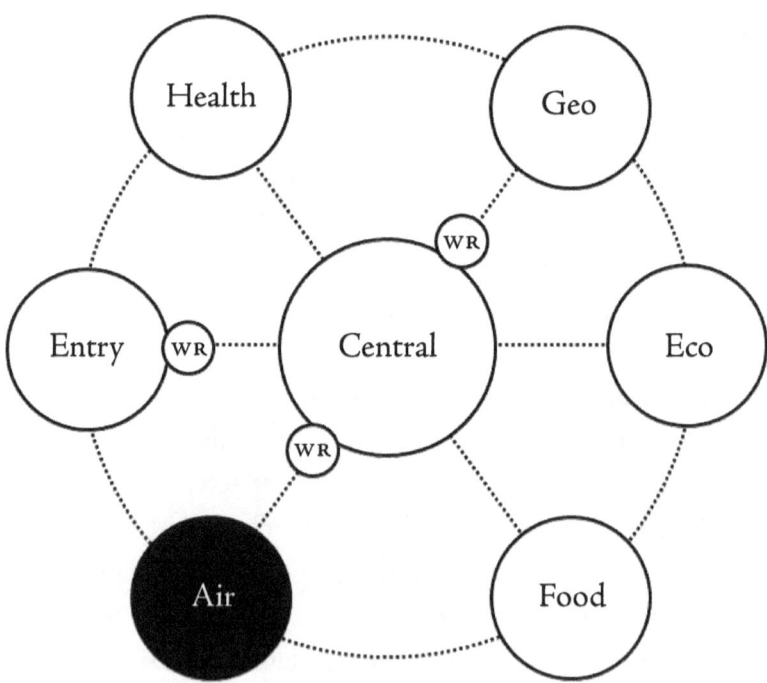

23

Comfort

Though it had been touch and go, a major calamity had been averted. The tremendous relief that followed gave way to a few days of euphoria, and then life went back to what passed for normal in the Shell. The women soon forgot the air purifier debacle and returned to their routines.

Larry, however, didn't. Try as he might, he couldn't stop blaming himself for the near-catastrophe. He was the one who had designed the Shell and chosen its efficient-but-complex air purification system. Something less fancy, he now realized, would have been more robust. And why hadn't he ensured a bigger supply of valves, which cost almost nothing, or provided some means to manufacture them, such as a 3D printer? If he erred in this one regard, what other design flaws had he been guilty of? When would they start revealing themselves? Though the others—including his erstwhile critic, Jessica—strongly and emphatically rejected his self-criticism, he couldn't let himself off the hook.

Normally a sound sleeper who enjoyed pleasant dreams, he now started having nightmares of catastrophes happening in the Shell. The fuel store exploded. Giant rats ate up their food reserves. Black-masked intruders broke into Central and kidnapped his family. Though in the clear light of day he could see these dreams as absurd, they often caused him to wake up in the small hours, his chest thumping and his hands clammy. Soon his appetite diminished and he had trouble holding down food. Dark hollows appeared under his eyes. His voice grew hoarse.

It was obvious that Larry wasn't doing well. It was also clear what the problem was—his sense of responsibility for them and his fear of letting them down. What wasn't obvious was the remedy. The others did all they could to cheer him up, but in vain. Anna's teasing, Jessica's scolding, the reassuring words of the older women—none of it made a difference. Even the valium that Nicole forced him to take didn't help. Something direct and dramatic was needed to shake Larry out of his mood, they felt, but what?

About three weeks after the failure of the air purifier and the closure of the Air dome, while Larry was busy elsewhere, the others held an emergency meeting in the clinic.

"We have a problem," said Nicole.

"You bet," said Jessica. "Larry."

"Our dear leader is in a funk," Anna said. "And sinking deeper each day."

"Poor dear, he's looking terrible," agreed Elizabeth. "He's lost so much weight, yet he barely touched his food today!"

"And he hardly sleeps. At this rate he's heading for a breakdown. And yet, there's nothing physically wrong with him."

"The man's an idiot!" Jessica exploded. "Still blaming himself for that stupid purifier."

Elizabeth shook her head. "I think it's more than that. It's as if ... as if all the stress and responsibility of the past few years has suddenly caught up with him."

"We've tried consoling him, baiting him, even yelling at him," said Anna. "Nothing works."

They sat around in worried silence. "Too bad you and he aren't the pair of lovebirds you used to be," Anna said to her mother finally. Until now, the end of Nicole's romance with Larry had never been discussed.

Jessica nodded. "A romantic interest might have diverted his mind from pointless self-blame."

"You may be right," admitted Nicole. "Unfortunately, we aren't lovers anymore. We are like brother and sister now."

Anna directed a searching gaze at her mother. "Mum, here's something I've always wanted to ask you. Why did you guys, you know, break up?"

Nicole sighed. "Our relationship simply ran its course. We were once attracted to each other, but I am not his type. I'm too brisk and practical. He'd have preferred someone gentle and caring."

"Like Grandma?"

"Exactly." Nicole gazed into space for a few seconds. "But to be honest, he isn't my type either. He's too sober and serious for me. All the men I saw before him, including your father, they were on the wild side. They had their faults, big ones, but my chemistry with them was much stronger."

Jessica stared at her. "Are you serious? You're saying you and Larry were mismatched?"

"Yes. That's why our relationship was fun for a while but then ended naturally."

"I used to think you were made for each other," Anna said.

Elizabeth sighed. "It's shocking how little we know about the people living under the same roof."

Glum silence prevailed for a few moments.

"You've helped so many people, Grandma," Anna said, wiping away a tear. "Couldn't you do something for him?"

"I've tried, dear. But he refuses to admit he has a problem. I can't help him unless he opens up to me."

Another short silence ensued, then Jessica sprang up from her chair, a gleam in her eye. "I know how to make that happen, Grandma."

"Make what happen?"

"Make Larry open up to you."

"Then tell us, dear."

Jessica's eyes twinkled with mischief. "I'll tell you what to do. But I'm not sure you'd be willing."

"Dearest, you know I'd do anything for him."

"Anything? You really mean it?"

"Yes, of course. Tell me what you want me to do."

Jessica continued to hesitate and spoke only after being urged by the others. "Well, it's a radical idea."

"We've exhausted all the non-radical ones," Nicole said. "Tell us."

"It will shock you."

Nicole laughed without mirth. "Sweetheart, we're living in a tiny bubble on a dead planet. Humanity has ceased to exist. We barely escaped freezing before we got here and have been flirting with death ever since. We're much less shockable than you think."

"Are you sure?"

Anna clicked her tongue. "Damn it, Jessica! Stop teasing. Tell us your bloody idea if you really have one."

Jessica made a gesture of surrender. "Okay, but consider yourselves warned." She paused to choose her words carefully. "Let's go back in time to our very first day in the Shell. Do you remember everything about it?"

"Yes, and how!" said Anna. "As if it happened this morning."

"The chopper ride, the race to the Shell, the shower, the tour, the food …," said Nicole.

Anna nodded and turned to her sister. "And the meeting where you kept challenging Larry. How I wanted to pull your hair to make you stop."

Jessica giggled. "I was snippy, wasn't I? That's all water under the bridge. Larry and I are besties now. But coming back to the meeting, remember what he said at the end?"

"Not every word, no, but I can paraphrase. Screw the old rules. To survive, we might have to do some crazy stuff."

"Bravo! And did you agree with what he said?"

Anna paused to think. "I did. But it seemed to be more like a theoretical idea than, you know, something that we'd actually have to do. And so it has proved. I can't think of a single occasion … okay, maybe the shower we took together that first day, that felt weird, but it was Grandma's idea, not Larry's. And perhaps our sleeping arrangement is a bit unusual. But we've done nothing, really, you could call *taboo*."

"Larry said we'd need to do that only when our survival was at risk," Nicole pointed out.

Jessica nodded her head impatiently. "But isn't our survival at risk now? Due to Larry's health?"

The others digested this thought for a few moments, moving uneasily in their chairs. Finally, Anna said: "Well, now that you point it out, Larry's health does threaten his survival and ours too. If he died, I wouldn't want to continue living."

Nicole and Elizabeth nodded assent.

"Our own survival apart, we owe it to him," Elizabeth said. "He saved our lives. We should be willing to do anything to save his."

"Anything, Grandma? Glad you said it, because you'll have the starring role."

Elizabeth's eyes grew wide. "Starring role? How, dear?"

"Okay, let's approach it this way. Would you agree something drastic needs to happen to jolt our friend out of his crisis?"

"Absolutely."

"And what are the most drastic social weapons? The most primordial instincts? The most basic forces?"

"The most basic forces?"

Jessica clicked her tongue. "How dense you are! Okay, think of it this way. What's *not* allowed in movies for kids?"

"Well … sex and violence, I guess."

"Exactly! Those are the basic forces. And that's my plan."

Elizabeth looked at her in bewilderment. "Are you saying we should … use *violence?*"

"No, not violence."

It took the women a second to catch her drift.

"*Sex?*" exclaimed Anna. "Are you crazy?"

"Yes, I mean sex. And no, I'm not crazy."

"It's the craziest idea I've heard."

Jessica waved her arms impatiently. "Why is this so hard to grasp? I'm suggesting we use lovemaking to get Larry out of his funk."

Anna made a face. "This discussion is getting too icky for me."

Jessica sighed. "Look, this isn't easy for me either. I'm not immune to the ick factor. But I can't think of anything else that might work."

Nicole laughed incredulously. "You talk as if we could press a button and order a lovemaking session. You know he and I are not a couple anymore."

"I wasn't thinking of you."

Nicole stared at Jessica. "Of all the crazy ideas … are you suggesting that you or Anna …?"

"Close, but no cigar," said Jessica. "We'd do anything for Larry, but I don't think he fancies us that way, does he, Anna?"

Anna had recovered from her initial shock at her sister's idea. "Larry and one of us?" She laughed. "No dice. For a while, I used to wonder … but I figured out that's not what he wants. He sees himself as a father figure."

"Yes, he's a fraud," said Jessica. "For all his tough talk about taboos, he'd sooner die than break that one."

Anna nodded. "And what happens if we get pregnant? We haven't had our tubes tied like you, Mum."

Nicole had recovered her composure. "I see where you're going with this. You two are out of the picture and so am I. Which leaves us with …"

Mother and daughters turned their gaze to the remaining member of the quartet.

Elizabeth gasped. "Surely you can't be thinking of *me*?"

"Yes, we are!"

Elizabeth blushed a deep scarlet. "You must be joking, dear! An old crone like me?"

"Old crone, my eye. Healthy, attractive older woman. Isn't she, Anna?"

"Absolutely! Sultry and sensual in a way that the rest of us can only envy. Don't you agree, Mum?"

Nicole paused to marshal her thoughts. Jessica's idea was shocking and radical, but the more she thought about it, the more it made sense. "Well, I did mention a few minutes ago that your Grandma would be a much better match for Larry than me." She turned to Elizabeth. "And I should confess that I was always a tiny bit jealous of you. The way Larry looks at you sometimes, the way he never looked at me, with such admiration. Like the other day when you were bending down to put something on his plate ..." Elizabeth stared open-mouthed at Nicole, who turned to Jessica: "So yes, if we follow your crazy plan, Grandma would be the right choice. Assuming she agrees."

Jessica looked at Elizabeth, who was sitting with a stunned look on her face. "Will you do it, Grandma?"

It took Elizabeth several seconds to find her voice. "Well!" she faltered. "I ... I don't know what to say."

"Say yes!" pleaded Anna.

"Will you at least consider it?" Nicole asked.

Elizabeth gazed at her daughter and granddaughters for a long moment. Her stupefied look gradually dissolved into her habitual untroubled expression, the hint of a mischievous smile on her lips. "Dear children, would you be shocked if I told you ..."

"Told us what, Grandma?"

"That I've often fantasized … about what you're suggesting?"

It was Nicole's turn to look shocked. "Really, Mum!"

"I'm sorry, dear. It's wicked of me. But I've always had a thing for Larry."

Nicole and her daughters sat in stunned silence until Elizabeth spoke. "Do you really want me to carry it out?"

Nicole was the first to recover. "Desperate times call for desperate measures," she said, and the girls nodded vigorously. "None of us can bear to see Larry fall to pieces before our eyes. I don't know if it'll work, but I can't think of anything else."

"Nothing to lose by trying," said Jessica.

"Very well, I'll give it a try." Elizabeth looked at Nicole thoughtfully. "But what makes you think he'll respond? Even if he's attracted to me, as you claim?"

Nicole took a deep breath and exhaled. "We all know how much regard he has for you. I think he cares about you even more than he cares for me or the girls. I've been really worried about your health, and so have the girls, but Larry has been the most concerned. In fact, sometimes I think your health worries him more than our problems with air, or energy, or anything else. If you could show him that there's life in those old bones of yours, that would reassure him more than anything else."

Elizabeth smiled, but looked doubtful. "But what will he think about taking advantage of his companions?"

"It doesn't apply to you. You're a woman of mature years, not a girl he has nurtured into adulthood. Further, if you couched it as a dying woman's last wish, I don't see how he could refuse you. A little white lie would be all it takes."

Elizabeth giggled. "What a wicked mind you have, my dear! I am finding all these hidden sides to you. Very well, you've convinced me."

"You are a sport, Mum."

"So when should we …?"

"How about this afternoon?"

"So soon?"

"If we're going to do something crazy, it's better to do it before we change our minds. Besides, every day that we wait is one more day that he suffers."

"Then say no more. I'll try my luck this afternoon, unless you have second thoughts."

"No second thoughts," said Nicole firmly. "Jessica's plan sounded crazy at first, but the more I think about it, the more I'm convinced that it's the only thing to do. It's either that or watch the man we love destroy himself."

"Let's hope it works."

"It will."

"I must admit that I'm getting excited about it already. It feels wicked, but I can't wait to do it."

"After all you've done for us, you deserve to have some fun, too. Besides, I have another motive."

"What?"

"Your health. I know you love to meditate, but I'm worried that you're overdoing it. Didn't you tell me that your master in Nepal began to meditate more and more in her last year or two, and one day never came out of her trance?"

"Yes, that's what happened. Fancy your remembering that."

"So with our little scheme we can kill two health birds with one stone—you'll meditate less and engage more in an activity that gets your heart pumping and your endorphins flowing."

"You silly thing!" giggled Elizabeth, blushing.

"I'll be there to monitor you with my stethoscope. I'll make sure your pulse rate stays in the safe zone."

All four women collapsed into giggles that turned into peals of laughter until tears flowed.

Later that afternoon, as Larry slumped wearily over his notes and calculations, Elizabeth came up to him.

"Larry, do you think you could come to my room? I wanted to ask you something personal."

"Certainly," said Larry, welcoming a break from his air and energy worries, and followed her down to her chamber. As the two went downstairs, Nicole and the girls exchanged a meaningful glance.

"If they're not back in five minutes our plan's a success!" said Jessica.

"Lucky Grandma!" sighed Anna.

It was nearly two hours before the pair returned from their tryst. Elizabeth had a gleam of mischief in her eyes. Equally, Larry—he of the calm, steady, even keel—looked blissful, guilty, and sheepish in equal measure.

"Success!" Jessica whispered to her sister.

And a success it proved over the next few weeks. Larry came out of his funk with a spring in his step; he ate well, slept soundly, and regained his cheerful spirit. But he became more than the Larry of old. For someone normally sober and poised, he often sang or smiled for no apparent reason, and acted playful with Anna and Jessica. The girls rolled their eyes at each other and took a while to adjust to the new Larry, but when they did they decided they liked him even better now. He had always been kind and competent and strong; now he was actually fun to be with. "RIP stuffed-shirt Larry," Jessica told her sister.

Elizabeth, too, was transformed. In the past, though she never spared herself when taking care of others, she often appeared to be struggling against a natural lassitude. She always did more than her share of everyday chores and activities, but it was obvious that, left to herself, she would prefer to just *be*. Though she was always available to help anyone, and was a wonderful listener, her eyes rarely lost their look of dreamy abstraction. A part of her seemed to dwell in some mystical realm where the cares and sorrows of life didn't penetrate. Now, though as placid as ever, she was also alert and engaged. She endured the girls' chaffing with good-natured indulgence.

About four months after Larry's recovery, the geothermal well started to cool again.

24

Heating

THE GEOTHERMAL WELL functioned perfectly until the end of November in Year Five, when its output fell by three percent over the course of a few days. Unlike most alternative energy sources, geothermal doesn't fluctuate much, so only minor fluid pressure adjustments were necessary to keep the energy output constant. A three percent drop was within specification, so Larry did not give it much attention until he observed a few weeks later that it had fallen another percentage point. By the time of the air-quality crisis, it was down five percent, but even that didn't raise alarm. At that rate of cooling, Larry thought, the well would remain hot and productive with at least fifty percent capacity for several more years. Furthermore, their austerity measures had reduced energy needs by six percent. And as Jessica had predicted, the failure of the Air dome proved to be a blessing in disguise for the power situation. Switching off the purifier and shutting off the heat to that dome reduced their power requirements by another twelve percent. By the time all this happened, their energy capacity exceeded their consumption. They seemed to be ahead of the game, and the well seemed to have stabilized.

Around mid-January of Year Seven, however, the well began to cool again. Until then, they were using less energy than the well's maximum output, but now they were losing that advantage. The cooling this time was more rapid than before. By mid-April the well had cooled by another fifteen percent. They were now using eighteen percent less energy than before, but the well had cooled by a total of twenty percent—their energy use was in the red again. The deficit was now beyond the capacity of the automated systems to correct, so Larry increased fluid pressure manually until their power needs were met.

The family held a meeting to discuss the falling energy output. Larry explained how their earlier energy conservation measures and the closure of the Air dome had bought them several months of extra time.

"Can't we deal with that by increasing fluid pressure?" Nicole asked, remembering an earlier discussion about how they were maintaining constant temperature in the living areas despite the cooling of the well.

"Yes, we can." Larry grimaced. "Unfortunately, at this rate, we will hit maximum fluid pressure in another month or two."

Nicole stared. "What happens after that?"

Larry avoided a direct answer. "At present the well seems to be cooling by about five percent every month. It seems to be a compounded decrease."

"What's that in plain English?"

"As the well cools, its rate of cooling should slow down," Jessica explained.

"And is that good or bad?" Nicole looked from one to the other.

"Compounded cooling is slower than linear cooling," said Larry. "But not slow enough for us."

"Then how much longer do we have?"

Nicole's question caused everyone to tense up. Larry tried an evasive answer, but she pressed him until he admitted that they would have just a quarter of their energy capacity in a couple of years. The well at that point wouldn't be hot enough to run the generators, and any heat from it would be lost in transmission. "It will be pretty much useless at that point," he concluded.

There was a short pause as the group digested the unwelcome news. A few years ago, such an announcement might have triggered exclamations of dismay. Now it elicited only grim silence. Having weathered other crises before, the Shellmates had an almost blind faith in their ability to deal with this one as well.

"Any suggestions?" asked Larry at last. He had gradually stopped making decisions by himself and now sought consensus. He relied on input from the girls and increasingly let them take the lead in policy discussions. *If there's going to be a future outside the Shell*, he told himself, *it'll be theirs.* It seemed only fair that they be allowed to lead. Besides, Anna and Jessica weren't the callow teens of their early days in the Shell; both were now mature, smart, and competent women.

"We could tighten our energy belts some more, you know—shower less often, or stop boiling water for tea. But I guess that wouldn't be enough," said Anna.

"Nope," said Jessica. "We'll have to shut down another dome."

The others stared at one another and then looked away. "But which one?" asked Nicole.

"We can't close Geo or Central. Air's already closed, and Entry's never been heated since we got here."

"We could close Health," Nicole said. "Which will mean no more gym."

Jessica shook her head. "It won't be enough, since it uses energy only when we're there."

"We'll close Health anyway and move the essential medical stuff here," Larry said. "But, as Jessica said, that won't be enough."

"Which leaves us Food or Eco. Pick one."

"Right. Any thoughts about which one we should close?"

"I'd hate to lose either," said Nicole. Elizabeth nodded.

"You decide," Jessica told Larry. In her earlier incarnation, she would have opted without hesitation to close Eco, which had been her least favorite dome, but she had begun to appreciate it much more. Besides, she had now learned to do something she would never have in the past—consider her sister's feelings.

Larry hesitated before responding. "I think it's a question of portability. Food has mostly portable stuff, while Eco doesn't."

"But where would we move it?"

"What if we move the stove, pantry, and the washer to Eco? It'll be a tight fit there, and Anna, you may need to crowd your plants together more than you'd like, and maybe shift the hydroponics downstairs to the hex, but it'll allow us to shut off power to Food."

"What about water?" Elizabeth said. "the pond is in the Food hex."

"Of course, we'll need to make a daily trip there. We could break off chunks from the pond and thaw them in Eco."

There were nods of agreement. "Yeah, that could work," said Anna.

Jessica turned to Elizabeth for approval.

"What do you think, Grandma? As the big boss of the Food dome?"

Elizabeth assumed a stern voice. "What? Close mah dome? Over mah dead body!" Then she laughed and resumed her normal tone. "What the rest of you decide is good enough for me, dear."

Anna giggled. "You're becoming a clown, Grandma."

"It's Larry's influence," said Jessica.

What had started off as a grim meeting ended in grins and chuckles, but the mood was serious during the following weeks as the plan was carried out. Many unforeseen difficulties cropped up—rerouting the plumbing turned out to be particularly tricky—but, on the whole, the move went well. On May 22 of Year Seven, Elizabeth began cooking in her new kitchen in a corner of the Eco dome, located as far from the manure buckets as possible. Having the food area right on top of the bioreactor was not ideal, but the family were amazed at how quickly they got used to it. Later that day, after a round of inspection, Larry turned off the heat to the Food and Health domes, which reduced their energy load by twelve percent and put them in surplus once again.

But the well continued to cool.

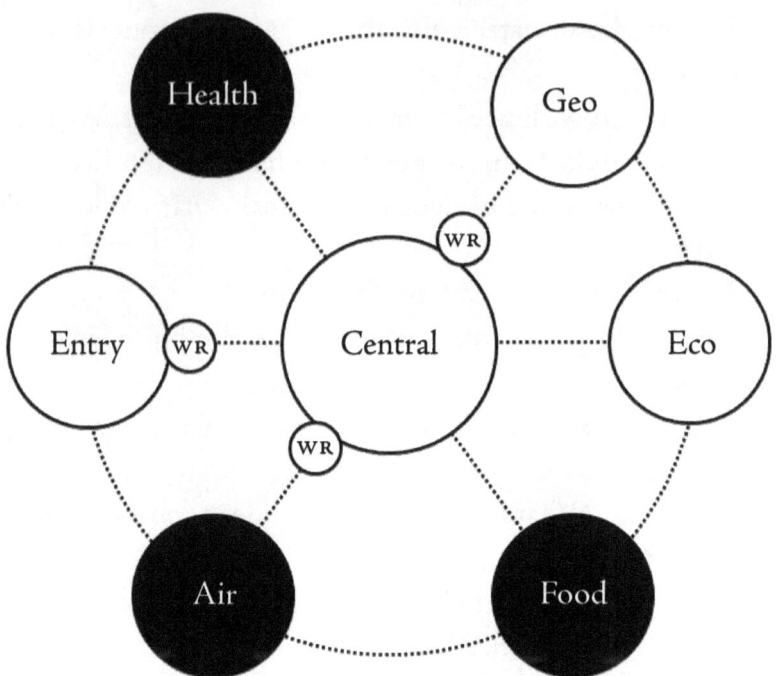

25

Backup

A FEW MONTHS after the Food dome had been shut down, Larry brainstormed with Jessica in the Geo dome. She had taken her sister's slot there after Air's closure, freeing Anna to devote all her time to her precious chlorella. Jessica didn't have as much of a feel for the power plant as she did for the air purifier but was coming up to speed so quickly that Larry increasingly relied on her judgment.

"Your Highness, can I get your opinion?" Larry's tone was light but his expression serious.

"On what?"

"The energy situation."

"Stable but precarious." Jessica wiped her hand on a rag and picked up a chart. "Look at this. On the positive side, the well's cooling more slowly. It's almost stable at seventy-two percent of the original output. Consumption is down to seventy percent, so there's a two percent surplus. But then again, we're at max fluid pressure."

"What's your gut feel?"

"Queasy. We don't know why the cooling started and why it's slowed down. If it speeds up again, we're screwed."

They looked at each other for a moment. "That's why we need to consider our plan B," said Larry.

"What's that? Shut down another dome?"

"That's become plan A." Larry laughed without mirth. "We'll have to do that soon anyway, but that won't be good enough."

"What then? Shift from Central to here?"

"Well, it's certainly warmer here, but what about air quality, with all the steam and sulfur?"

"Nasty."

"You and Anna have been wonderful about not complaining, but I can't see Lizzie surviving a month here."

"Lizzie?" Jessica raised a quizzical eyebrow.

Larry blushed and stammered something.

"Don't worry, I'll only tell everyone. Anyway, what's your plan B?"

"Remember the Air dome hex?"

"Of course. Packed floor to ceiling with diesel."

"Right, we have 120,000 liters of it. That's about 100,000 kilograms. We could shift all of it to the Entry hex and run the diesel-based generators in the dome above."

"But what about the food store under Entry?"

"We shift it to Air."

Jessica looked unconvinced. "Okay, then what? Shift all ops to Central, including clinic and kitchen?"

"Exactly. And some plants, too. So we'd be down to maintaining just two domes."

Jessica reflected for a moment. "Hmm, I'll buy it. Not that there's any choice. But how long can we carry on like that?"

"My guess is three years, but you could make a more precise estimate."

"Will do." The Jessica of old would have asked *what happens after the diesel runs out?* Like the others, however, she had stopped agonizing over their long-term prospects. As long as there was no immediate threat, she was happy. Her time horizon had shrunk; an additional three years of survival felt like an extra lifetime.

A thought struck her. "Where are the design docs for the diesel backup? I never saw any."

"Design docs?" Larry looked down and sighed. "We don't have any."

"*What?*"

Larry looked troubled and guilty. "Unfortunately, I didn't ever get to designing and installing a diesel-based backup heating system."

"But that's crazy!" Jessica stared at Larry. "You never created a backup? Why the hell not?"

Larry flinched from her accusing glance. "It was partly lack of time and partly overconfidence. I simply stocked up with fuel and figured I'd worry about it later. I'm so sorry, Jessica."

She was immediately contrite. "Sorry, I didn't mean to yell at you." She hugged him, somewhat awkwardly, and held him close for a few seconds. "You did everything for us. I've no business finding fault."

"It's okay. Don't give it a thought."

"You're not mad?"

"Only at myself."

"Stop that. Don't start blaming yourself again. Look how much trouble we had last time!"

Larry blushed, remembering the "therapy" he had undergone. "I won't, I promise."

"Good, let's go ahead and build the backup."

"Sounds good. But as we were talking, I realized there are two big catches we need to address."

"There always are! What's number one?"

"Diesel exhaust. What do we do with it? We've been rather spoilt by the geothermal well. All that clean heat! All we had to deal with was a bit of hydrogen sulfide, some carbon dioxide, and steam. But with a fossil fuel ..."

"We'll get emissions—boatloads of it."

"Yes. I think about three kilos of carbon dioxide per kilo of diesel."

"Hold on, let me check." Jessica queried the computer database and found the answer. "You're close. It's 3.16 kilos of CO_2, and about half as much steam."

"And that's a lot. The steam will condense, and we can collect it and even drink it, but the carbon dioxide ..."

"... will suffocate us."

"Yes."

"Couldn't we use some of the energy to turn it back into carbon and oxygen?" Jessica asked.

"Unfortunately, no."

"Why not?"

"Thermodynamics."

"I don't get it."

"Can I get into lecture mode for a second?"

"Isn't that your *normal* mode?"

Larry grinned despite his tension. "When you burn diesel, the carbon in it burns into carbon dioxide, giving off energy in the process. To reverse that process, or any exothermic reaction, you'll need to supply at least as much energy as is produced. That's the theory. In practice you need much more energy to split open a CO_2 molecule than the energy that came from burning that atom of carbon."

"Bummer." Jessica was quiet for a few seconds and then had a thought. "Wait a minute. Doesn't diesel have hydrogen as well as carbon? Couldn't we use energy from burning the hydrogen portion to pay for carbon dioxide reversal?"

"Hmm, that's a thought." Larry chewed on a pencil for a few seconds and then shook his head. "But if I remember right, only a third of the energy from diesel combustion comes from the hydrogen component. So you'll still be in the red."

"What about chlorella? Couldn't we set up a hundred more panels of it to soak up the extra carbon?"

Larry nodded appreciatively. "That's another idea. But again, I don't think it's practical."

"Thermodynamics again?"

"Indirectly. Let me go into lecture mode again. Plants and algae and cyanobacteria do fix carbon, using it to grow. And they do it very efficiently. But you need to consider two things. Firstly, they're biological organisms and can't grow very fast. Secondly, they'll need loads of sunlight. So, more chlorella will certainly help, but we'll never grow enough to keep up with combustion."

"Silly me. If it was that easy, global warming would've solved itself."

"Exactly. Let's say we use a hundred kilos of diesel every day. That means a daily output of three hundred kilos of carbon dioxide. Fully grown chlorella can fix up to half a kilo of carbon per square meter per day. So we'll need about six hundred square meters of it for our needs."

Jessica snorted. "Good luck finding the space for that. Not to mention the six hundred solar lamps and six thousand watts of electricity."

"Right. Also, the chlorella won't soak up other pollutants in the diesel exhaust such as nitrogen oxides and sulfur dioxide. And though diesel emits less carbon monoxide than gasoline, given enough time even that will accumulate to toxic levels."

"Okay, Mr. Engineer, you've made your point! So we have to vent the exhaust out."

"Right. And lose most of the heat in doing so."

Jessica groaned. "It's hopeless. No wonder they call it *exhaust*."

"You should leave the bad jokes to your elders," Larry chuckled.

"Now a different question. How did you plan to get heat from Entry to Central?"

Larry grimaced. "That's what I should've worked out *before* dragging you all here. But I think we could modify the piping system we have now. Hot fluid will go from Entry to Central, transfer heat, and then return to the heat source in Entry. Continuously."

"A closed thermal circuit between Entry and Central?"

"Exactly, once we close all the other domes."

Jessica flipped through a sheaf of papers and picked out one that had a diagram of the piping system. She studied it for a while and then looked up. "What if we dumped the fluid and ran the exhaust through the pipes?"

"Say that again?"

Jessica repeated her idea, and Larry sprang up in excitement. "Now that's an idea that might work! It would certainly transfer heat very effectively from Entry to Central." Then his face clouded. "But the capacity of the pipes is limited. In a few hours they'll be at full pressure and won't take any more exhaust. What happens then?"

"Then we vent out the cold exhaust and put more hot fumes in."

"Hmm." Larry's brows creased in thought for a few moments and then his face lit up. "You know what? I think we finally have a plan. It'll need a huge amount of re-engineering, we'll need to change the piping and install new vents, but I think it might actually work."

Jessica beamed with pleasure. She was no longer tormented by conflicting feelings when praised. Though for old times' sake she would deflect a compliment with an ironic quip, it was now more out of modesty than perverse sentiment.

"It will work if a hundred things don't fail," she said.

"No, we can make it work. There's one more catch, however."

Jessica groaned. "God! Just when I thought I'd saved us all from eternal cold. I should've known it was too good to be true."

"Your idea is brilliant. We just need to consider one more thing."

"Okay, let me guess. Engineering issues are often symmetric. First was exhaust, so second has do with intake, right?"

"Right again! It's the second problem with burning fossil fuels—it not only produces carbon dioxide, it also uses up oxygen. So to run the generators, we'll have to install vents to draw in cold air from the outside. Nothing fancy with valves and gauges, just a crude arrangement of piping. But the air outside, at minus 127 degrees, will have to be pre-heated to plus 50 degrees, the flash point of diesel. In this case, what will the net energy output be?"

Jessica made a face. "Much lower, I'll bet."

"I think so, too. Could you work out some answers? And estimate how much energy we would need to heat the two domes?"

"Will do, Chief."

Jessica went to work that afternoon and remained busy with her calculations for several days. She used a blend of mathematical calculations and computer modeling to arrive at the answers. A few days later she shared her results with Larry.

"Good news and bad news," she said. "The good news is we need to preheat air only to minus 30 degrees, not plus 50."

"Good news, indeed! How did you reckon that?"

"The air can be colder, because the diesel itself will be inside the dome and relatively warm."

"Well done, Jessica! You're smarter than you look." Larry tried to dodge a well-aimed pencil stub. "And how long will the diesel last?"

"That's the bad news." Jessica retrieved her pencil. "The efficiency of the system is only about thirty percent. The main problem is the cost of preheating, as you feared. We can reduce it somewhat by capturing heat in the spent exhaust, but that won't be enough. Preheating will need a lot more energy. Between that and various losses, barely a third of the energy from diesel will be available for our use. If we assume we need the heat from a hundred kilos of fuel per day, we'll actually have to burn close to 350 kilos. Which means …"

Larry finished her sentence: "… we have only a year's worth of fuel."

They gazed at each other for a while in silence.

"Should we break it to the others?" Jessica said eventually.

"What do you suggest?"

"Let's wait. Tell them the good news that we have a diesel backup plan."

"And if they ask how long it'll last?"

"Tell them it's hard to estimate."

Larry looked at her thoughtfully for a moment and nodded. "I agree. A white lie is the best policy for now. No sense in causing premature alarm."

"And the well might stabilize."

"Yes, let's hope we never have to use the diesel option."

"You bet."

26

Diesel

As if to allay their concerns, the well remained true for a while. The spare energy from it went to the Entry dome where Larry and Jessica spent several hours each day on their diesel project. After some puzzlement, the others accepted this effort as a prudent backup measure. Only Larry and Jessica knew the true situation; the others felt reassured by the well's seemingly stable energy output.

Work in Entry posed a new set of challenges for Jessica.

Her earlier stint at Air had exposed her to a mechanical system far more complex than anything she had seen before. Though she would never have admitted it, Jessica, like her sister in Eco, was terrified by the burden of the responsibilities on her young shoulders. At least Anna had some leeway; if she botched up and lost her plants, she could plant some more. The loss would be only temporary. With her, on the other hand, the stakes were higher. Air and heat being vital for survival, any slipup in her work—an over-tightened valve, an incorrect pressure setting, an accidental reversal of electrical polarities—could have lethal consequences. Although

Larry assured her that the system had many checks and safety mechanisms that made it resilient to human error, Jessica was engineer enough to know that the blunders you *don't* plan for are the ones that will get you. Many historical engineering failures attested to this. The Challenger space shuttle debacle, for instance; as Richard Feynman famously demonstrated, it all came down to a rubber seal that failed because of the unexpectedly cold weather on launch day. Then there was NASA's 125 million–dollar Mars orbiter that broke apart before it could start its mission because the agency's contractor mistakenly used imperial instead of metric units. Not to mention innumerable other exhibits in the engineering Hall of Shame—Exxon Valdez, Deepwater Horizon, Columbia—that showed how simple, preventable flaws could have lethal consequences. When even seasoned pros made such Titanic blunders, how could a novice like Jessica avoid them? On top of these fears, in the past she'd had other struggles, such as adapting to life inside the Shell and learning to work with Larry.

Now, in Year Seven, the situation was different. She had matured into a skilled engineer, confident in her ability to handle any situation that arose with her machinery. She was also confident that any error that occurred wouldn't be due to her incompetence. And she now got along with Larry like a house on fire. He let her make all the major design decisions, content to play a supporting role. Her theoretical knowledge of air flow, heat transfer, and fluid dynamics now exceeded his. On practical matters he still held the edge thanks to his two decades of experience in getting systems to work. Even here, though, she was no laggard. Her apprenticeship in the

Air dome had paid off, and she was as dexterous with drills, saws, and other tools as any skilled craftsman. Larry was only too happy to acknowledge her abilities. In their early days she had been turned off by what she considered his arrogance; now she was touched by his humility. For a self-made billionaire, he was amazingly free of ego. And now he actually "got" her jokes and occasionally even made a neat jest of his own. She grew so fond of him that she would have indignantly denied ever disliking him. Together they made a fabulous team, she thought. If anyone could get the diesel backup to work, it would be the two of them.

On the flip side, however, she had even more responsibility than before, and the work of creating a new system was far trickier than her previous task of maintaining an existing one. The Entry dome, previously left cold, now got some heat from Geo. But not much could be spared for them, so they had to work in below-freezing conditions most of the time. Drilling holes for the new intake and exhaust vents, though tedious, was not too complicated. But the moment they broke through the dome's outer shell, an intense blast of glacial air from the outside struck them like a body blow. Hands would freeze and lungs would burn before they could put a temporary plug in the vent. Compounding her physical misery was the constant reminder of the ghastly world outside. Under normal conditions, she, like the rest of the family, could afford to insulate her mind from it. Now that cold dark reality was inescapable. Back with the others at the end of a grueling day's work, however, she couldn't talk too much about that for fear of alarming the others.

If the extreme conditions made work unpleasant, they also spurred Larry and Jessica to work harder and faster. By mid-October of Year Seven, the two had finished the initial construction and were ready for a test run.

Testing the system offered its own challenges. All heat to Central would need to be shut off for a day or two to get rid of the residual effects of the well, and the heat would remain off for a few more days until the trial run was completed. This meant relocating everyone to Eco during that period. The conditions there, already crowded, got even more cramped. There was barely any place for them to sit, let alone sleep, and the uncarpeted floor was colder than ice. But no one uttered even a murmur of protest. By now, their cohesiveness as a team was absolute. Larry was moved to tears by their instant cooperation and cheerful stoicism. On Nicole's suggestion, she, along with Anna and Elizabeth, donned spacesuits and went to the closed domes to salvage any bits of carpet or other floor covering they could find. Back in Eco, they toiled for several hours to move the plants around and set up a viable living and sleeping space. When Larry and Jessica returned each day after their testing, half-frozen and shivering, noses running, hands stuffed into armpits, they had a nice, snug spot to relax in.

"I can't thank you enough," Larry said the first evening.

"Thanks a million—" Jessica began at the same instant.

"Shut up you two and snuggle up," Anna cut in. "No thanks allowed here."

Larry and Jessica had to make scores of modifications and adjustments to their system. The number and configuration of pipes, the gas pressure through them, the rate of fuel combustion—all that took several trial-and-error cycles before the system would work. Then more iterations to optimize it. But by the fifth day of testing, the Central dome had begun to warm again, and by the seventh it was nearly as warm as it had been before.

"Success," said Jessica.

That evening they celebrated with another bottle of champagne that Larry produced from his mystery location. He gave Jessica the credit for the success, a compliment she accepted with modesty. *She has acquired grace*, Elizabeth thought with a smile.

Their test completed, they shut down the diesel system and switched the Geo heating back on at Central. Life resumed its normal course. The well remained stable. Their makeshift kitchen in Eco ran smoothly. They resumed their routine activities: games, classes, films. To compensate for the loss of their gym, they danced for an hour or two every day. Larry, as the only man, was in demand. He divided his attentions between the two girls and could never decide who was the better dancer—Anna, light and swift, was a delight to twirl around, while Jessica, slightly heavier and slower, nonetheless had a languid grace that was equally pleasurable. Nicole and Elizabeth danced the slower numbers together, using the opportunity to recycle anecdotes from the pre-Shroud days. Life was good.

And then, in May of Year Eight, seven months after the successful diesel test, one of the leaves of the avocado tree turned blue.

27

Blight

I<small>T WAS</small> E<small>LIZABETH</small>, in the midst of her chores on May 22 of Year Eight, who saw it first. The avocado tree, a dwarf variety, sat next to a makeshift kitchen counter rigged up near the stove. Elizabeth had enjoyed being able to just reach out and pick the ripe fruit before they sat down for their meals and, on that day, had already plucked one. As she examined the tree to see if she could find another, she noticed a bluish stain on one of the leaves. It looked like a splash of paint, but she knew there was no paint in the Shell—or indeed, any other volatile chemical except a can or two for emergencies. She was puzzled but forgot about it as she busied herself getting their lunch ready. It was only at the end of the meal that she said casually: "Anna, did you see the avocado tree today? One of its leaves is blue."

Anna's silence caused the others to put down their forks. "A *blue* leaf?" she said eventually. Her face had gone pale. Without waiting for a response, she got up and ran over to the tree. When she came back to the table, she was so ashen that the others exchanged looks of puzzlement and alarm. What was all this fuss about a blue leaf?

Larry felt his heart pound. "What is it, Anna? Something wrong with the tree?"

Anna's normally laughing countenance had set in grim lines. "If it's what I think it is ... something's wrong with, like, *all* our trees."

Exclamations of surprise and consternation rang out.

"Come over and take a look," Anna said and pointed to the blue-stained leaf that had drawn Elizabeth's attention. To the others it didn't look ominous at all. It was a rather pretty azure color, Jessica thought. *Like the skies of the distant past.*

"I dearly hope I'm wrong," Anna continued, "but the blue stain might be *Phytophthora nitrophilis.*"

"Phyto what?" asked Larry.

"*Phytophthora nitrophilis.* It's a fungus that thrives in polluted waters. It mostly affects aquatic plants, and causes a disease called marine blight."

"I've never heard of it."

"It's rare. Remember the Great Irish Famine of the 1840s, caused by potato blight?" The others nodded. "*P. nitrophilis* is like a close cousin. Though it sends its oospores all over the planet, it rarely affects land plants. But when it does, it's very serious."

There were more exclamations of concern.

"That sounds a bit like strep or staph," said Nicole. Seeing some puzzled looks, she explained: "Bacteria that hang around in our bodies innocuously, but sometimes run amok."

"It's something like that. Once this fungus manages to infect a plant, it spreads like wildfire to other plants in the vicinity."

"Bloody hell!" said Larry, shaken out of his composure. "But if it's so widespread and so deadly, why doesn't it strike more often? Why have we never heard of it before?"

Anna shrugged and spread her palms. "Probably because the attacks die down almost as quickly as they start. Why that happens is still a mystery. One theory is that other organisms in the environment sense the threat to their food supply and produce counter-toxins."

"Nature policing itself?" Jessica asked.

"Sort of."

"So can we hope that it'll happen here as well?"

Anna shook her head gloomily. "No, I don't think so."

"Why not?"

"Our ecosystem might be too small and constrained for the blue fungus to have natural enemies. I can't be absolutely sure, of course."

Larry raised his hand. "Hold on, before we panic we should find out for sure if it's really that. Couldn't the blue stain be another organism? Something harmless?"

Anna shrugged. "I hope so, but frankly I'm not too hopeful."

"When will we know for sure?"

"In a day or two. If it *is* marine blight the avocado tree will become all blue. Most of the other plants here will have blue leaves as well. After that …"

"After that?"

"After that they'll have only weeks to live."

There were gasps of shock followed by a long, anxious silence.

"Couldn't we do something to protect the other trees?" Nicole said eventually. "Move them to Central, or cover them?"

Anna laughed grimly. "It's too late for that. By now, the spores will have spread all over Eco and tagged along with us to the other domes as well."

Jessica banged her spoon on the table. "We can't just sit here and do nothing while plants die!"

"But what can we do, dear?" Elizabeth said, casting a worried look at her. "Anna has already explained that the blight would've spread everywhere."

"Can't we spray them? I know Anna hates pesticides, but surely now …?"

"Do we even have any here?" asked Nicole.

"No, this is a completely organic facility. Right, Larry?"

Larry avoided Anna's eye. "Actually, we do have a few for emergency use," he admitted. "Pesticides, and fungicides too. A range of them, in fact."

Jessica uttered a sharp bark of laughter. "Thank heavens for pragmatism!" She turned to her sister. "Would you consider using them just this once?"

"I'm not the fanatic you take me for!" Anna snapped. "I'd rather have a live plant than a dead one, organic or not. We should try fungicides. In fact, try any chemical we have."

"But there's a catch, right? I can tell."

"Yes, there's a catch, and a big one. No known fungicide kills *P. nitrophilis*."

Larry cursed under his breath. "Shall we test them anyway?"

"Yes, let's do it right now."

Jessica sprang up. "Hey, wait a minute! What about the chlorella?"

Larry, Nicole, and Elizabeth grew pale, but Anna stayed calm. "The blight doesn't infect algae. And the chemicals won't hurt them either, if we use them just this once."

Four simultaneous sighs of relief followed her words. Since the air purifier had breathed its last, the health of the chlorella bio-oxygen panels had become as important as their own.

"I hadn't even thought of the chlorella," said Larry. "We're lucky to have the two of you to keep us older folks on our toes."

Anna was quickly regaining her composure. "Come along, you fogy, and show me where you keep the toxic stuff," she said to Larry.

They hurried from Eco and returned in minutes, each carrying two large, bright-orange canisters bearing the logo— Jessica noted with secret amusement—of a leading agribusiness firm that had been the *bête noire* of ecological activists worldwide. Meanwhile, the fungus-blighted avocado tree had been shifted to the part of the dome farthest from the kitchen. After donning face masks, Anna and Larry sprayed the tree liberally with all four compounds.

"How long before we know if this stuff works?"

"Let's give it overnight. If we see more blue leaves we're, like, out of luck."

Back in Central, after dinner, they tried to engage in their customary diversions, but their thoughts kept straying back to the blue leaf.

"How do you think the fungus got in here?" Jessica called out to Anna, who had been glued to her computer since dinner.

Anna shut off the laptop and rejoined the family. "Not from the outside, at least, not recently," she said slowly. "We have a closed ecosystem here. Besides, everything outside is dead anyway."

"So it was here all the time?"

"Must've been."

"Then why now, and not earlier?"

Anna sighed. "I'm not sure. According to our database, past outbreaks have happened in the vicinity of sewage treatment facilities. But not just any facilities. The ones affected were located on agricultural land that'd seen heavy nitrate fertilizer use. One theory is that the combination of phosphorus-rich sewage sludge and nitrogen-rich soil creates the ideal conditions for the fungus to grow—a high concentration of phosphorus and nitrogen in the soil. Something similar may've happened here."

Jessica seemed unconvinced. "Okay, we use sewage as manure, so there's your P. But we don't use nitrate fertilizer. So where's the N coming from?"

"Something to do with our diet?" said Nicole.

Anna thought for a moment and nodded. "Could be. In the early days we ate mostly fresh stuff. But we ran out of that. Lately, we've been eating tinned stuff, especially fish, lentils, and spinach. They're high in nitrogen. And what we eat ultimately passes into the plant food chain."

Jessica digested her sister's words for a moment and then asked: "So we've been dumping a ton of nitrogen into the soil?"

"Right. I did observe an increase in nitrogen when I checked the soil chemistry a few months ago, but I thought it was, you know, within safe limits. I was wrong. Perhaps we've just crossed a threshold that lets the fungus break out. In my defense, this type of infection is considered extremely rare."

"How could you have known?" said Larry. "Besides, what option did we have? It was either fertilize the soil with manure, or let the plants die from lack of nutrition. No, Anna, you've done absolutely nothing wrong. The fungus, like the valve failure in the Air dome, is one of the unknowns that Jessica warned us about. There's no way to anticipate them."

"That's right," agreed Jessica, putting her arm around her sister and holding her tight for a few seconds. "The only thing to do is adapt. We've done it before, we can do it again."

Years ago, such optimism from Jessica and kindness toward her sister would have been unthinkable. Now it seemed natural. Elizabeth mused at the irony of her family members growing emotionally closer as their living situation worsened. *Too bad it took the Shroud to bring us all together,* she thought.

That night, for the first time, Jessica opted to sleep in the middle between her sister and Larry. She felt that Anna, despite all their assurances, blamed herself for the blight; a little sisterly support might comfort her. Having Larry's big, reassuring presence on her other side was an added bonus. *So this is what I've been missing all these years!* she thought.

In the morning, nobody was keen to go to the Eco dome. The moment of truth was at hand, and everyone feared it would be a bitter one.

And so it turned out. Not only did the avocado tree sport several blue leaves, so did the mango and the peach. Most of the other plants had blue-flecked leaves as well. Anna's shoulders slumped in defeat. The others took turns to hug her and murmur soothing words in her ear. But her feelings over-flowed into silent tears, and then into big, racking sobs. The family knew how much the plants meant to her. Her grief at their loss would be mingled with remorse for letting the team down. There was nothing to do but hold her close and wait for her to recover. It took several hours before they could coax a smile out of her. Failures and losses, however painful, could never keep Anna down for long, and in a day or two she had recovered some of her cheerful spirits.

As if to rub it in—or as a parting gift—the Eco dome yielded its most bountiful harvest during the next few weeks. The leaves grew bluer and the branches withered, but the trees offered the most succulent fruit ever. Everyone agreed that their final batch of fruit was not only the best grown in the Shell, but the best they had ever consumed. The peaches were sweeter and juicier than they had ever remembered eating, the avocadoes richer and nuttier, and the mangoes simply ambrosial.

By July 6 the avocado tree was dead. The peach and the mango soon followed. The citrus bush was the last to go. It held out against the fungus as long as it could, but one day in August of Year Eight the Shellmates ate their last orange.

28

Limericks

THE DEATH OF their plants and trees left the family with only tinned and preserved foods to eat. Although both nutritionally and gastronomically these were a pathetic substitute for fresh produce, nobody uttered a murmur of complaint. Nicole compensated for the potential loss of vitamins and minerals by giving everyone a daily supplement, while Elizabeth and Jessica experimented with new cooking styles and spice combinations to render their daily fare more palatable. But the family bond was now so strong that the main concern was not the diet but Anna's morale. Yes, she seemed to have recovered from her initial anguish, and seemed back to her old self—affectionate with her mother and grandmother, teasing with Larry, and feisty with her sister. But her companions watched her closely to make sure she carried no residue of sorrow or guilt over the loss of her beloved plants. Jessica was bursting with gibes about their new diet but refrained from voicing them. It was left to Anna, finally, to tire of the kid-gloves treatment and get her companions back to their normal selves.

With this goal in mind, she organized a competition for the funniest Shell-related limerick. Each round would last twenty minutes. At the end of the allotted time, the contestants would read out their poem, and Jessica would decide the winner. Her own poem would be judged by the others. Black humor would get extra points.

Larry went first:

There was once a place called Shell
Snug amidst a desert colder than hell
The five inside
Would stay till they died
Or got no more heat from their well.

"Nice," said Jessica. "But more factual than funny. And the fourth line is clunky."

Nicole went next:

There was a family that moved to a Shell
Where they continue to happily dwell
Will they live in this state
Until the end of Fate?
Hopefully not, but it's too soon to tell.

"Lacks humor, but I like the ambiguity in the last line," Jessica said. "The end could be from revival outside or collapse inside. Okay, Lizzie—Grandma, I mean—it's your turn. Make me laugh, or be harshly judged."

"Oh dear! This is my very first limerick ever, so don't be too unkind," Elizabeth said and then read aloud:

There was once a man who built a warm bubble
For his family, while the world turned to rubble
Inside, it was great
Except what they ate
Their diet! That was their real trouble.

"Not bad!" said Jessica. "Too laudatory toward Larry—you know how quickly flattery goes to his head. But the food reference made me smile. I'd say this is the best one so far. But I'm still waiting for humor. Anna, hit me."

"Well, black humor isn't my forte. But perhaps some of your flair may have rubbed off on me. So here goes:"

There was once a man called Larry
Who kidnapped all the girls he could carry
Once in his Shell
They fell under his spell
For who else could they expect to marry?

The women roared with laughter, and Larry had the grace to blush. Teasing him was a popular pastime with the girls, with the older ones often joining in. Larry, though sometimes bashful, was nevertheless pleased by their humor at his expense. Anything that kept their morale up was welcome. Besides, he found the girls delightful, a fact that he tried to hide from them—no sense in losing the tiny shred of authority he had left!

"Full points for humor!" said Jessica. "You've exposed him for the rake he is. The Shroud is obviously something he engineered just to get us into his clutches. Confess it, Larry!"

"If so, I don't regret it," said Larry, recovering quickly. "A dead planet is a small price to pay for your affections."

"You bastard, when did you learn to make repartee?" said Jessica. "Coming back to your poem, Anna, it's funny, but not dark enough. Here's mine."

> *The Shell was a place that lifted your mood*
> *The air was fair and the food was good*
> *Until the air went stale and the pond went dry*
> *And the well went cold and the plants did die*
> *But it was there that Larry chose to raise his brood!*

"It's nice and dark," said Anna. "And the last line's funny. But the meter is off, isn't it?"

"True," admitted her sister. "And the rhyme in the second line isn't great either."

"The first four lines remind me of a poem in *Fall of the House of Usher*," remarked Larry, and quoted from it:

> *In the greenest of our valleys,*
> *By good angels tenanted,*
> *Once a fair and stately palace —*
> *Radiant palace—reared its head.*
> *But evil things, in robes of sorrow,*
> *Assailed the monarch's high estate;*
> *(Ah, let us mourn, for never morrow*
> *Shall dawn upon him, desolate!)*

"Perhaps you could expand your poem into a longer piece, Jessica?" asked Elizabeth. "Not as a funny poem, but a serious one?"

"Call it *Fall of the House of Shell!*" Anna said.

Jessica laughed. "So I guess the winner today is Anna?"

"No question," said Elizabeth. "Here we were all worried about her morale, and the dear girl comes up with something like that."

"You can't keep her down," Nicole agreed. "Not when she gets to indulge in our favorite sport of Larry baiting."

"I ought to be angry with her, I suppose," Larry said.

As he said this, Anna was reclining with her legs on his lap, and Jessica was leaning against him. Though Larry treated them both as adults and rated their abilities above his own, a part of him continued to think of them as children who needed to be indulged and protected. They were often playful with him, like frisky little kittens, while he assumed a gently chiding, fatherly demeanor. He loved their attentions, but it only made him all the more conscious of the grim reality awaiting them outside and strengthened his determination to move heaven and earth to keep them safe. They were beyond precious to him.

"Good luck with that," said Jessica, rolling her eyes. "I won't hold my breath."

The daily limerick competitions continued with great success. Anna, who displayed an unexpected flair for light verse, was often the winner, though once Elizabeth beat her with this effort:

In the desert built Larry his dome humongous
Into which he grabbed and boldly flung us
"You're safe from the cold!"
"No more worry!" we were told
Until his plans were undone by a fungus.

Nicole and Larry managed to turn out decent rhymes, though they tended to be factual rather than funny. Jessica

continued to work on her longer poem and finally came up
with this:

Safe in their nest, on planet Earth
In the eternal cycle of death and birth
Warmed by the miracle of solar fire
The human race had all it could desire.

And one fine day came a distant cloud
That brought not rain, for its name was Shroud;
It was darker than dark, blacker than black
No more fine days would ever come back.

Starting at first as a greyish haze
The cloud got thicker at a deadly pace;
As it wrapped the Earth in its drear embrace
Of the Sun there soon was left no trace.

Left in the dark with the Sun unseen
The planet's cooling was swift and mean;
It got chilly at first, then chillier still
Then colder yet, then cold enough to kill.

But humanity, to its utter shame
Did nothing more than scoff and blame;
By ignoring the Shroud until far too late
The human race thus sealed its fate.

It mattered not if they were weak or strong
They couldn't escape a planet gone wrong;
They died on the roads, they died in their beds
They froze in the fields, they froze in their sheds.

Billions of lives, wiped out in a trice!
Billions no more to know virtue or vice!
Billions of humans who'd never get older!
Yet the planet only got colder and colder.

Soon came the end of the last human life
No more would man know joy or strife
And yet did the cold keep marching on
Until Nature herself was dead and gone.

"Brilliant!" said Anna. "This is the best poem I've heard in my life. And on this high note, I pronounce myself completely cured."

So Anna was fine. But on September 17 of Year Eight, Nicole couldn't get out of bed.

29

Existence

With her natural empathy and professionally-trained emotional antenna, Elizabeth always kept a watchful eye on her family. She knew only too well how even the healthiest people could fall apart under stress and how psychological problems could derail even the best-organized social groups. Jessica's rebellious spirit had been an early concern, but that was now history. Anna's fragility had been another potential worry, but she too had outgrown her teenage diffidence and vulnerability. Both had matured into strong, confident women, calmed and toughened by their Shell years. Larry's excessive concern for the family's safety was another worry, but they had found an effective—if unconventional—remedy for that. No, Larry and the girls were fine, or at least as fine as they could be under their circumstances. And Elizabeth was too old a campaigner to worry about herself. She had always been tranquil, and now, thanks to her new relationship with Larry, she felt rejuvenated.

The problem was with the fifth member of the family. Elizabeth had long been aware that things were not all right at *Maison Nicole*. Her daughter was the one who had lost the most and gained the least in the move to the Shell. The girls had blossomed from gawky teens into charming women, with Larry as their adored and adoring protector. As for herself, she now enjoyed delights that surpassed even those of her days with George. But Nicole? She hadn't gained much and had lost a great deal. She no longer had patients to treat. And although she had never been a doting mother, in the pre-Shroud days she did have her parental responsibilities. Now her grown-up daughters no longer needed her mothering. Her romance with Larry had sustained her in the beginning, but that was over years ago. Likewise, her concern about her mother's health had kept her engaged for a few years, but now that too had receded. Elizabeth was now much healthier—her cardio figures were now in the safe range thanks to medications, and she brimmed with energy.

Nicole therefore had nothing to occupy her. And into this void came troubling thoughts.

Nicole's had been an unexamined life. The death of a patient would give her the occasional twinge of existential unease, but such feelings rarely persisted—there was always the next patient and the next one after that. Then back home for a late dinner with the family, an hour of television—a sit-com, crime drama, or cooking show, something entertaining rather than challenging—and then off to bed for a few hours before the next day's busy routine. The advent of Larry made only a minor change in her lifestyle. She would take the occasional afternoon off when he was in town or go in to work an hour or two later than usual. Her life became more enjoyable, but its core remained unchanged.

Her hectic overcommitted life in pre-Shroud Simpsonville had kept her grounded in immediate needs and left her no time to dwell on fundamental questions of life and death. But now, deprived of her work and family responsibilities, she couldn't avoid confronting them. Initially, she'd been content to have an occasional chat with Larry or Elizabeth, but those conversations had stimulated rather than soothed her. Though sympathetic, Larry was unable to offer much practical help—the two of them were not in the same boat. While Nicole felt herself spiritually adrift, Larry was firmly anchored to the practical realities of their existence. He had his mission in life, which was to keep them all safe and happy. He was down to earth and pragmatic—*hopelessly left-brained*, as he put it. All he could do was to advise her to talk to her mother.

Elizabeth did her best. She had long conversations with her daughter where she shared insights acquired over a lifetime of spiritual exploration. Elizabeth had grown up in a secular household. Her parents and siblings were more interested in education, career, and community work than religion. But very early in her life, when she was still in school, she had felt the need to seek a deeper meaning in life beyond the purely material. As a teenager she attended church regularly, but as she grew into adulthood she found her pastor's sermons simplistic and unconvincing. She briefly experimented with drugs, and while they did occasionally help her glimpse an inner bliss inaccessible through her conscious state, such experiences were fleeting. It was only when she plunged into Buddhism, meditation, dream yoga, and other Eastern spiritual disciplines that she found what she was looking for. They helped her bypass her conscious mind and senses to find something profound and meaningful deep inside her psyche. Thus began a lifelong practice of looking inwards, leading to a career as a spiritual counselor. She was not qualified to teach specific meditative techniques, however, so instead she engaged her patients in discussions and suggested a number of religious, philosophical, and spiritual works where they might find answers to the questions troubling them. This discussion-oriented approach had worked remarkably well with the disturbed youths who were her principal clients, and she had hoped it would help Nicole too. But in this she was disappointed.

Nicole did enjoy her chats with her mother. It was a relief to articulate thoughts which, she now realized, had troubled her for a long time, even before the Shroud. Their discussions were an intriguing journey into hitherto unexplored spiritual domains. But in practical terms she came away empty handed. Her mother was unable to provide the mental peace she now desperately sought. Elizabeth had a naturally serene temperament, and in her own dreamy way was as pragmatic and down to earth as Larry. She was willing to accept the collective spiritual wisdom handed down by her teachers. Nicole, unlike her, had a restless mind that wouldn't accept second-hand wisdom. She needed answers. What was the purpose of existence? Was there a Creator? Why did pain and suffering exist? Why wasn't happiness universal and permanent? Why would a benevolent God create the Shroud?

Conventional religions offered no answers. Discourses by spiritual teachers—Augustine, Krishnamurti, Trungpa— weren't much more enlightening. Nor did the works of Descartes, Russell, Sartre and other philosophers prove very helpful.

Although the questions and doubts churned away at the back of her mind, Nicole initially kept them to herself. She tried to maintain a normal level of interest and engagement in their day-to-day activities, but she found them increasingly meaningless. Living this "double life" wasn't too difficult at first. It wasn't until the beginning of Year Eight, when she started telling Larry and Elizabeth about her inner turmoil, that anyone else knew about her thoughts. Even then, the others took it as a not-unusual reaction to their perilous situation. No one realized how central, how all-consuming those thoughts had become. Even Elizabeth didn't grasp the extent of her daughter's spiritual crisis.

Then came the blue fungus that killed all their plants. Anna, the plant lover, recovered, but Nicole, who had no special interest in plants, didn't. To her the die-off was the last straw, the final thread in the shroud that smothered her faith in a meaningful world. Her inner questions now became deafening. She felt a weight of hopelessness, of despair, that she couldn't shake off. With a superhuman effort, she continued to perform her daily tasks, forcing a cheery optimism that rang increasingly hollow. She secretly dosed herself with anti-depressants; the drugs gave physical relief but didn't quell her spiritual agony.

One September morning in Year Eight found Nicole still in bed while the others were up and about, sipping coffee and waiting for her to get up and join them. But she couldn't. She tried to call out, but her voice refused to rise above a whisper. It seemed as if a heavy weight was pressing down on her. *Am I dead?* She immediately dismissed the thought—she could still see and hear the others, and even smell the coffee. *I've had a stroke* was her next thought, but she had enough sensation in her limbs to convince her otherwise. Nor did it feel like a heart attack. Whatever the cause, she could barely move her fingers and toes. Getting up was out of the question. She lay there in silent misery, waiting for someone to notice her plight.

She didn't have to wait long. Just after 7:00 a.m. Jessica came to wake her, took one look at her face—saw the stream of tears, the dribbling saliva, the ashen pallor—and screamed. Everyone rushed to Nicole's side and gazed at her in shock. Nobody knew what to do.

"She's trying to say something," Anna said, and Larry knelt down beside Nicole and brought his ear close to her mouth.

"Help me up," Nicole whispered. "Please."

Lifting her gently, Larry brought her to the couch and held her on his lap as the others took turns to kiss her, stroke her hair, and murmur endearments. After a few seconds, their practical side asserted itself. Anna and Elizabeth, both trained in nursing by Nicole, took her vital measures. "BP 100 over 60, a tad low but okay, and pulse is normal," Anna said. Elizabeth drew a blood sample and ran it through an analyzer from the clinic. They waited impatiently as it performed a gamut of tests. "It's all looking good," Elizabeth said finally. "Glucose, electrolytes, everything." Nicole's reflexes seemed normal, her pupils contracted nicely, and her heartbeat sounded fine. But she slumped wearily against Larry's chest, unable to move.

Larry and the others looked at one another anxiously. "Any thoughts?" he said.

"Beats me," said Anna. "Her vitals are great. It's definitely not heart attack or stroke."

"Some form of paralysis?"

"Her nerve functions are normal."

"So the poor dear *could* get up if she wanted to ..." said Elizabeth hesitantly.

"Then why doesn't she?" asked Anna.

Everyone stared at Nicole, who was slumped against Larry with blank eyes and slack jaws.

"Can you hear us?" Larry shook her gently. "Can you get up?"

Nicole didn't respond. Their words didn't seem to be registering on her.

"Maybe she doesn't want to get up," said Jessica at last.

"What?"

"Logic. She can get up but won't. Ergo, she must not *want* to get up."

"That's crazy!" Anna stared at her sister. "Why wouldn't she want to get up?"

"I don't know," Jessica sighed. "Forget it."

Elizabeth suddenly sat up straight and grabbed Jessica's arm. "I think you might be on to something."

The others stared at her.

"On to what, Grandma?" said Jessica. "I was just shooting my mouth off as usual."

"No, no, darling, you never do that. Everything you say has a point. And in this case, I think you might have hit upon the cause of your poor mother's problem."

"What cause?"

"This is just a wild thought, but I'm wondering if her inability to get up is a symptom of something more fundamental."

"Like what?"

Elizabeth hesitated. "I know this is going to sound crazy, but I'm wondering if she's lost the will to live."

The others gazed at her in shocked bewilderment.

"That's absurd!" Larry cried, holding Nicole close and fighting tears. "How can you even say such a thing?"

Elizabeth flushed under his scrutiny, but spoke firmly: "Haven't you noticed how dull she's been lately? I know she's been a good sport and has tried to engage in everything. But didn't you notice that she seemed to be deriving no pleasure from anything, just going through the motions?"

They looked at Nicole for a few seconds, as if hoping she would deny it. But she showed no sign of having heard them.

"Yeah, I did notice that," said Anna, after a pause. "She seemed to be, you know, just pretending to be cheerful."

"Forced smiles," said Jessica, nodding. "I could tell a mile away."

"So could I," Larry said in a low voice, looking down. "I kept asking her if she was troubled by something, but she always denied it."

"We should've done something," Elizabeth said. "We should have acted sooner."

Larry shook his head in puzzlement. "But first tell me *why*, Elizabeth. Let's assume you're right, that she's lost the will to live. But why? How?"

Elizabeth stared into space for a few seconds before replying. "I can only guess. I think she might have lost a sense of purpose. Perhaps she thinks we don't need her."

There was a long, shocked silence. Jessica might overstate a concern for melodramatic effect, but not Elizabeth, and her words carried utter conviction. The moment she finished speaking, every other concern was forgotten. All their activities, all their worries, all the disasters they had weathered— the air purifier that failed, the plants that perished—all of

that paled into insignificance beside the urgent, overpower-
ing need to rescue Nicole from whatever inner demons were
plaguing her and make it clear to her beyond the slightest
doubt that she was absolutely vital to all of them. That, without her, *they* would have no will to live.

"But how did it happen so fast?" asked Larry, almost plead-
ingly. "I know she wondered about the meaning of existence
and things like that. But losing the will to live? How did that
happen?"

Elizabeth sighed deeply. "I think I'm to blame. She used
to come to me with her questions, and I tried to help her as
much as I could. But my knowledge is so limited—I've always
been content to rest my faith in the great spiritual traditions.
This poor girl, on the other hand, had the burning need to
find out for herself. I knew that my answers didn't satisfy her,
and all the books I recommended weren't much help. I failed
her!" Elizabeth wept, and her granddaughters rushed to
embrace and console her.

"But what could you have done, my love?" Larry said. "I'm
no expert on spiritual matters, but it seems like she needed to
go on her own inner journey and find her own answers."

"That's where I could have been of real help to her,"
Elizabeth said between sobs. "Instead of giving her theoretical notions, I should have taught her how to meditate …
how to look inward for answers. But I didn't."

"Why not, Grandma?" Anna asked.

"Because I never got permission from my Master to teach
her techniques. But I shouldn't have been so hung up on that.
I'm such a fool."

"Don't cry, Grandma! You just followed rules, that's all."

"Is it too late?" asked Jessica. "To teach her some of your spiritual tricks?"

Elizabeth's weeping subsided, and she smiled through her tears. "No, it might not be. My Master said she could teach even a zombie to meditate."

"Then so can you," said Larry. "But first things first. We can't do anything if we don't get her up and about. How do we do that?"

"Give her a stimulant, maybe?" suggested Anna. "You know, amphetamines or something."

Larry looked at Jessica and Elizabeth, who both nodded. "Just this once can't hurt," Jessica said.

"Let's go for it."

After some discussion and examination of the drugs available in the clinic, they administered an intravenous cocktail of methamphetamine and modanafil, boosted with a stiff dose of caffeine. Within a minute the stimulant began to take effect. Nicole opened her eyes and blinked at her family.

"Did I pass out or something?" she asked. Her voice was weak, but now audible. Larry gently helped her stand up and take a few tentative steps with his support. She was obviously relieved to sit down again. Her daughters snuggled up to her, with Jessica stroking her hair while Anna placed her cheek against hers. Both girls were weeping.

"What's wrong with me? I've never felt like this."

The others looked at one another, wondering how to give her their diagnosis and how she would receive it.

"Your vitals are all great, Mum," said Anna, snuggling close.

"Then why do I feel like jelly?"

Larry cleared his throat. "Dearest, we suspect that your problem might not be physical."

"Then what?" Despite her weakness, Nicole said with some spirit: "Are you saying I'm *depressed?*"

Larry looked to Elizabeth for help, but she motioned him to continue. "It's deeper than that, we think," Larry started hesitantly. "It might stem from your spiritual longings. You seem to have lost a sense of purpose." Nicole gasped and shook her head feebly in protest, but Larry continued: "You seem to have lost the will to live."

The others waited in anxious silence to see how Nicole would react. The silence stretched for so long that Larry was about to repeat his words, but Nicole finally responded: "It's true that I've not been feeling good lately. Perhaps you're right. I seem to be feeling a lack of …" Her voice trailed off.

"I guess none of us realized how dark it was for you, the … the emptiness you must've been feeling inside."

Nicole sighed, and after a few moments managed a weak smile. "Talking of emptiness inside, how about a bit of breakfast?"

The others beamed with relief. They would have to watch her carefully, but for now Nicole seemed to be out of danger.

Over the next few weeks, the family's customary activities were suspended in favor of the pre-eminent goal of restoring Nicole's health. It took her a week to start walking by herself, and another month before she could participate in more strenuous physical activity. Even though she was a shadow of her former energetic self, still needing a daily shot of stimulant to start her day, she was obviously "back." But her improved physical condition only served to highlight her inner turmoil, which she could no longer conceal from the others. She now openly admitted the troubling questions that had taken over her mind.

"Pity that Mum had to nearly die before we realized what she was going through," Jessica commented.

"I should've been more forthcoming," said Nicole. "But I'm so used to taking care of others' health that I hated the idea of making a fuss about my own."

"Now that the spiritual cat is out of the bag, it's time to treat your ailment," said Larry. "Do you agree, Lizzie?"

"Yes, the sooner the better."

That very day, October 29 of Year Eight, Nicole's meditation lessons started. They didn't go well initially. She could not sit still for more than a few seconds at a time and felt unbearably restless in any position. She also proved to be uncharacteristically irritable. Her mother's plea to *breathe deep, let the tension out, and let the healing thoughts in* only seemed to exasperate her. Once again, Elizabeth realized her limitations as a spiritual advisor to her daughter. Naturally calm herself, she could sit quietly in any position for hours on end without discomfort. Meditation came almost naturally to her, and that made her a poor teacher for her daughter, whose restlessness she couldn't relate to. "I'm like a dolphin trying to teach a human to swim," she sighed.

After the failure of their first few sessions, Elizabeth asked the others for suggestions. She observed that her daughter's nerves seemed to be in an extreme state of irritation. "Until we help her overcome that, she can't get into a relaxed state."

"And the stimulants probably aren't helping," said Anna. "But I guess we can't stop them until she's better."

"How about some counter-irritation?" asked Jessica.

"Counter-irritation? What do you mean, dear?"

"I get it!" said Anna, who by now had such close sympathy with her sister that she could decode her thought processes well before anyone else. "We make her feel some other sen-sation—put ice cubes on her back, say—to keep her nerves busy while you work your spiritual magic. Like those sleep machines that produce a steady rushing sound that drowns out all other ambient noises."

"Exactly!" said Jessica. "I was thinking of putting pressure on her hands and feet."

Larry rubbed his chin doubtfully. "Hmm … I can't see how that would help."

"I find it soothing when someone grips my hands very hard and then lets go," Jessica explained. "Pain is actually calming."

Larry pondered her idea for a moment and then nodded. "Okay, let's give it a try."

Elizabeth approved the plan. At her next meditation lesson she had the girls dig their nails into Nicole's calves, while Larry pinched her arms.

"Pinch hard," she told them. "do you feel it, Nicole?"

"Ow!" she said.

"Pinch harder!" Elizabeth ordered. They did, and Nicole screamed.

"Okay, girls, ease off just a bit and hold it. Now Nicole, I want you to close your eyes and breathe deeply. Feel the pain."

Nicole breathed deeply. The pain was intense.

"Now Nicole, *be* the pain."

As Nicole continued to breathe, the pain took over her entire existence. At that moment nothing else existed. Her focus was absolute. As she sat and breathed, her pain gradually receded and she was aware of a strange calmness. It lasted only a minute or two, but during that short interval, her questions didn't nag her. She felt more peace than she had in a long time.

She opened her eyes and saw that her loving torturers had stopped the pinching. They were now anxiously gazing at her.

"Well?" asked Jessica.

"I think it worked," Nicole replied. "Just for a bit, but things seemed to get quieter inside."

"Thank heavens for your cruel streak, Jessica!" said her sister, hugging her. Jessica stuck her tongue out, but she was perilously close to tears. Elizabeth, fighting tears herself, decided to give Nicole a few more doses of the treatment, pinching her at a different spot each time. By the end of their two-hour session, Nicole had managed to stay calm for a full five-minute stretch. They had two sessions the following day, and for several days after. By the third week, Nicole's arms and legs were black and blue all over. But soon she no longer needed to be pinched and was far more receptive to her mother's coaching. It took her another two weeks, until early December of Year Eight, to experience her first meditative state. After that, there was no stopping her. She spent several hours each day downstairs in her room practicing the various techniques her mother had taught her and discovering some of her own. Her questions never went away—looking inward produced no more answers than looking outward. But somehow it didn't matter anymore. Her inner journey often conjured up such bliss that her intimate moments with Philip and Larry paled in comparison. She emerged from each session as recharged as her mother after her "sessions" with Larry.

"To each her own," Jessica murmured to her sister with a wink.

By the middle of January of Year Nine, Nicole had been fully restored to health. The period after her recovery was

one of the happiest in the Shell. Nicole, revitalized by a deep
inner joy that she had never experienced before, was in the
highest of spirits. Her joy was infectious, and soon everyone
went around with a smile. Even Larry, who thought his brain
lacked a right hemisphere, started dabbling in meditation. The
sight of him sitting uncomfortably cross-legged and chanting
Ommmm would send the girls into paroxysms of giggles.

This happy period lasted nearly four months. Then one
morning the heat failed to come on.

30
Cooling

AFTER CAUSING THE closure of the Food dome in
May of Year Seven, the well cooled more slowly for
a few months and then remained stable for a year
and a half. Indeed, it behaved so well that it lulled the family
into a false sense of security. Jessica and Larry even wondered
if their heroic efforts to install the diesel backup had been
worthwhile. But on May 13 of Year Nine, they had the
dubious satisfaction of seeing their fears confirmed.

The first inkling was the failure of the heat to come on at
its scheduled time of 5:00 a.m. The unexpected chill caused
everyone to oversleep, and it was past 7:00 by the time the
family woke up. And when they did, they had a nasty surprise in store: a thermometer that stayed obstinately at zero
degrees. Jessica rushed to the Geo dome—by now, the rule
about never moving about alone had long been suspended—
and immediately found what the problem was. It was not, as
she hoped, a blocked pipe or broken thermostat—serious but
fixable problems—but what she and Larry feared the most.
The well had cooled and was continuing to cool.

Back in Central, the group met with a feeling of déjà vu. By now everyone knew the drill: close another dome, lower the thermostat, and hope for the best. The choice of which dome to close was obvious this time, as they had only one besides Central and Geo in operation. Nevertheless, Larry consulted Anna first. Her beloved plants were dead, her bio-reactors were idle, but she was still the mistress of the Eco dome. The green light would have to come from her.

"Well, there's nothing *eco* about it now, is there?" she said in a resigned voice. "Let's move the kitchen and chlorella panels in here and shut the damn thing down."

Jessica went over and hugged her. A few years ago she might have downplayed or even mocked her sister's loss; now all she felt was empathy.

The rest of the day passed in moving the kitchen and pantry to Central. It was gloomy, laborious work, made more tedious by the extra layers of clothing they had to wear against the now biting cold. By dinnertime, the move was finished. Eco was shut off for good. Before long, that dome, like Air and Food before it, would be just a memory.

It was a somber family that sat down to dinner that evening. On the positive side, Central was slowly warming up again. Their living quarters, though, were now really cramped. The kitchen and pantry took up most of the office space, while the chlorella panels stood in the living area, squeezed against the medical equipment relocated there after the closure of Health. Their sleeping tent had to be pulled down since it took up too much space. And with all that, the energy situation remained precarious.

"Is there anything more we can do?" Elizabeth asked Larry.

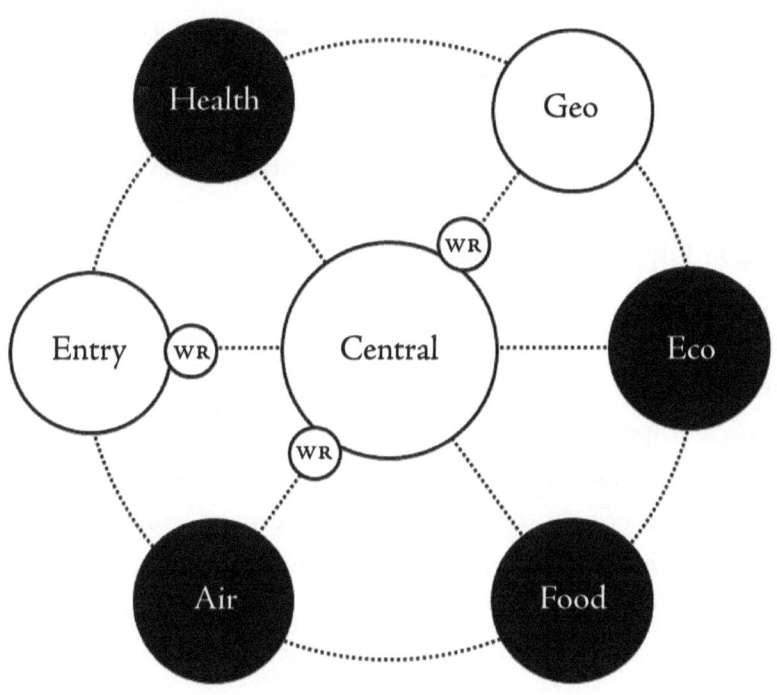

"Nothing I can think of."

Closing the Eco dome got them a few weeks' respite. Morale, gloomy at first, soon rose again. Their games, dances, and other activities were now seriously circumscribed, but the family took it in their stride. They invented games that took advantage of their peculiar living situation. They played hide and go seek with the lights off. Larry was an ace at seeking, until it turned out he was cheating by using infrared goggles to detect body heat. Another favorite game was walking from any object in the dome to another blindfolded without bumping into anything. Jessica, with her strong spatial memory, reigned supreme until Larry cheated again by moving objects while she was approaching them. Limericks came fast and furious, darker and funnier than Jessica could have ever hoped for. Impromptu skits, music sessions, and dances helped them while away their time. "This feels like the most incredible holiday ever," Anna remarked. "A bit surreal, but who cares?"

On July 2 of Year Nine, without any further warning, the geothermal well simply went out. In the space of a few hours its core temperature dropped from about 800 degrees to several degrees below freezing. ("*Well* below freezing," as Jessica quipped.)

Once again, a blast of cold hit the family at dawn. They knew instinctively that this was no ordinary cooling. Jessica went to Geo and hurried back to confirm what they feared. "The well's history," she said.

"It could've given us more notice," was Anna's only comment.

Larry and Jessica had anticipated the event, judging by the rate of cooling of the Geo well. A few days previously they had already switched on the diesel heating system at its lowest setting. Now they cranked up its power. By noon, Central was warm again.

"It's down to us and Entry," Larry said, adding to himself: *and we are living on borrowed time.*

"How long will the diesel last?" Elizabeth asked Larry, as always giving him an opening to talk about something unpleasant but necessary.

"About a year," he said.

"And after that?"

"After that, we'll have to stay in our spacesuits. That won't be much fun, I'm afraid."

"Yikes," said Anna. "And how long can we survive in them?"

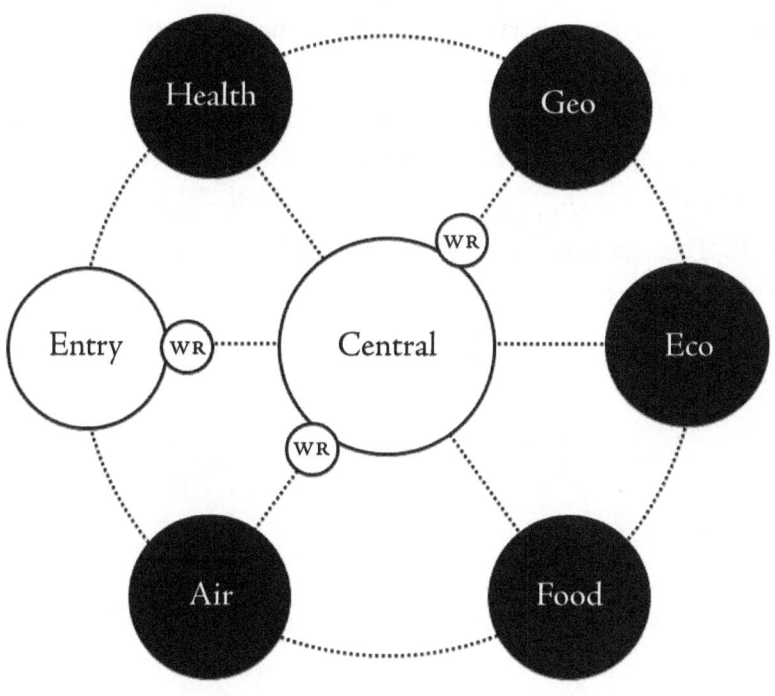

"A week or two."

"Ouch."

The family members digested the news in silence. If Larry had expected his companions to express dismay or fear, he was proved wrong. Once again, he was amazed and touched by their courage and stoicism. Anna expressed the group's sentiment: "We have like a year before we run out of fuel. Let's enjoy it as much as we can."

"Yes, let's party like there's no tomorrow," Jessica said. "Literally."

Animated by this spirit, the family resumed what became their latest version of a normal existence. Maintenance and housekeeping chores mingled with fun and frolic. Morale remained high, camaraderie stayed solid, and optimism held strong. Having only twelve months of heating left was a grim prospect, but to a bunch of humans surviving against all odds on a dead planet, any future other than instant annihilation was to be celebrated. And they did.

Very soon, they no longer spoke about the geothermal well. "Let's pretend it never existed," said Larry.

That turned out to be a mistake.

31

Fracture

WHILE THE FAMILY worked and played and loved in blissful ignorance, deep below them the Earth's core had been slowly but steadily losing its titanic thermal battle with the Shroud-cooled surface. For a while, geothermal heat moving upward and outward from the Earth's interior held its own against the cold front bearing down from the surface. Gradually, however, as the Earth's surface grew colder, its internal warmth fled further inward. And when the cold front from the surface reached the Geo well's heat source, the Shell lost its primary energy supply.

That was catastrophic enough, but the failure of the well presaged a deadlier problem.

As the family figured out later, when a large, complex, and heterogeneous object contracts, the process isn't uniform. Some parts shrink more than others. Eventually, the thermo-mechanical stress causes the object to break apart; if the object already has holes or cracks, that's where the fractures tend to occur. In the case of the Shell, the bedrock underneath had one large, deep hole—the geothermal well—along with several cavities that accommodated the hexes and subterranean tunnels connecting them. It also had the water well and a number of narrow, deep holes in the washrooms intended for the disposal of non-recyclable waste. The rock had several possible routes for fracture, but the path of least resistance lay along the imaginary line joining the Geo, Central, and Air domes as well as the two main washrooms. There was almost as much hole as solid ground along that path. That's where the break occurred.

The trouble arrived on September 1 of Year Nine and, as always, came in the small hours of the morning. It announced itself with a deafening crack and a blast of cold that seemed to come from the frigid reaches of outer space. Everyone woke up instantly in bewilderment and shock. Nicole was the first to recover. She struggled up and was about to step forward into the darkened room when she heard Jessica scream, "Mum, stop!" Larry switched on the flashlight he kept near the bed. The sight that greeted them was pure nightmare.

It was not a sight, but an absence of one, a void, a ghastly, dark emptiness where their office should have been. For just inches away from the foot of their sleeping area was an abyss that went down as far as the eye could see. The kitchen, office, and washroom were gone. The passages to the Geo and Air domes had disappeared. All that was left was the part of the floor where they had slept, their living space with the chlorella panels, and the door to the Entry dome. Most of their roof was gone as well. They were now out in the open.

What saved them, ironically, was the failure of the well. Since that catastrophe, the thermostat had been turned all the way down at night to conserve energy. In the sub-Arctic conditions that resulted, the family had taken to sleeping in

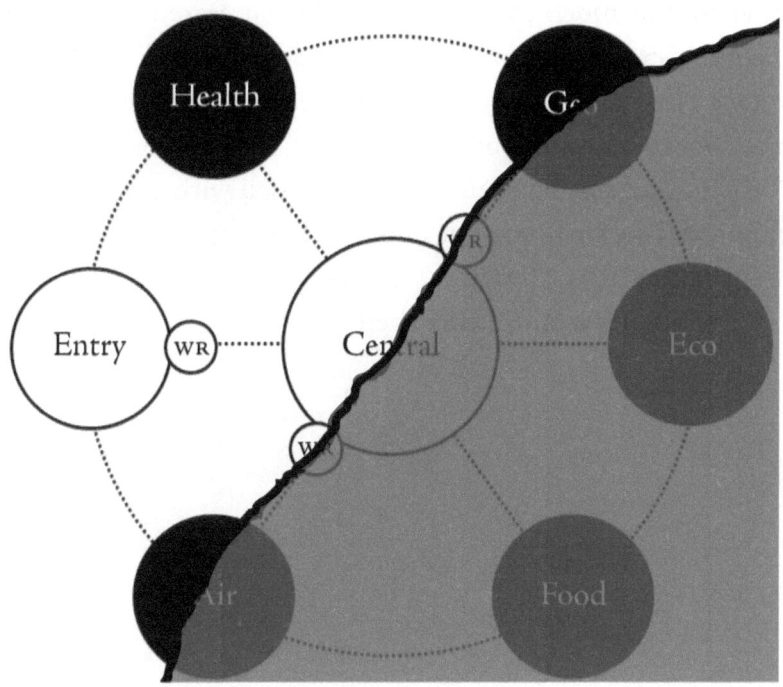

the warmest clothing possible, including thick gloves, socks, and ski masks. But for that, they would have frozen instantly. Even now, they were only seconds away from death.

"Quick! Into Entry!" Larry shouted. His voice sounded tinny and appeared to come from a great distance.

Entry was mercifully intact. It took them only seconds to get to its safety, but those seconds felt like an eternity in the hellish cold. Once inside, Larry, Jessica, and Anna put on their spacesuits and fetched the chlorella panels and solar lamps from Central. They made one more trip to salvage what else they could—pillows, blankets, journals—and turned off all heat to the shattered dome that had been their home for the past decade. Larry did a quick check of Air. The door to it opened, but much of the dome had been erased by another yawning crater. Jessica likewise tried to see if Health was intact but found that the Fracture had irreparably jammed the doors leading to it on both levels. It, too, was lost for good.

They had started their stay in the Shell with a big Central dome and six smaller outer domes. They were now down to a single outer dome, Entry.

The Shell was now just a shell.

32
Post-Mortem

THE FAMILY HUDDLED together on fragments of carpet salvaged from Central. Larry produced a bottle of brandy kept for emergencies in every dome. Using fuel container caps as makeshift tumblers, he poured out measures of the amber liquid for each of them.

"Well, Jessica, you were right as always." Larry coughed as the fiery liquid burned in his throat. "The unknown got us."

"But what the hell happened?" said Anna. "I still can't believe what I saw! What is it, a crevasse?"

"It certainly looked like one," Larry replied. "But how and why, I've no clue."

"Earthquake?"

"Unlikely. We're nowhere near a fault."

"Jessica, any idea?"

"Differential contraction."

The other women looked puzzled, but Larry nodded. "Could be," he said and added for the others' benefit: "Jessica thinks the cold might have made the rock under us shrink unevenly."

"That's right," Jessica said, and outlined a theory of how the cold could have caused the ground below to fracture.

The family digested this idea for a few moments. "So what's our situation now?" Nicole asked Larry.

Larry took a deep breath. His heart still pounded from the excitement and alarm of their narrow escape. "Our situation is dire, I'm afraid." His heart brimmed with despair as he looked at the grim, anxious faces of his companions. *How do I break it to them? Haven't they suffered enough?* With infinite weariness he said: "We've lost most of our food and water. The Air dome has cracked open, and our food store has vanished into the void. The Food dome and the pond under it are on the other side of the chasm."

"They might as well be on the other side of the planet," said Jessica.

"Yes, they're forever out of reach. Perhaps we should've left half our food here, but like an idiot I had us shift most of it to Air to make way for the fuel."

"*Most* of it?" Nicole said. "That means we have some food here?"

"Yes, but not much. About five hundred kilos of tinned stuff that we couldn't find room for in Air."

"Well, that's something."

"Yes, but with the loss of the pantry, we've lost all our sugar, salt, and condiments."

"Hell."

"Yes. And as for water, our only source now is the condensate from the burning diesel."

"Yikes, that doesn't sound like much."

"It isn't. Each liter of fuel will give a liter of water at best."

"Any more bad news?"

"We've also lost our computer database, radio equipment, and virtually all tools and spare parts."

A long, gloomy silence followed.

"On the positive side, we're all still alive," Elizabeth said at last. "That's something to be grateful for."

"Right," said Anna. "If the fracture had taken out Entry—"

"—we'd be icicles now," Jessica finished for her.

"Bloody hell," said Nicole. "More brandy, please."

Larry doled out another measure and the family sipped in silence for a while. "Talking of positive things …" he said eventually.

"Fuel?" Jessica said.

"Yes. Before the Fracture, we had enough for a year. Now, since we don't have a Central dome to heat, our diesel supply will last longer."

"How much longer?"

"About a third. Something like 16 months."

Nicole voiced the collective sentiment: "Then we must make sure that our food and water—and *we*—last that long."

33
Journals

Larry's Journal

TODAY IS DEC. 31 of Year Ten. It's been exactly five years since I last took up my pen to write an entry in this journal. When we all agreed to write one at the end of the first day, first year, fifth year, and every fifth year after that, I honestly didn't expect to reach the third milestone, let alone the fourth. But here we are, still alive, still moving, breathing, talking, and thinking.

I referred to our first five years here as the Steady State period. Everything seemed to work well then. Our well ran hot, our air blew fresh, our plants grew strong, and our food tasted great. All our domes were operational—it's hard to believe that now, squeezed as we are into a single outer dome.

I was prepared to have things fall apart slowly, a gradual attrition, a steady increase of entropy. That's the universal law. And that's what happened during Years Six to Nine, as our systems failed one by one. Each of these was painful, but we adjusted. The Air dome failure and the plant deaths caught us rather unprepared, but we managed to cope. One could call this period the Decline.

Then, on Sept 1 of Year Nine, came the Fracture. To say we were unprepared would be the understatement of the century. Hardened though we were to single-system failures, to have our habitat split open like an eggshell was something else. In that single instant, we lost so much—food, water, supplies, information, living space—that I can think of only one word to describe the event: Collapse!

So we have spent the past sixteen months, post-Fracture, huddled uncomfortably in the Entry dome. We keep the temperature below freezing to drag out our precious fuel reserves as long as possible. The heating isn't uniform, as it was during our Geo days. The space next to the walls remains bitterly cold. There's one spot that's tolerably warm—or not too unpleasantly cold—near the middle, about two by three meters, right among the diesel engines, which is now our living and sleeping area. The noise of the engines was bothersome at first, but we no longer notice it. The girls and I have rigged up a species of tent there and layered it with our salvaged carpet fragments to shield us from the icy floor. We almost never leave this cocoon except for hurried trips to fetch food and water.

As for calls of nature, we initially used the loo just outside the door to Central, but as that grew too cold and painful to reach we set one up in a corner of Entry itself using empty containers with lids. It's so cold there that our wastes freeze and don't reek.

We live in semi-darkness during the "day," with all our available light keeping the ever-important chlorella alive.

Being unable to move around much is probably not a bad thing, as we have to be less active now to avoid getting too hungry or thirsty. Water is scarce—we've been able to condense and collect only a fraction of the water vapor from the diesel exhaust—and food even more so. So no more exercise or dancing, leave alone intimate moments! The only physical activity we do, apart from essential chores, is a bit of tai chi in the mornings and yoga in the evenings. The lessons we've taken from Lizzie on how to relax our breathing and slow down our metabolism are now paying off. We stay wrapped in as many layers of clothing as we can wear. We sleep a lot. There isn't much else to do. I would use the dreaded H-word to describe the situation, except that the bear—unlike us—has the good sense to stuff itself with salmon and build a thick layer of fat before it goes off to its cave to sleep out the winter.

Talking of food, we're now subsisting solely on canned beans, tuna, and spinach, because that's all we have. It's unappetizing and monotonous. The girls use the heat from the diesel engines in ingenious ways to heat our food, and even boil water. But it's still tedious. And there's no coffee or tea to go with the hot water.

All in all, not a pleasant existence. But no one ever complains. Could there ever be a more wonderful family than the Millers? Each of them is more admirable, more adorable, than the other. I could write volumes about them and only scratch the surface of their virtues.

But sometimes I wish they were less wonderful. Then it would be easier for me to face the grim prospect that looms ever closer.

Nicole's Journal

At Larry's urging, I'm taking up my pen—literally, because we've only one laptop, and Jessica's using it—to put my thoughts down on this tenth anniversary of our Shell life. I'm sure the others will talk about our living conditions here and our diminishing future prospects. Let me write about what's been going on *inside* me.

I never understood until I came to the Shell why some people spend all their lives searching for meaning—giving up their jobs, abandoning their families, tormenting themselves. Now I realize it's the only goal that matters, work and family being nothing but pleasant distractions on this journey. This realization has come as a great shock, completely overturning everything I believed in. It must have been an even greater shock to my loved ones, but they've accepted it, as they've always accepted everything, without complaint or reproach. Indeed, they've positively embraced my spiritual quest, seeing how vital it was to my wellbeing. I bless them all, as I embark on a journey where they can't follow.

Questions, questions, questions. They were driving me crazy. It was only when I stopped looking outwards—to Larry, to Mum, to philosophy, to religion, to spiritual traditions—and started looking inward that I found answers. Or rather, I didn't find answers per se, but learned what questions to ask, and why the answers didn't matter. I learned to tap into that quiet magical oasis of tranquility deep within me, where the quest for meaning becomes irrelevant. Everything goes still there. From that spot, it's a struggle to tear myself away and return to what people call *reality*. I now understand why Mum used to spend nearly all her free time enjoying that special inner sanctum.

I guess our physical lives are going to end in a few weeks once we run out of diesel. Death. And what comes after we die? That used to be one of my big questions. Now it doesn't seem to matter. We all seem to carry that mysterious, deathless place deep inside us. The loss of the physical body is immaterial.

Anna's Journal

Ten years! It feels like we've been here for an eternity, yet time has flown by incredibly fast. Yes, that's a contradiction, but so's our existence here. We're all alive—barely—while the rest of the planet is probably dead. We've survived for ten long years but are now down to our last few weeks here. Should I curse the fate that's in store, or should I celebrate the miracle of being alive against such odds?

Perhaps celebration would be more apt. Don't we celebrate a triple century, even when the batsman goes out a few balls later? Don't we cheer him as he walks back to the pavilion? Our current situation may be a shambles, and our future without hope, but what an innings it's been!

Our survival has been miraculous. But there's so much more to celebrate. Could anyone be blessed with more fabulous company than I've enjoyed these past years? Mum, always kind and cheerful, now such a serene presence. Grandma, warm and nurturing, now with that look of sweet mischief. Jessica, now my bestie—how did I ever manage without her friendship? No matter how dire the situation, she manages to find something amusing, some silver lining. I used to be the chipper one in the family. Now, I can count on her to cheer me up whenever I need it. And last but not the least, Larry. Can I finally say what I've always wanted to—that I have a terrible crush on him? (And so does Jessica, I suspect, though she might deny it. Mum, with all her spiritual yearnings, still has a special place for him in her heart. And as for Grandma … !!!!) And how can I not? How could anyone *not* be madly in love with him?

I guess my biggest reason for celebrating would be my good fortune in having such wonderful people in my life. And that's my best consolation for what's to come. I may soon be dead, but I will have spent the last ten years of my life with the most wonderful people ever.

Jessica's Journal

It looks like our time is finally running out. Had to, some-time. I guess the end, or the beginning of the end, happened far more quickly than expected. Im supposed to be the pessimist in the family, but even I didnt expect something quite so brutal as the Fracture. Thats exactly the kind of unknown Id feared when we 1st came here. Unfortunately, its exactly the kind of unknown that we cant prepare for. We can only react, recover, & adapt.

I must say its been a fun ride. Crazy, weird, surreal. Sounds incredible, but Ive had far more fun inside the Shell than I ever did outside. Indeed, if the Shroud had never come into our lives, I would be much less happy than now. If, in some parallel Shroudless universe, my doppelganger is leading a "normal" life, I bet its far less fun than mine. It will be interesting to meet her & compare notes. Perhaps we *will* meet in some spatio-temporo-spiritual setting—who knows what comes after death?

As this will most probably be my last journal entry, a word or two about my fellow Shellmates. Ive never been one to pay compliments, assuming that the others are as embarrassed by them as me. Besides, what words could do justice to my family? Even Anna, w/ her flair for words, would find it challenging. But Ill try. Mum—nicer than ever, now so tranquil too. Anna—the best sister & the best friend, period. Grandma Lizzie—dearer & sweeter w/ every passing day. Larry ... I remember a time when I found him annoying.

Now, when hes holding me in his arms, I forget everything
else. Ill leave it at that.

Life is short, but if you have the right company its good.
Not much else to say.

Elizabeth's Journal

The end of life's journey is approaching. In the past, I've often
wondered about what I'd feel at this point. Would I be sad
to leave the earthly plane behind? Would I be excited about
what's to come? Would I be afraid?

What I feel now is a mix of emotions. Gratitude for these
ten merciful years of "society, friendship, and love, divinely
bestowed upon man," as the poet put it. Regret for having
to say goodbye to my beloved companions. Curiosity, even
some eagerness, to see what comes next. Some nervousness
about how exactly the dying will happen. Will it be prolonged
and painful? Or could we do something to make it swift and
relatively painless? I should ask Larry. I'm sure he's thought
about it, and maybe planned for it, but for obvious reasons
that's not a topic he'll want to raise himself.

Our survival this long on a dead planet has far exceeded
Larry's expectations, he confessed to me a few days ago.
What's exceeded *my* expectations is the way this family has
come together. From being loving but disparate individuals
with divergent interests, we've grown closer and closer over
these years in the Shell, to the point that we're now close to
being just one body, mind, and soul—a superhuman, with
Larry's strength, Nicole's skill, my serenity, Anna's vitality, and
Jessica's intelligence. Is this a foretaste of what the union with
the Infinite feels like? If so, I can't wait.

34
Celebration

O N THEIR TENTH anniversary evening, the family held a celebration. They usually kept the Entry dome cold and dim to conserve energy, but today they turned all lights on and cranked the heat up to a toasty 15 degrees. Larry produced yet another miraculous bottle of champagne and served everyone in makeshift flutes shaped from diesel can lids.

"Larry, you missed your true vocation," said Jessica.

"She's right," said Anna. "You should've been a sommelier in a Parisian restaurant."

The other women chuckled, and Larry smiled. He had been unsure about the mood of the family. It was a relief to see everyone in lively spirits. They would need all their cheerfulness to receive the status update that it was his unpleasant duty to make. But he was in no hurry, letting everyone savor the moment. It was great to shed some of their cumbersome layers of clothing. The broad-spectrum solar lamps they had salvaged from Central, normally used just on the chlorella, now bathed them with a bright, warm glow. The champagne, though long past its expiry date, fizzed deliciously in their mouths. It was a golden moment.

After about half an hour of pleasant conversation, snuggled up together, with the champagne all gone, it was time to turn to more serious matters. They couldn't afford to keep the heat blasting and the lights blazing for much longer. The women looked at Larry expectantly, but as always he hesitated until Elizabeth came to his aid.

"Larry, this is lovely, but it falls upon me to ask you—what's our situation?"

Though Larry had long renounced his leadership role and left the decision making to family consensus, for old times' sake the others still looked to him to take the lead on discussions. He wondered how he should deliver the news. Better state it plainly, he thought.

"We have six more weeks of food. The fuel situation is worse, I'm afraid."

"How much time?"

"Another two weeks at the most."

There was a long silence. No one could think of a suitable comment. They could stretch their food and water out longer, but not their fuel—they had already cut their consumption to the point that Anna and Nicole were showing early signs of frostbite.

In two weeks, we'll start freezing to death. Larry's thought transmitted itself to the others as if by telepathy.

"Last two weeks of warmth," Jessica said.

"What about the spacesuits?" asked Anna.

"The suits won't be much use, I'm afraid," Larry said.

"Why not? Didn't you tell us we could wear them if the heating failed?"

"The suits will reduce heat loss from our bodies. At some point, though, the air will get too cold to breathe."

"So we'll freeze anyway," Jessica said. "Just more slowly and painfully."

During another long silence, Nicole remembered the oxygen cylinders transferred to Entry during the closure of Health in Year Seven. Scanning the dome with eager eyes, she found the corner where the cylinders lay and pointed toward them. "What about using those?"

Larry's eyes lit up for a second and then grew somber again. "No, that won't work either. The oxygen will also attain the ambient temperature."

"So we'll breathe cold oxygen instead of cold air," Jessica said.

Nicole thought for a moment and nodded. "I see. We've got two more weeks to live."

Nobody spoke for a few minutes, each deep in reflection.

"Larry," said Elizabeth, finally. "I don't know how to put this ... but freezing to death seems like a slow and terrible way to go. Is there some way to ... make it less unpleasant?"

Larry looked at her for several seconds, a gentle smile playing on his careworn face. "Lizzie, my love, I don't know how you do it, but you always manage to voice the thought I lack the courage to express. But yes, we can make it fast and painless."

"Cyanide pill?" said Jessica.

Nicole and Elizabeth grimaced, but Anna nodded. "Yeah, astronauts used to get one, didn't they? In case they got stranded in space."

"It's not so different from our situation."

Larry followed the exchange between the sisters with a tender smile and shook his head. "I don't think astronauts got suicide pills. Spies did, maybe. Anyway, we can do better. Bundle up and follow me downstairs. There's something I need to show you."

Dark, cold, and forlorn, the Entry hex seemed to foreshadow what lay in store for them. Their footsteps echoed in the near-empty chamber.

Anna shivered. "Geez, this place could be a horror movie set."

"Like *30 Days of Night*," Jessica said. "Cue a horde of thirsty vampires springing out of the dark."

"Not a jolly place, this," Larry admitted. "But here's what I wanted to show you."

His flashlight revealed a door innocuously marked Cleaning Supplies, which he slid open, revealing a closet with two shelves. The top one was empty except for two bottles of champagne. The lower one was covered with a dark glass screen.

"Larry, you sneak!" said Anna. "So this is where you hid your bubbly all these years."

"True," admitted Larry. He explained that he'd had the champagne specially bottled in containers of his own design, made from space-grade glass guaranteed to withstand ultra-low temperatures. He told them how he had had to thaw out each bottle slowly and carefully before he could pour out the liquid it contained. "But what I want to show you is in the lower shelf. Excuse me while I break open the screen."

The lower compartment displayed a number of syringes, IV apparatus, breathing masks, and innumerable containers of drugs, ranging from familiar-sounding ones such as opium, morphine, and barbiturates, to several whose names had meaning only for Nicole. "Wow, what a collection of opiates and anesthetics!" She turned to her mother. "This is what you were looking for. Everything you need for a painless, even pleasant death."

"Really, dear?"

"Yes, really." Nicole picked up a vial of thiopental and shook it. "Take five grams of this and you could walk out the door into the desert, smiling."

They picked up vials at random and tried to read the information printed on them in the dim glow of the flashlight.

"I'm sorry I had to show you this," said Larry. "Perhaps we won't need it. I'm still hoping something will turn up."

"Like Mr. Micawber," remarked Jessica, eliciting a smile from Larry. He knew she had read *David Copperfield* in the early days just to have something to say to him.

Back in their warm circle upstairs, the group was silent. With two weeks left, death was staring them in the face. Larry's suicide equipment had only made explicit what they all knew but had avoided thinking about until now.

"Before we break up this meeting, I have one question for all of you," Larry said, breaking the long silence. "And I want you to give me an honest answer."

Everyone nodded. Only Jessica suspected what was coming.

"I made several poor decisions in designing this place. Instead of dedicating each dome to a single function, I could've made each dome self-sufficient. Then, no matter where we were, we'd have all the basic facilities. I could've stored more diesel and installed a proper backup heating system, instead of dumping the problem on Jessica. I could've installed 3D printers to make replacement valves. I could've provided us with better winter clothing before we made that crazy helicopter trip here, and I could've come a week earlier to fetch you. I could've installed vibration testers to monitor the health of the bedrock below us. And I didn't anticipate any of the failures—plants dying, air exchanger going kaput, the well cooling off suddenly. But my biggest error, as Jessica rightly pointed out early on, was not taking you all into my confidence when building the Shell. Had I used our collective wisdom, instead of relying on just my own, we might not be in the dire situation we are now. Perhaps, as Anna once suggested, we should've built an undersea habitat, or even moved into a nuclear submarine, rather than construct a shelter on land. So my question for you is this. Tell me honestly—did I make a mess of things?"

"Of course you made a mess of things, Larry," said Jessica, "and I hate you for it!" This, with her arms around him, her cheek against his, and tears streaming down her face. The others looked suddenly bright-eyed, and Larry himself felt a pricking sensation in his eyes. If he didn't control himself ... but it was too late. He felt the tears well, and in a few seconds was sobbing his heart out. Everyone held each other close, their tears streaming unchecked. Ten years of shock and sacrifice and suffering sweetened by a few moments of domestic bliss while death tightened its implacable grip—it all flowed out at that moment.

Everyone knew it would be their last cry.

35

Preparations

THE NEXT TWO weeks raced by. Having accepted the inevitable, the Shellmates stopped checking the diesel level. Instead, they decided to enjoy their last few days as much as they could, with jokes, poetry, music, dancing, and cuddling. Finally, it was January 17 of Year Eleven, the day that the heating would stop for good around midnight. Exit Day, as Jessica termed it. That evening they held one last meeting.

"Should we do it now?" said Anna.

Jessica went to check the diesel level one last time. "Hold on, there's something strange here," she said a couple of minutes later.

"What, are we out of fuel already?" Larry cried.

"No, relax. Just the opposite. We seem to have another week's worth left!"

"How's that possible?" Larry said. "Did we count wrong?"

"No, we counted fine. We're using fuel slower than we thought."

Anna felt a surge of hope that died at once. *Wasn't it merely delaying the inevitable?*

"Let's go ahead with our plan," she said. "Why drag it out?"

The family reflected for a few seconds.

"Oh, dear! It seems a pity to end it when we still have some fuel left," said Elizabeth hesitantly. "Another week of life …"

"You, Nicole?" asked Larry.

Nicole sighed. "I'm in two minds. I do see Anna's point. But I can't disagree with Mum, either. Where there's life …"

Larry nodded. "Perhaps then each of us should choose our own time to … call it quits?"

"Third possibility," said Jessica. "Why don't we go out with a bang?"

"With a bang? How?"

"Crank the heat and light up. Live warm, bright, and snug for couple of days. *Then* call it quits."

"I love that idea!" cried Anna.

"It's a great compromise," Nicole said.

"I like it too," said Elizabeth after a pause. "How about you, Larry?"

"It's a terrific plan. In fact, let's stop rationing food and water as well."

"Deal." Jessica beamed at the enthusiasm for her proposal. "Let's end our existence as civilized humans, not as wannabe polar bears."

"Yes, and don't forget those two bottles of champagne!"

The next two days passed in riotous celebration as the Shellmates cherished their last moments of life on Earth. They woke up both days in high spirits and enjoyed each moment with songs and games and general silliness. At night, pleasantly exhausted, they cuddled tight and drifted off into sweet, dreamless sleep.

By the evening of the second day they had used up almost all their food and water. They had just enough fuel to keep them warm until about ten o'clock the following morning.

"Let's do it at nine," Jessica said.

36
Lamp

O N THE MORNING of January 20, the revised Exit Day, Nicole was the first to open her eyes. She lay still for as long as she could, but then fidgeted and stretched and woke up the others as well. "Larry," she complained. "You could've let us sleep a little longer. This is our last opportunity to sleep in."

"But I didn't wake you." Larry switched on the lighting and rubbed the sleep out of his eyes.

"You turned the ceiling light on too early."

Larry, who had been stretching and yawning, sat up bolt upright and stared at her. "What did you just say?" he said.

His tone was so sharp that it was Nicole's turn to stare at him. "I said I was woken up by a lamp. That one." The others stared at the point at the center of the dome she indicated. "You can't see it now, with the other lights on."

"But there's no lamp up there."

"Larry ..." Jessica's voice was so tight that the others stared at her. "Can I turn all lights off for a second?"

"Sure, but what for?"

Instead of replying Jessica sprang up, ran to the master switch, and flipped it off. The dome should have gone pitch dark but didn't—what appeared to be a dim red lamp at the very center of the roof remained on.

"See?" said Nicole. "That's the one. Odd that it didn't go off."

"But how could that be?" cried Anna. "Where's that light coming from? What's up there?"

Larry and Jessica looked at each other for several seconds. Then Larry heard himself speak, slowly and distinctly, in a voice he could barely recognize: "Up there, right in the center of the ceiling, is a circle made of glass that's clear all the way to the outside."

The silence stretched on and on. Everyone stared spellbound at the ceiling, afraid to blink lest the spell be broken.

It was Jessica who finally spoke, her voice a hoarse whisper. "Sunlight!" she said.

"*Sunlight?* Can it really be …?" whispered Nicole.

"I think it is. No, I'm bloody certain it is!" Larry's voice rose to a jubilant shout.

Elizabeth's eyes were already streaming. "Too bad I've said *miracle* so often before. Now I have no words left."

Suddenly, everyone was hugging and kissing and weeping joyous tears, looking up every few seconds to stare incredulously at the reddish orb up above them.

"Anybody interested in a little spacewalk?" said Larry.

In minutes everyone was suited up and ready at the airlock, Jessica with a thermometer clipped to her suit. Having remained shut for ten years, the door's electric mechanism had long stopped working from cold and disuse. With the girls helping him, Larry tried to open the door manually.

They had to pull the handle with all their strength before the airlock would budge. It opened slowly, creakily, as a recovering invalid might resume activity after a severe illness and a long convalescence. But it finally gave in to their combined efforts. They stepped out into the open, a place they hadn't set eyes on for ten long years, except for a few panic-stricken seconds after the Fracture.

And the sun was shining.

But only in a manner of speaking. All they could see around them was an orange glow, as would have appeared in the pre-Shroud era on a cloudy, foggy day. But it was enough for them to see around them, to feast their eyes on the desert they had last seen years ago. To the west, things didn't seem very different from what they remembered. But to the east, stretching out as far as the eye could see, was a crevasse of such gigantic proportions that the Grand Canyon would have been a mere gully in comparison. Precariously perched on its near edge was the broken shell of Central, next to which stood Entry, their pathetic, insignificant dwelling. It was only then that the full realization hit home of how close to the brink they had lived for the past year.

Cautiously approaching the edge, they peered down, but could see no bottom. Looking ahead, only the sharper eyes of the girls could discern the farther edge of the canyon, which they reckoned to be a couple of kilometers away. Miraculously, the Eco and Food domes still stood there. Slowly, the group retreated from the yawning pit and reassembled near the Entry dome.

"The temperature is minus 50. I can't believe it!" Larry said, glancing at Jessica's thermometer. "It's almost 80 degrees warmer than it was." His voice, coming through the audio system built into their suit helmets, brimmed with excitement.

"We stopped checking years ago," Jessica said.

"It must have started warming the past few days, hence the extra diesel," Anna said.

"Now that the sun is out it'll keep getting warmer, won't it?" asked Elizabeth.

"It should," said Larry. "But we can't tell how much or how fast."

"Right," said Jessica. "So don't put on your T-shirts yet."

37

Desert

B ACK INSIDE, DIVESTED of their suits, the group sat in a close circle. Everyone looked expectantly at the others, waiting for someone to speak. It was Anna who finally voiced the collective sentiment.

"Today gets my vote for being the craziest, merriest, loveliest day ever!"

Everyone started speaking at once. Waves of hope, joy, gratitude, relief, and disbelief flowed from them. It was only much later that Larry struck the business note.

"Dear team, it looks like we may not die today after all. But our troubles aren't over yet."

The mood grew sober.

"Right," said Jessica. "Minus 50 is bloody cold, and we're out of fuel here."

"What are our options?" Nicole asked after a pause.

"Stay here or head to town," said Larry. "In either case, we should set out immediately to find fuel. Where to look, I'm not sure."

"What was that place, that little village to the west? It's been so many years that I don't even remember its name now," said Elizabeth.

"Wallabin?"

"Yes, that's the one I was thinking of. Perhaps we could try the filling station there?"

"But Wallabin's thirty kilometers away! How do we get there?"

"We sure can't *walk* that far," Jessica said.

"Didn't you have your truck parked in a garage nearby?" Nicole asked Larry.

Larry made a face. "Yes, but it's on the other side of the chasm. Right next to Eco."

"Scratch that idea, then."

"What about the helicopter we flew in?"

Larry grunted. "Yes, the chopper is perhaps our best bet."

Jessica laughed incredulously. "Seriously? You want to fly that bird? It's been sitting out in the open for ten years."

"It's worth a try. It got damaged on landing but might still fly."

"That's insane! With cold and dust and rust and fuel evaporation—"

Larry dismissed her objections. "Dust can't get into the engine. There's zero moisture in the air, so no rust. And in the cold, fuel will freeze, not evaporate."

"But how will the engine start? It's almost as cold as when we flew in, and it stalled then."

"We'll have to figure out some way to start it. Once it starts, it'll fly." Larry tried to sound confident.

Jessica shook her head. "Okay, but how far will it take us? The fuel tank was nearly empty even then."

Larry was silent.

"Didn't we have some octane here?" said Anna. "Couldn't we use that?"

"All gone," said Jessica. "Burned along with diesel. And what's left in the tank can't take us ten kilometers, let alone thirty. What do we do then? Walk the rest?"

Larry had no answer, and the family's elation gave way to the grim realization that they weren't out of the woods yet. A twenty-kilometer walk in sub-Arctic weather would be borderline suicidal. At the very least, they could expect to lose some fingers or toes to frostbite. And how would they get the pump at the filling station to work when the fuel was frozen solid?

"Or," said Jessica, and everyone turned to her eagerly.

"Or what?" Anna saw the gleam in her sister's eye. "Tell us!"

"Fly the chopper across the chasm to the truck. That's just two kilometers. Then drive the truck to town."

A stunned silence ensued. This obvious solution hadn't occurred to anyone else. Then, wordlessly, they hugged her, one by one.

✳ ✳ ✳

It was just past noon when the team suited up and left, giving them about eight hours of what passed for daylight. They carried near-empty fuel cans and the last of their provisions to the helicopter and thus completed a round trip they had started ten years ago. Conditions were eerily similar— the same dim light, the temperature just a shade warmer. But the mood of the walkers couldn't have been more different. Then they had been on the verge of panic; now, despite their cumbersome suits, they walked with eager anticipation.

When they reached the helicopter, Larry measured the fuel level by inserting a stiff wire into the tank and subtracting for tank thickness. He reckoned they had enough to get them to the other side of the chasm and back. As he feared, the fuel was frozen.

"Damn!" Larry growled. "This is supposed to be a special cold-weather fuel ..."

"We need to thaw it before we can fly the chopper?" Anna asked.

"Yes, but how?"

"Light a fire under the tank," said Jessica.

Anna let out an incredulous guffaw, but Larry looked at Jessica for a second to see if she was joking, saw she wasn't, and nodded. "We still have a few liters of diesel left in our cans. We can pour it on the ground under the tank and light it up."

Nicole gasped. "What if the tank explodes?"

"It's too cold for that. Anyway, we have no choice. Empty out your can, Jessica."

But the moment the diesel hit the ground, it froze solid and refused to ignite.

"We should burn it straight from the can, not pour it on the ground," Anna said. "You know, cut off the top half of the can first."

Larry agreed. "But even that might not be enough. The air is still too cold."

Then Nicole came up with a suggestion. "How about using the oxygen tanks we have back in the Shell? The ones near the heaters?"

"Excellent idea!" Larry said after a moment's consideration. "Yes, let's try that. You all stay here and think warm, positive thoughts while I fetch a couple of cylinders."

Larry set off at a trot and returned a few minutes later from his errand. Anna and Jessica, meanwhile, had just sliced open a diesel can and were stirring it to keep it from freezing. They slid it under the tank.

"Won't the oxygen cool as it comes out, though?" Larry asked Jessica as he tore the seal from a cylinder.

"It'll still be warmer than the air. Besides, diesel burns better in oxygen."

And so it proved. Encouraged by a blast of pure oxygen, the small pool of diesel in the can caught fire almost immediately and sent its flames shooting up against the tank. After a few minutes, Larry dipped the wire into the tank and confirmed that the fuel had melted.

"Okay, I'm going to try the engine now," he said. "If it starts, get in at once!"

Warmed by the fire beneath and now fueled by liquid aviation gasoline flowing into it, the engine came alive. Slowly and reluctantly, it sputtered into life. Larry and his passengers were soon airborne.

The short flight over the chasm was both thrilling and terrifying. Looking straight down into its abyss, they could faintly discern the bottom several kilometers below them. A few spots on the rock floor where the magma had broken through glowed yellow. *I'm going to hike down there someday,* Larry promised himself. Though he was tempted to swoop down and take a closer look, he dared not risk it with the fuel they had and an engine that might stall at any moment.

All too soon, they had landed on the other side near the garage. They broke open the door and found Larry's truck standing inside, alone and desolate on the frozen ground. With great exertion, they shifted it into neutral and pushed it into the open. It too refused to start until it got a few minutes of the direct-fire treatment. *How did I ever manage without the Millers,* Larry wondered. He used an oxygen cylinder to press the gas pedal all the way down. With the heaters on at full blast, the interior took about forty minutes to turn toasty warm. Spacesuits quickly came off, allowing for another round of embraces, but accompanied by laughter and excitement now rather than tears.

Compared to the squalid living conditions of their previous year, the truck seemed obscenely luxurious. It had a large, full fuel tank as well as several reserve cans; their fuel worries were now history. It also carried a modest store of snacks and drinks. Everything was frozen solid but they used the truck's electric heater to turn frozen canned coffee into a piping hot liquid, their first in more than a year. It was a generic brand from the supermarket, but it tasted more delicious than anything they could remember. Everyone sipped their drink slowly, savoring each mouthful, and swallowing with reluctance. Then they attacked the quickly thawing nuts, crisps, chocolate, and other snacks. "I never knew junk food could taste so heavenly!" Anna said.

"Okay, what now?" Larry said, when the first wave of gastronomic ecstasy had abated and everyone was sitting back in the special warm glow that comes from satisfying a long-denied appetite. "Do we take the fuel back with us to Entry? Or shall we head straight to town?"

"To town!" said Jessica.

Nobody challenged her.

"No offence, Larry, but I think I've had as much of the Shell as I can take in this lifetime," said Anna. "I vote we go into town and, like, never look back."

Larry joined in the laughter. "No offence taken! I feel the same. Besides, we've been lucky with the chopper so far. What if it doesn't start tomorrow, and we're stranded on the other side?"

38
Town

OTHER THAN THE muted sunlight that infused everything with an orange glow, their drive to town felt rather normal at first. The terrain didn't look much different from what they remembered from the pre-Shroud days. It had been a hot desert then; it was a cold one now. Larry drove slowly while the girls kept a wary eye for cracks in the road. It was only when they turned into the main road near Balindoo that the familiarity evaporated. What should have been a bustling highway was now dead silent. Stalled and abandoned vehicles cluttered their path, many with drivers and passengers still inside. Some of the people were huddled into positions that suggested the horror of their final moments, but the majority appeared strangely calm and lifelike.

"Oh, dear God," said Elizabeth. "This is appalling."

"Why did so many of them end up in their cars?" Anna said.

"Unheated homes," said Jessica grimly.

"Yes, I think so too," said Larry. "Initially, their cars with the engines running and heat on would've been warmer. At some point, the engines would've stopped, and then it would've been too cold to leave the car."

"It dropped from minus 20 to minus 100 in a few hours," said Jessica. "No time to go anywhere and nowhere to go."

"How appalling," said Elizabeth. "How terrible to be stuck in their cars, to freeze to death like that."

"One consolation," said Nicole. "At those temperatures, they wouldn't have suffered too long. Death would have been swift."

At first the family stopped at every vehicle they saw and bemoaned the fate of its passengers.

"I feel almost guilty at having survived," Elizabeth said.

"If I see anyone I know, I'll want to die," said Anna.

"I wish I could grab the Shroud by the neck and wring it slowly, painfully," Jessica growled.

Everyone felt the same futile mix of guilt, anger, and sorrow. This weighed them down so much that, at some point, they had to avert their eyes from the carnage around them. As they drove on toward Simpsonville, the family's morale gradually returned.

"I could use a limerick session," Jessica said.

"Me too," said Anna. "Along with some booze."

Nicole and Elizabeth echoed the girls' sentiments.

"That's the spirit," said Larry. "We can't avoid such terrible sights, but we've got to stay upbeat."

Progress was slow. Several times during their journey Larry had to use the full power of his truck to nudge aside vehicles blocking their path. It was nearly 7:00 p.m. and the orange sunglow was fading by the time they approached the town center. Here they saw fewer derelict vehicles. But bodies lay all around on the sidewalks, some still holding items of food that hunger had driven them to seek in the deadly cold. After gazing at them in horror and pity, Larry turned away and kept driving. Some minutes later he pulled into the parking lot of a supermarket and stopped the truck, leaving the engine running.

"Okay, here we are," he said. "What now?"

Nobody had any immediate idea.

"I'm not sure," Elizabeth said hesitantly. "When we faced death from freezing or starving, it seemed obvious what we should do. But now that there's no immediate danger ..."

Jessica sat silent. In moments of crisis her brain worked overtime, but now she appeared dazed.

"Perhaps we should think of, like, basic necessities," said Anna. "You know, food, water, warmth."

"And look for a place to stay," Elizabeth added. "This truck is nice and snug but might start feeling cramped."

Larry nodded. "Yes, that's what we should do. Find a good shelter. Some place we can call home for a few weeks while we figure out our long-term plans. But where?"

"Any place would do if we make it livable." Nicole said.

Jessica entered the discussion. "Since we own the entire planet, we have options."

Anna snorted. "Don't write off the rest of the human race yet."

"Could we go back to our old home?" said Elizabeth.

Suddenly everyone's mood lightened.

"Brilliant idea, Grandma!" said Anna. "The last time we saw it, the house was, like, the coldest ice box ever, but perhaps it's come along since then."

The suggestion found immediate favor with Jessica. It would be wonderful to be back home, she thought, even if that word no longer meant much. It wouldn't be too far to go, and there would be books and photographs and clothes there. "Zero points for imagination, Grandma, but a perfect ten for good sense." Elizabeth pinched her cheek, and Nicole smiled. "What does boss man say?"

"Boss man he say—what women want, he want," Larry replied. He mused wryly on his fallen standards—he who used to read Dickens and Thackeray, now exchanging badinage in pidgin English! His pre-Shroud persona would have been mortified. On the plus side, however, his old jokes had always gone unappreciated, while his new, cruder sense of humor elicited chuckles from Jessica, his erstwhile critic. "Let's go there in the morning, though. It's almost dark now."

"Sounds good," said Nicole and added, after a pause: "Any ideas on how we should spend our first evening of freedom?"

"Raid a supermarket," said Jessica promptly. "Especially the liquor section."

"Zero points for honesty, but a perfect ten for imagination," mimicked Anna, ducking away from her sister's playful punch to her jaw.

The suggestion met with unanimous approval. The space-suits came back on, and soon the five were inside the store, navigating their way with difficulty through the lightless aisles. Their flashlights revealed a scene of panic-stricken disorder frozen in time—dozens of customers lay sprawled or huddled amidst scattered groceries and collapsed shelves. The family quickly salvaged the items they would need to cook their first post-Shell meal: milk, eggs, salt, condiments, sugar, coffee, oil, frozen fish, and vegetables, along with basic utensils.

"Yuck," said Jessica, as she opened an egg carton and showed it to the others. The insides of the eggs had spilled out of their shells while freezing and congealed into an unappetizing mess.

"Bring them. They should still be edible," said Anna.

The inner room with the liquor stocks was almost intact. Evidently, the panic-stricken shoppers had survival in mind, not intoxication. Most of the bottles had cracked open with the cold, but a few were undamaged. The family members chose a bottle each of their favorite tipples: Bordeaux for Nicole, Kahlua and Cointreau for Anna and Jessica, sherry for Elizabeth, and an 18-year-old Glenlivet for Larry.

Leaving the others to their liquor search, Jessica wandered off into the appliance section and returned a few minutes later carrying a device that looked like a cross between a barbecue grill and an acetylene torch. "Look what I found!" she said. "A Vapemit stove."

"A what?"

"Vapemit. A smokeless stove. It burns hydrogen and emits steam. Perfect for indoor cooking."

"Brilliant! That solves the problem of where to set up the stove."

Back at the truck, Larry cleared out the space behind the rear seat, dumping all the cans, tools, and equipment out on the parking lot. The floor was thickly and comfortably carpeted. They lit the stove and began their dinner preparations with eagerness. Larry thawed out the Scotch and poured them all a drink.

"To planet Earth," he said, raising his glass. The others echoed his toast. With so many hands working in smooth unison borne of a decade of survival-level, high-stakes teamwork, dinner was ready in the blink of an eye. And what a meal it was! If their earlier snack in the truck had tasted heavenly, this went far beyond into a zone where adjectives couldn't follow. Blissful silence reigned as the family relished their meal.

"Not bad," said Jessica when the meal was over.

"Yeah, not too terrible," agreed Anna. "Though it can't compare with the delicious tinned stuff we've been eating for the past year, lukewarm and sans condiment."

"And the best part? No cleaning up," said Larry. He collected their plates and utensils and dumped them in a bin outside.

Dinner over, a pleasurable drowsiness stole over the family. It was cold and dark outside. But inside the truck with the engine running and the heat and reading lights on, it was bright and warm. They rearranged the seat cushions to make a snug little nest. A large sheet of canvas salvaged from the store made for a passable blanket, and they made themselves comfortable under it. There was so much to talk about, so many questions. Why was the Shroud thinning out now? How much longer before things got back to normal? How would their new life be, with no one else but themselves? What would happen to all the dead bodies? But all that could wait for another day. Before the family knew it, muted daylight was streaming in through the windows.

39

Home

IT TOOK THEM quarter of an hour to drive to their old house. They had to negotiate the by-now-familiar obstacle course of derelict vehicles and dead bodies, but, on the flip side, they had no moving traffic or signals to deal with. Driving time inside town hadn't changed much from the old days, it seemed. On the way they stopped at a sporting goods store. They shed their suits and slipped into the warmest long johns, hooded parkas, and ski pants they could find.

"Whew, what a relief!" said Nicole.

"I never want to see the inside of a bloody spacesuit again," said Anna.

In the dull orange glow of the morning sun their old home looked surprisingly normal, as if patiently waiting for its occupants to return. They felt a wave of excitement and nostalgia as they approached it. Anna had a fleeting irrational thought that once they stepped inside everything would be back to normal, and the Shroud would have been just a nightmare. The illusion held for a few moments even after they entered. Walls, floor, ceiling, windows, and doors were still intact. There was little dust—a thin sooty layer on the floor and furniture was the only sign of the Shroud's visit.

"Everything's exactly how we left it," said Anna. "How lovely!"

But reality set in quickly.

"We could move in here right away," said Larry. "However—"

"Too cold," Jessica cut in, tapping her gauge. "Minus 47."

"Ugh," said Nicole. "Though the ski things are a million times better than the suits, I'm dying to get out of them."

"Me too," said Larry. "We need to find some way to heat this house. The old heating system is useless without a supply of gas."

"Re-engineer it to run on diesel?" said Jessica.

Larry considered her suggestion for a moment and then shook his head. "Maybe, but it would take weeks to do it."

"Right," said Jessica. "We need a quick fix we can rig up in a few hours."

A short silence ensued as the family pondered the problem. Then Anna had an idea: "Couldn't we turn the house into the inside of a truck?" Seeing the mystified glances around her, she explained: "You know, find a way to suck the hot air from the truck into the house."

Jessica's eyes lit up. "Now there's an idea! Run the engine and heater full blast, open the rear and jam it against the window."

"Would that work?" Anna asked Larry.

"Hmm ... it might, but to heat a house this size we'll need more than one truck. More like half a dozen, all running at the same time."

"No problem!" said Jessica. "Just drive around and grab 'em."

Larry smiled. "Any objections to a bit of larceny?" The others shook their heads emphatically.

"We have four windows at the ground level and one in the basement," said Nicole, catching the enthusiasm. "So five trucks?"

"One for each of us!" said Anna. "That should do the trick."

"If we're going to prison for auto theft, we might as well go as a family," said Elizabeth.

When the laughter had subsided, Larry sprang up. "Let's do it then. While we're stealing the trucks, let's also break into a hardware store and steal as much foam insulation and duct tape as we can find. We want to make tight seals between the windows and the trucks."

"Also steal a nice, big diesel generator," added Jessica. "To get the lights back on."

"Great idea," said Larry. "Let's go!"

They set out enthusiastically, full of the spirit of adventure. Elizabeth was the first to spot a candidate truck—a Toyota Land Cruiser SUV, looking as if it had just been driven out of the showroom. Larry and Jessica got the driver's side door opened. Inside, with a calm, faraway look in his eyes, sat the driver, his seat belt still buckled.

Anna screamed. "Oh, God, that's Mr. Lodge."

"Who?"

"Mr. Lodge. My piano teacher." Anna's voice choked, and tears began to stream behind her mask. "He looks like he's just sleeping."

Jessica put an arm around her. "So sorry, love, so sorry." She held her as close as their bulky clothes would permit. "How absolutely terrible."

They stood indecisively for a few seconds, and then Larry said: "Let's do this later. We'll find other trucks."

Anna shook her head. "No, I'm okay now. It was just a shock. And I guess we should get used to this. Let's ease him out."

After some hesitation, they unclipped the frozen driver's seatbelt and pulled him out. They laid him on the sidewalk, still hunched in a sitting position. No one spoke, but Anna's gentle sniffling wafted through the silence.

The truck, predictably, wouldn't start. They tried the fire-under-the-tank technique, which melted the fuel in the tank, but the engine still refused to start. Jessica wanted to repeat the procedure under the engine, but Larry came up with a better method. Connecting a length of rubber hose to his truck's tailpipe, Larry placed the other end in the engine compartment of the SUV. "Let's give it a few minutes and try again," he said. The two of them then returned to Larry's truck, where they sat in gloomy silence.

"Feels like grave robbery," Jessica said at last.

Elizabeth sighed. "Yes, it seems horrid, stealing from a dead man and throwing his body on the sidewalk." She paused a moment and then added: "But, as Anna said, we need to harden ourselves to this. We can't save these poor people. We can't even give them a decent burial, there are too many of them and, besides, the ground is frozen. All we can do is try and make our own lives a bit easier."

"Totally agree," said Jessica. "Old scruples don't apply."

"Nicole?" said Larry.

"I agree," she replied. "What would've been unthinkable before feels almost normal now."

The family lapsed into silence.

"Time for another try," said Larry after about fifteen minutes. The third time proved the charm, and the SUV started with only a token protest at being woken up from its decade-long slumber. Larry turned the vehicle's heater to maximum and drove it to the house while the others followed in his truck. They repeated the foray four more times, each time driving back with a new truck. Soon, five extra vehicles were parked around their house.

Over the next few days, the team worked hard to turn their house back into a home once again. By the end of the third day, two of the five heater trucks had been mated with a window each using generous amounts of foam and duct tape, although they had a good deal of difficulty getting the tape to unspool and stick at the ambient temperature. By the fourth morning, the house was noticeably warmer. Two more trucks got plugged in that day. Within hours, the ground level of the house was warm enough for them to shed their padded outfits, and a day later it had reached a pleasant 20 degrees.

The fifth truck was then connected to the basement window to make the entire house livable again. Larry and Anna, who had figured out how to melt and pump the diesel from a nearby filling station, made periodic refueling trips to keep the trucks running. They also figured out clever tricks to keep the fuel in the trucks from freezing and prevent the engine and battery from getting too cold. Meanwhile, Jessica had been busy at work with the generator, and soon the lights came on as well. Camp stoves replaced the gas range in the kitchen. By the end of a week, the house was fully functional, except for the plumbing. Jessica set up a rudimentary water boiler using a diesel heater and bottled water. It wasn't enough for showering—that luxury was still a dream—but sufficient for a much-needed sponge bath each day. The wastewater simply ran out through a pipe into a ditch where it instantly froze.

By the eighth morning after their arrival in town, the family had transformed their old house into a home again. The planet outside might have changed beyond recognition, but they had learned to survive in it. And they were overjoyed to be back home.

"Travel is overrated," said Jessica.

40

Outlook

"STOCK-TAKING TIME," SAID Larry, on the evening of January 25, about a week after they had moved back into their old home. "How is everyone?"

The five of them were seated on the floor on several layers of rugs, surrounded by pillows, cushions, and bolsters, all acquired from nearby furniture stores on the deferred-payment plan. It was luxurious to the point of opulence.

"Sitting pretty," quipped Jessica.

"We've managed to make this house nice again," said Elizabeth.

"It almost feels like we're back in the early days of the Shell," said Anna. "You know, boxed-in but snug. But with a leader who's not quite the despot he used to be."

"Yes, I miss the old Larry," said Jessica. "This one doesn't give me enough reason to complain."

"You silly things!" said Larry. "To get serious for a minute, let's look at our prospects. We don't have to worry about food and fuel for the time being. There are enough houses, stores, and petrol stations around to keep us warmed, fed, and watered for a long time. Agreed?"

"Yes, Chief," said Jessica. "No worries about food, water, fuel, or shelter."

"So we're safe for the moment, which is wonderful," said Elizabeth. "But what comes next?"

"Yes, what's the climate going to be like a month from now?" Nicole said. "Or a year?"

The questions were addressed to Larry, but he raised an inquiring eyebrow in Jessica's direction.

"The temperature's going up slowly, but steadily," she replied. "It was minus 127 during the Shell. Then minus 50 the day we stepped out, and a week later it's just crossed minus 45." She gestured toward the windows, though the view was blocked by the trucks jammed against them. "It's technically summer now, so solar radiation should remain steady or increase slightly for the next two months. After that we'll get less heat from the sun in autumn and winter, but, to compensate, the Shroud may have thinned out further."

"What does all that add up to?"

"Daytime should go just above freezing by October."

"Wow, that would be just a little colder than a normal winter day," said Anna. "Won't that be something!"

"How fast do you think the Shroud is thinning?" asked Nicole.

"The light meter readings are going up slowly," said Jessica. "But we can't draw conclusions from surface observations alone. We'll need to know what's happening higher up."

"But if you were to guess, how much longer will it take for the Shroud to go once and for all?"

"At this rate, another year."

"How I wish I could, like, snap my fingers and make it happen," said Anna. "Just imagine being able to step outside and soak in the sunlight!"

"Just one problem," said Jessica. "Thawing."

"I'm sorry?"

"What will happen when dead bodies—people, dogs, rats—thaw?"

Anna, Nicole, and Elizabeth gasped, and even Larry caught his breath. This concern had been at the back of everyone's mind, but the deep-freeze conditions had helped them avoid confronting it.

"Good God," said Larry. "Everything will start to rot *en masse*."

All eyes turned to Anna, who shook her head, and then to Nicole, who considered the question for a few seconds before replying. "Thawing *is* a concern. But the picture isn't too bleak."

"No?"

"I think not. Do you remember the lectures Anna and I gave on how organic matter degrades?"

Larry frowned as he tried to recollect Nicole's teaching. "Let me see. You told us that a corpse at room temperature will start to decompose within minutes by the combined action of …"

"Germs plus their own enzymes," Jessica finished.

"Good to know you were listening!" Nicole chuckled. "That's correct. Normal decay is partly microbial and partly biochemical. But I'm not sure how that will play out here. Biochemical decay will take off like crazy once the deep freeze goes. Cellular structures will break down, turning tissues into sludge. As for the microbial process, I suspect it'll be really slow."

"But why?"

"Because the deep freeze will have wiped out most bacteria and fungi. The entire microbiota of the planet might be living in our bodies right now."

There were gasps of astonishment and incredulity.

"Really?" cried Jessica.

"Mum's right," Anna chimed in. "Minus 100 kills all microbes—okay, maybe not all, some hardy ones might've survived. You know, the ones that form spores. And extremophiles, and so on. But those bugs will take a long time to, like, recolonize the planet."

Jessica looked unconvinced. "So corpses will turn squishy, but not foul?"

"Exactly," said Nicole. "They'll look disgusting but won't stink or breed disease."

Larry wiped his brow. "Whew. That's one less thing to worry about."

"Yes, and something to be grateful for," Elizabeth said, "Though it'll be distressing to be surrounded by decomposing bodies."

"Dump them into the chasm," said Jessica. "We don't have to watch them turn to goo."

As with many of Jessica's ideas, it took the family a second or two to be sure she wasn't kidding.

"That's a thought," said Larry. "It'll be a huge effort to shift the bodies, but maybe we could clear out this neighborhood at least."

Anna quickly embraced her sister's idea. "We could also find a tow truck and clear the roads at the same time!"

Her idea found ready acceptance, and the family discussed logistics for a few minutes.

"So much for cars and bodies," said Larry during a pause. "Coming back to our prospects, it looks like we can expect a reasonably normal climate within a year, maybe sooner. The lake should thaw, the pipes should open up, and we can have running water again. What else could we work on?"

"Get the local powerplant up and running," said Jessica. "They kept tons of coal in reserve. With just five of us, it should last forever."

"Perhaps by next summer we could do some planting as well," said Anna. "Won't it be lovely to have some greenery around? Imagine seeing a coneflower bloom again, or even an apple ripening on a tree! The botany department at the Uni used to have a fantastic collection of seeds."

"Anything else we should do?" Larry asked.

"What about other survivors?" asked Nicole. "Are there likely to be any?"

Until now the discussion had been sprightly and animated, but the word *survivors* had an immediately sobering effect.

Larry took a deep breath and sighed. "Yes, we talked about this a few years ago, and the picture hasn't changed. The Scandinavians are still our best bet. Once we have our lives under control, we could try contacting them."

"How do we say 'hello' to people halfway across the globe?" asked Nicole. "It's not like we can phone or send email."

"Shortwave radio," said Jessica.

Larry nodded and turned to Anna. "Didn't you intern at a radio station once?"

"Yes, fancy your remembering that!" Anna smiled. "Yes, when I was fresh out of high school. I was just a paper-pusher, though, and they never let me go on air." She pouted in mock anger.

"It's their loss, dear, I'm sure you'd have made a lovely host," said Elizabeth.

"No question about that," said Larry. "But tell me, Anna, did they have a shortwave service?"

"Sure they did. They had listeners as far away as Alaska."

There were exclamations of surprise.

"Guess where we'll break into next?" said Jessica.

"The radio station," said Anna without missing a beat.

"Wrong," said Larry. "First we break into the university library to steal every book on radio transmission we can find for Jessica to read. *Then* the radio station."

"Trust you to create work for me and Anna," said Jessica.

"Yes, while the three of you relax, as always," Anna added.

"Age has its privileges," said Larry.

"And youth has its responsibilities," smiled Elizabeth.

Jessica made a face, but she and Anna were clearly excited about the idea.

41

Year One AS

THE SHELLMATES' FIRST year After Shroud was a period of hard work, steady progress, and high spirits. The knowledge that they now owned the entire continent, perhaps the entire planet, never ceased to amaze them. The freedom to go anywhere and take anything was a thrill that never waned, especially for Anna and Jessica. Larry, normally the soul of rectitude, was amazed by how quickly he fell in with their marauding spirit. Nicole too showed herself to be an enthusiastic bandit and scavenger, often finding creative ways to break laws that no longer existed. If a building she needed to get into had a locked door, she had no qualms about smashing it open with an ax. Even Elizabeth enjoyed plundering the houses and stores in the neighborhood for essential items. With an entire continent to pillage, the five survivors knew they would never again lack basic necessities.

By the end of May, they could leave the house without their ski outfits, wearing just normal winter apparel. By mid-August it was just slightly colder than a normal winter's day. Two trucks, one in the basement and one above, now provided sufficient warmth. The lake began thawing. Larry found an empty wine tanker that he and Anna pumped full of water from the lake. With some clever engineering from Jessica, it became their source of hot and cold running water. She also reconnected the drains to the now-thawed sewers.

"Heavenly," said Anna after her shower. "Just heavenly."

The next major task was to start the powerplant. This proved relatively easy. Though the plant ran on coal, it was modern in other respects. All it took to turn its systems back on was flipping the main switch a few times. The ignition system, dormant for ten years, now spat out a tongue of blue flame. Lumps of coal caught fire and in a matter of hours the plant was back online. Its reservoir held a vast reserve of coal, but in the interests of frugality and safety they cut off all the outgoing circuits except the one feeding their immediate neighborhood. Only their house, the nearby streets, and the stores in their neighborhood had power. If they wanted power elsewhere—in the library or university, for instance— they could turn the relevant circuit breaker on as needed.

Meanwhile, Nicole and her mother took on the unpleasant task of clearing the nearby streets of cars and bodies. They towed the vehicles to the curb, hauled their passengers into a salvaged garbage truck, and dumped the bodies into various spots at the outskirts. In about two months, the streets around their house were almost clear. Then began the more difficult task of clearing out the bodies from the houses and shops and other nearby buildings. Here the others pitched in as well, helping to carry the now thawing bodies down to the curb from where they could be lifted onto the garbage truck. By November, they had cleared out all bodies within approximately one square kilometer around their house.

Surrounding this area on all sides was a short stretch of parkland, which had now turned brown. Everything that lay beyond this area—vehicles, buildings, corpses—they simply torched to the ground after salvaging whatever food, equipment, and supplies they could lug back to their neighborhood and store in nearby buildings. It wasn't long before the entire town was corpse-free, except for a few well-preserved specimens that Nicole put in cold storage at the hospital for study purposes. She grew wiry and strong with the hard physical labor and could soon lift almost as much weight as Larry or the girls. Even Elizabeth, now in her seventies, became exceptionally sturdy for her age.

The weekly calendar had no real significance any more, but for old times' sake the family took the weekend off to explore the town and its environs. Larry found a helicopter in working condition, which he taught the others to fly, and soon they were making sorties into the desert. They flew down the chasm a few times, marveling at the awful grandeur of the geological cataclysm wrought by the Shroud. They even went back to the remains of the Shell on the other side.

"That odd structure, ladies and gentlemen, is what remains of the Shell," said Anna, assuming a tour-guide voice. "Can you believe this place housed the legendary Miller family during the last year of the Shroud? Designed by a crazy inventor called Larry Brandon, notorious for his weakness for whiskey and women."

"If only this chopper had an ejector seat!" said Larry.

The hardships of their final year in Entry having now faded from their minds, they were able to view their old habitat with equanimity. On an impulse they decided to camp out in the dome one night, hoping to recapture a thrill of horror from the past. But it felt strange and oddly hostile now. They couldn't believe that in that very place they had come within a whisker of annihilation.

"This might become a museum someday," said Jessica.

After retrieving a few mementos, they left the next morning and never returned.

During a three-week period in November, a faint odor of rotting bodies registered on the sensitive nostrils of the girls whenever the wind blew from Adelaide. Though the air then grew fresh again, suggesting that the decay process had finished, the family decided against visiting nearby cities for the time being. They had disposed of thousands of corpses in their neighborhood, but could they handle millions?

The farthest they ventured was an hour south by helicopter to the famed wine-growing region of Barossa Valley. In the cellar of one of the estates there they were delighted to find barrels of vintage Shiraz in excellent condition and got roaringly drunk for the first and only time in their lives. They flew back the next morning carrying as much wine as they could. Then it was back to their routine of work, rest, and play.

On weekdays, the group split up in the morning to go to their individual tasks, staying in touch by walkie-talkie. They met briefly for lunch and sat together for dinner at the end of their day's work. Ravenously hungry from the long hours of manual labor, they demolished huge amounts of food at every meal, washed down by the Barossa estate wine as long as it lasted. All five were now as skilled at cooking as they were voracious in eating. Initially, they made do with groceries scavenged from the stores nearby. As the weather grew warmer, Anna resumed her love affair with horticulture.

Using seeds, fertilizer, and equipment borrowed from the university's department of botany, she soon covered every inch of open space in their neighborhood with her plantings. She commissioned another water tanker for her own use and made frequent trips to feed and water her saplings. Soon she brought fresh greens and herbs to the table, followed by tomatoes and chili pods a few weeks later. "By this time next year you'll have your first cherries," she promised.

After a hard day's satisfying work, a hot shower, and a huge, delicious meal, sleep was as deep and sweet as it could ever get. The house was now warm enough that they could have gone to their individual rooms, but they continued to camp together on the living-room floor—it just felt more natural. During the evening, Nicole and Elizabeth went off to one of the other rooms to meditate. Other than that, they enjoyed staying together in the living room.

"When you have harmony, your need for personal space diminishes," Elizabeth noted in her diary.

42

Doubts

AFTER SOME MORE discussions early in their first year AS, the group decided to wait a bit before trying to make contact with other survivors. Partly this was from lack of urgency. They were very comfortable now, enjoying their ever-increasing freedom as the planet warmed and the sun shone brighter. Besides, they needed some time by themselves to adjust to the new world.

Their hesitation about advertising their presence also stemmed from a fear of the unknown. If there were other survivors, what kind of people would they turn out to be? Friendly, neutral, hostile? The Shellmates hadn't just survived their ten years of close confinement under the most trying of conditions— they had emerged as better human beings. Each of them had gained something: Jessica empathy, Anna strength, Nicole peace, Larry vivacity, and Elizabeth health. They had lost none of their strengths. Jessica was just as smart as before, Anna just as delightful, Nicole just as competent, Larry just as strong, and Elizabeth just as loving. And they cherished and enjoyed each other like never before. They had all been very lucky, as Elizabeth pointed out, because things could have gone wrong for them in a hundred different ways. They could have fallen ill. They could have succumbed to rage, fear, or hate; giving in to such negative emotions would have almost certainly sealed their fate. If, despite all that, they had survived, they might have emerged from the Shell embittered, vicious, or psychotic. The shock of finding a lifeless, corpse-ridden planet would only have made things worse.

Given these scenarios, wasn't it possible—even likely—that other survivors would bear at least some emotional scars from their ordeal? What if they turned out to be warped or crazed? Perhaps they might have undergone some kind of brutal power struggle; the ones that survived would then be either viciously tyrannical or abjectly servile. They might have sunken into savagery, cannibalism, or worse. They might carry foul diseases.

No, it was better to wait for a bit.

In the meantime, Jessica continued to bone up on the fundamentals of communication theory, antennas, and radio transmission. She and Anna spent several hours familiarizing themselves with the equipment at the local radio station. The mass of circuit diagrams, consoles, wires, and switches in the control room looked daunting at first, but no more so than the equipment at the Air and Geo domes they had mastered. They soon felt confident enough to operate the station. As a trial run, they transmitted a piece of music on an FM frequency, while the others back home tuned in to listen. After a few failed tries, a piece by Mozart and then a raga played by Ravi Shankar came over the radio to the intense delight of Larry, Nicole, and Elizabeth. Switching from FM to shortwave AM was now just a matter of flipping a set of switches.

On Nicole's suggestion, the group also began regular training sessions in self-defense. Larry, initially hesitant about this, was eventually persuaded. If there were other survivors besides themselves, sooner or later they might meet face to face. If the encounter was friendly, their training would have provided merely some exercise and amusement. If it turned out to be hostile, on the other hand, their ability to defend themselves might be a matter of life and death. Larry, who knew some kung fu, and Nicole, who had learned basic self-defense during her college days, proved able instructors in unarmed combat. They also tried out various firearms borrowed from the nearby police station. Though none of them had fired a shot before, they became moderately proficient in using guns.

"You can now defend your honor if need be," Larry teased his companions, "and save yourselves from a fate worse than death."

"What if the others turn out to be, you know, man-hungry amazons?" asked Anna. "Then you'll be the one playing defense!"

"He might not want to," said Jessica.

"Having more admiring women around him will be terrible for his ego," said Anna.

"You little twits!" scolded Larry. "Seriously, I hope we never have to use any of this training."

While preparing themselves to face the world, they checked the shortwave frequencies daily to see if anyone else was transmitting. They consistently drew a blank.

Were they alone, after all?

43

Sermon

O N JANUARY 17, the first anniversary of their return, the group held another celebration. This time, the mood was unrestrainedly cheerful. Death from freezing or starvation no longer threatened them. They had a whole continent to explore, a land that was now returning to life. They were in peak health, got along famously as a team, and had no shortage of tasks to challenge their physical and mental powers. The house was warm, the windows open, and the air fresh and pollution-free. The streets around them were clear and quiet. All the tennis courts, swimming pools, theaters, and libraries were theirs to enjoy. Life was great.

On the flip side, drinkable champagne was now impossible to find, so the family had switched to gin and bitters.

"Not too bad as celebratory libations go," said Jessica. To tease Larry, she would sometimes assume a snobbish accent and vocabulary. She did so well that over time the speech mannerism had become almost ingrained in her. Now she had to make an effort to recapture the slangy drawl and terse phrasing of her youth.

As always, the family enjoyed an hour of boisterous festivity before turning to more serious matters. Elizabeth gave Larry his opening: "It has been a wonderful twelve months. But what does the new year hold in store for us?"

Larry set his glass down and put his arms around his two most favorite tormentors sitting on either side. He was feeling pleasantly warm and mildly tipsy from the gin.

"Glad you asked. I've had many, many good years both before and during the Shroud, but I can safely say that the past one has been the best ever. May I be allowed to get preachy for a moment?"

"No way," said Jessica.

"Permission denied," said Anna.

"Please," begged Larry.

"Okay, perhaps just this once," said Anna.

"Thanks. My sermon is this—life is great as long as we have a goal and are making steady progress toward it. We can't stop striving, however, once we accomplish that goal. Because if we do, we'll stagnate and grow unhappy, even if we have everything we need. That's why it's important to keep finding new goals. Agreed?"

"It's better to travel hopefully," said Anna.

"Clichéd but true," said Jessica.

"During the Shell years, our goal was to survive. That was the destination we were traveling hopefully toward. The hope of deliverance kept us going and made our confinement bearable. A year ago, we attained that goal. We arrived at that destination. Then we found a new goal, which was to make this house into a home again and make the environs safe and pleasant. Our combined efforts have made short work of that goal as well. We now have every comfort of civilization: electricity, heat, water, even street lights. So now that destination too has been reached. Agreed?"

"Sure, Reverend," said Jessica. "If you say so."

"Preach away, Larry," said Anna.

"So we need to come up with some new goals for each of us, and perhaps some joint goals as well. Of course, we'll keep pegging away and making things around us more civilized. You know—clear more streets, plant more trees, all of that. We'll continue our studies and experiments. But these are incremental steps. By goals I mean something more fundamental."

He paused for a few seconds and addressed Nicole. "Let me start with you. Any thoughts on your goals for the future?"

"Hmm ... I can't think of any goals, really. I could resume my medical lectures with the equipment from the hospital. And there's plenty of cadavers to dissect, of course. But I guess you'd call these incremental goals."

"How about you, Lizzie?"

"Me, darling? I can't think of anything beyond my desire to be of use to all of you. Nothing else comes to my mind, I'm afraid. How about yourself?"

"As far as I'm concerned, my goals were to ensure the safety of all of you and create a space where you could develop your survival skills. I think I've done pretty well on the second one, to the point that each of you knows at least as much as I do, and often much more. Without flattery, each of you is now as strong or stronger than I am. There's nothing I can do that each of you can't do better."

"Actually, there's one thing," said Anna. Her sister giggled.

"I wonder what that is, but better not go there, perhaps. Anyway, I feel my work is done. I can now sit back and grow old. You know, putter around the house, read books, and keep trying to meditate. Maybe run a few simple errands. So that accounts for us old fogies. The three of us have pretty much lived our lives and are content to play supporting roles. Which brings me to these two lazy creatures sitting next to me. We can't let them off the hook so easily. They have their entire lives in front of them and can't afford to coast for too long."

"Count on you to make us do the heavy lifting," said Jessica.

"Slave driver!" said Anna.

"Have you thought of what you might want to do with your life?" Elizabeth asked Anna.

Anna looked at the floor. "Well, we've talked about this before." She sighed. "In the normal course of things, I guess I would've joined the Agri, got married, had kids. But what's the use of talking about all that? I might as well wish to travel to Mars."

Elizabeth looked at her tenderly for a long moment and turned to her other granddaughter. "What about you, dear?"

Jessica shrugged her shoulders and grimaced. "I had big plans too. Get a PhD, teach at the Uni, do research, win the Nobel prize. Maybe marriage, family. But now … it doesn't matter, does it?"

The discussion continued for a while but remained inconclusive. Larry had the last word on the topic: "Whatever you two decide to do I will support with all my ability. I think I can speak for your mum and grandma as well. From now on, you get to make all the decisions. The three of us will do our best to make sure it happens. The future is yours."

After this serious turn, the conversation resumed its jovial tone. Their prospects were limited, but they knew they had much to be grateful for. Dinner was an enjoyable affair. After some post-prandial card and word games, they slept like the dead.

Sometime during the night, the radio receiver came to life. Broken words in a foreign language came through for a few minutes, and then the transmission stopped.

44

Contact

A WEEK LATER, on January 24 of the second post-Shroud year, a transmission came through when the family had just sat down for breakfast. Intensely excited, their meal forgotten, the girls rushed to the radio and turned the volume up. They weren't alone on planet Earth after all! By the time the others came downstairs, Jessica had already started recording the audio signal. The female voice on the radio was speaking a language that Larry immediately recognized as Finnish, a language he knew slightly. The sounds seemed oddly familiar to Jessica too, and she knew why—they reminded her of the last transmission she had heard before fleeing to the Shell more than eleven years before.

The signal wavered in strength. Some words were clear—apart from *tulen pian* and *kartta*, Larry could make out the Finnish words for "person" and "contact"—while others were unintelligible. After about ten minutes the signal went dead and only static came through. The family listened as Jessica played her recording.

"From what I can make out, they seem to be looking for other survivors," Larry said. "They were specifying some way to contact them—on a special frequency, perhaps—but that part was too garbled."

"Since they're broadcasting in Finnish, are they looking for survivors only in their local area?"

"It's possible. It's also possible they have no English speakers left."

The family members looked at each other with uncertainty and hope.

"Perhaps they'll make other transmissions?" Elizabeth said.

"This might not be their first," Nicole added. "Others might have come through when we were asleep or away."

"True. Let's leave the recorder on. How many hours of audio can it store?"

"Hundreds. It's voice activated."

"That's great. Let's check every evening to see if something came through during the day."

After keeping the family on tenterhooks for the next three days, another transmission came through, this time in English. The audio quality was much better, and, despite the speaker's thick Nordic accent, his words were perfectly intelligible:

Message from surviving members of Finland cold shelter. We are group of twenty-nine men and forty-four women, composed of scientists, physicians, engineers, pilots, others. We have restored electricity, water, and other essentials to the Suomenlinna neighborhood of Helsinki. Hope to have at least one runway at the Helsinki airport operational. If you get this message, contact us by shortwave radio at 15.265 megahertz. Tell us about your group, skills, and situation.

The transmission threw the family into a frenzy of excitement, and they immediately gathered to discuss how they should respond.

"You get to make the call," Larry told Anna and Jessica. He and the two older women looked expectantly at them.

The girls gazed at each other for a few seconds.

"This is, like, unbelievably thrilling," said Anna finally. "But I can't decide what to do. We have a very happy life here, and I'd hate to upset it."

All eyes turned to her sister. "Same here," said Jessica. "Super, mega excited, but not sure we should respond. At least not at once. We should wait a bit until we can think straight."

The others exchanged glances.

"Sounds good to me," said Larry, and looked inquiringly at Nicole and Elizabeth, who nodded without speaking. "And as we said before, you two get to decide. The rest of us will embrace your choice, whatever it is."

Jessica rolled her eyes. "That's right, dump it all in our laps!"

Anna echoed her sister's sentiment. "You guys can't bail on this. Once we establish radio contact, we'll have to reveal our location. Maybe they'll know the location from the signal itself, who knows? Anyway, the next thing you know they'll be knocking on our door. Are we ready for that? What we decide will have, like, major consequences for all of us."

Larry turned to Elizabeth for help. "It *is* a serious responsibility," she told her granddaughters, "but one that the two of you can handle." Nicole and Larry nodded. The girls argued some more but finally conceded the point.

Over the next few weeks, while similar messages were received several times daily, the girls took long walks together to talk about their course of action. They made little headway.

On the positive side, both were of the same mind; the situation would have been delicate if one sister wanted to make contact while the other opposed it. On the flip side, they were both in an agony of indecision, torn between the thrill of the new and the comfort of the familiar. Over time, their excitement dwindled and inertia took over. Life was very pleasant now. Why rock the boat when the sailing was so smooth?

"We've decided against contacting the Finns," Jessica told them one day.

Larry felt a mix of disappointment and relief. He would have loved seeing the girls expand their social circle, enjoy other relationships, find romance, maybe marry and have kids, but he was also anxious to keep them from harm. *A father's eternal dilemma*, he told himself wryly. Despite his relief, he wanted to make sure the girls really knew what they were doing.

"Why not?" he demanded. "You were so excited when they first contacted us."

The girls looked at each other. Jessica spoke first. "If it ain't broke ... plus, too much to lose."

"Anna?"

"What Jessica said. Also, I'm a little nervous that we won't, you know, fit in."

Seeing Larry and the older women exchange puzzled glances, she explained: "We've been living this bubble life, just the five of us, we've grown up in such odd circumstances ... what I'm trying to say is that we've lived by ourselves so long that we're practically a separate species now, like those creatures in dark caves that lose their eyesight because they don't need it. I don't know how those folks will find us. Maybe they'll think we're dumb or weird or something."

Larry laughed incredulously. "Dumb? Weird? When I look at you I'm awed by what you've achieved and what you're capable of. I can't see anyone in the world, whatever bubble they come from, finding the two of you anything other than warm and caring and funny and resourceful and courageous. All my life, in all my travels, all my experiences, all my readings, I've never known two finer specimens of humanity than the two of you."

By the end of this speech both girls were weeping, and the others rushed to comfort them.

Elizabeth and Nicole echoed Larry's sentiments. In the end, however, Anna and Jessica stuck to their decision and life at the Miller residence resumed its pleasant rhythm. The initial disappointment faded away, and everyone felt relieved. The girls sometimes speculated about how the Finnish survivors were getting along—probably quite well, they figured. From their transmissions, they appeared to be a well-organized and resourceful group.

"You know what?" said Anna. "Deciding to be by ourselves should be depressing, but it actually feels warm and fuzzy. I love it here with all of you. I don't want to change anything. Let's all, you know, grow old and die together."

"Yep. Forget the Finns!" Jessica said.

EPILOGUE

UT THE BEST-LAID plans often go awry. On July 17, they heard a different message on the Finn broadcast. As if by design, the transmission came through when the family had assembled for a planning session.

After the standard request for survivors to contact them, the Finns added a postscript:

Survivors please note. Preliminary atmospheric measurements indicate extremely high concentrations of carbon dioxide. Levels in upper atmosphere will peak at 2,500 ppm in four years. Carbon dioxide is believed to come from combustion of carbon particles in Shroud, which explains shroud thinning and disappearance. Since normal biogeological phenomena such as photosynthesis and ocean cycling are now nearly nonexistent, dangerously high levels of carbon dioxide are likely to persist for decades. Runaway global warming is predicted. Planet's surface, once made uninhabitable by cold, might be made uninhabitable by heat in a few years. Survivors also note: insulating shelters that saved you from cold cannot protect from extreme ambient heat. Air conditioning equipment too will not work at anticipated temperatures. Only undersea habitats might be feasible.

The family heard the broadcast in stunned silence. Then, punctuated by exclamations of astonishment and dismay, an animated discussion went on for several hours. The outcome was a consensus that they could no longer afford to ignore the Finns. Later that day they sent out their first shortwave transmission on the frequency specified. The thirty-second broadcast ran at full antenna power, repeating every ten minutes:

This broadcast is from Simpsonville, six hundred kilometers north of Adelaide. We are four women and a man, ages 28, 30, 51, 71, and 49. Most likely we are the only survivors in Australia. Let us know if you have located survivors elsewhere. We are in excellent physical and mental condition and are living comfortably with no immediate problems. We have cleared the town of corpses and have electricity, running water, vehicles, machinery, plants. Our members have skills in engineering, computing, horticulture, medicine, mental health. Our group includes Larry Brandon, inventor of the Brandon satellite.

Larry was reluctant to include the last line, but the girls overruled him. "You saved the planet once and can do it again," said Anna.

"Now wait and see if it reaches them," said Jessica. "We may not have enough power. They probably have a much stronger transmitter."

"If they have a powerful antenna for transmission, they could use it to receive very faint signals as well," argued Larry. "Let's hope for the best."

The Finns did receive their message. An hour later came their reply:

Transmission from Australia received. Delighted to hear from you and to learn that you are in excellent health and circumstances. So far we have been unable to locate other survivors. Ten years ago, our seismograph recorded signal strongly suggestive of thermonuclear explosion at or near Cheyenne Mountain bunker in the USA. For this and other reasons we believe there are unlikely to be American survivors. China may be last remaining hope but we have picked up no signals from there so far. As you may have heard in our earlier broadcast, threat to planet is not over; on the contrary, we might face an even greater threat very soon. Your engineering and other skills, especially Mr. Brandon's knowledge of climate mitigation, will be of immense value to us all in days to come. Imperative, therefore, that you recommission your airport so we can link up and join forces. In the meantime, we urge you to remain in close communication so we can jointly design shelters that can withstand new imminent climate extreme.

The family sat in silence for several seconds, then heaved a long collective sigh.

"So much for your hopes of retirement, Larry," said Anna. "It's back to work for all of us."

"Yes," said Jessica. "Holiday's over."

THE END

ACKNOWLEDGMENTS

My journey as a writer has been a very rewarding one, thanks to all the wonderful people who have accompanied me.

My wife, Anu, has read every word I've written and has never failed to offer invaluable feedback. Our parents, siblings, and extended families have been equally supportive.

I'm grateful to Debbie Peikes and Ross Cutler for reading *Unlight* and offering constructive criticism. Paul Freedman, Carron Morris, and other members of the *Princeton Library Writers' Group* have offered valuable critiques, as have numerous fellow authors on *Writer's Café*. My Australian friend Gavan Murray Bromilow gave me very useful advice on making this novel accurate in its geographical and cultural details.

Despite umpteen rounds of proofreading, some typos managed to squeak through. I thank Malini Bhandaru, Balam Sundaresan, Jaykumar Srinivasan, and Radha Ramkrishna for pointing them out.

I am deeply grateful to readers at the *Online Book Club* for providing thoughtful reviews and feedback. Almost every day I receive one or more of these reviews, and I am always amazed at their quality and elegance.

My editors Elizabeth Law and Graham Clarke as well as professional beta readers Cat Skinner, Nicole Martin, and—in particular—Catherine Milos took turns to help me transform a *very* rough first draft into a finished novel that I could be proud of. Hari Ravikumar typeset the book with great care. My thanks to all of them!

Chandra Shekhar